Hope in the Highlands

Seduced in Scotland
Book 1

Matilda Madison

ARE YOU SIGNED UP FOR DRAGONBLADE'S BLOG?

You'll get the latest news and information on exclusive giveaways, exclusive excerpts, coming releases, sales, free books, cover reveals and more.

Check out our complete list of authors, too!

No spam, no junk. That's a promise!

Sign Up Here

www.dragonbladepublishing.com

Dearest Reader;

Thank you for your support of a small press. At Dragonblade Publishing, we strive to bring you the highest quality Historical Romance from some of the best authors in the business. Without your support, there is no 'us', so we sincerely hope you adore these stories and find some new favorite authors along the way.

Happy Reading!

CEO, Dragonblade Publishing

Additional Dragonblade books by
Author Matilda Madison

Seduced in Scotland Series
Hope in the Highlands (Book 1)

Gambling Peers Series
A Duke Makes a Deal (Book 1)
The Baron Takes a Bet (Book 2)
The Earl Breaks Even (Book 3)

Chapter One

H OPE SHARPE SAT at the dining room table, chin in hand, as she gazed out the window of the London terrace home. She was trying to ignore the stifling heat that had descended upon the city that week, as well as feign interest in her grandmother's overt excitement.

"Isn't she a dear!" the elderly Alice Sharpe said, fanning herself with the envelope of the letter she held in her other hand. The invitation had topped the small pile of correspondence brought to her just before breakfast. "Dorothea is so gracious to remember us."

The corner of Hope's mouth pulled up in a half-hearted smile, but it was difficult to get excited for yet another ball, to be part of yet another season when Hope had been through several already. It wasn't that she wasn't grateful to be invited to the events that clogged the social calendar at this time of year, but the oppressive, unseasonable heatwave that had fallen on London this spring was all Hope could focus on.

The housemaids had opened nearly every window to allow in the breeze, but Hope dreamed of the cool, breezy months of autumn. She simply wasn't made for heat. Her fair skin burned easily beneath the sun, which made her grandmother insist that she cover up so as not to freckle. But the extra layers of clothing that she was forced to wear were stifling. They may have kept freckles at bay but that was no compensation for the way they made Hope sweat.

But she didn't complain. No. Ever trying to be the dutiful granddaughter, she always did what was asked of her, unlike her younger sisters, Faith and Grace. But it wasn't because she was weak-willed. Hope merely believed in finding the best of situations.

Including situations like attending the ball of…of… Come to think of it, who *was* Dorothea?

"Dorothea?" Hope asked, facilitating the conversation.

She went to take a sip of her tea but abandoned it when she realized how hot it was. Frowning, she looked at her middle sister Faith, who lifted her glass of water in a mock toast.

"The dowager duchess of Spotsmore," her grandmother said. "She's always been a dear friend of mine. She's holding a ball in honor of her granddaughter, Lady Natalie Hawkins."

Although the Sharpes weren't exactly wealthy, they lived in relative comfort in a well-staffed London terrace in Soho Square that had been in their possession for several years. Not quite as grand or fashionable as Mayfair, but certainly a respectable neighborhood and Mayfair adjacent. Alice had still somehow managed to wrangle them an invitation to what was bound to be one of the most prominent events that season. The Spotsmore mansion was the jewel of Mayfair, and they always held the most fashionable soirees.

"Isn't Lady Natalie already engaged?" Faith asked, her brow creased.

"Lord Bartley hasn't proposed," Grace, the youngest Sharpe sister, interjected, not looking up from her book. Despite her grandmother's disapproval, Grace always read at the dining room table. "Not yet."

"Well, I'm sure this is Dorothea's very clever way of helping things along," Grandmother Alice said, eyeing Hope with purpose.

The small, telling gesture reminded Hope of the state of her own romantic prospects with one Mr. Jacob Pennington. The fourth son of a baron, and with the very little likelihood of inheriting said title, Jacob had attended school to become a lawyer. They had met three years ago during a picnic in Hyde Park, and had started their courtship that very day. But he was steadfast in his five-year plan and Hope knew he wasn't likely to propose until he made partner in his law firm.

Their pre-engagement was well known throughout London and almost everyone in society had taken to calling her *Hold-on Hope*, which she had always endured with a smile, not wanting to generate gossip by showing her true reaction. In reality, it irritated her to no end.

"Hope?" Alice said, interrupting her daydream. She faced her expectant grandmother, who sighed with disappointment. "Pay attention, Hope. Young ladies do not fare well when their attentions are so easily lost."

Hope nodded dutifully. Whenever she would complain about her prolonged courtship—with no engagement in sight—to her grandmother, she was merely reminded that patience was a virtue. Her grandmother would then say that Mr. Pennington would likely prefer a wife to be accommodating rather than peevish, which only added to Hope's agitation.

But then she would take a deep breath, count to five and remind herself that no good ever came from complaining.

"Yes, Grandmother."

Hope straightened her shoulders and focused her attention on her sisters' discussion about Lord Bartley. Hope had once had the unfortunate mistake of asking the gentleman his opinion on literature. He had superciliously stated that fiction was a frivolous waste of time and that she would be much better served by focusing on writings of *real* import. After that, she was forced to suffer through nearly an hour of his personal review of a mathematics book proving Brianchon's Theorem, written by Charles Brianchon.

It had been one of the most tedious hours of her entire life.

"Lady Natalie is a fine young woman and will make an excellent marchioness one day," her grandmother said, waving off a footman's attempt to fill her water glass. "She should be very pleased that Lord Bartley has chosen her."

"I hope she doesn't have a fondness for books," Hope mused quietly.

"Poor dear," Grace said, finally looking up. "I quite liked Natalie. It's a shame that she'll have to bear that marriage."

"Whatever are you all talking about?" their grandmother asked with a pinched brow. "Lady Natalie is fortunate to have found someone to marry. She's doing a sight better than you three," she said before giving Hope a pitying glance. "Well, except for you, my dear."

Hardly a shining compliment, but Hope tried not to be bothered.

"Why anyone would want to be tied to a man like Lord Bartley indefinitely is a mystery," Faith said as she buttered her toast. "He's an absolute toad, and I for one am very sorry for Lady Natalie's misfortune."

"Faith Sharpe, you'll watch your tongue," Alice scolded as a sudden cough escaped her throat. Her hand came to cover her mouth as her face scrunched up. "Lord Bartley... is a..." The tremor from her hacking caused her fine gray hair to loosen from its intricate style. "A fine..." She coughed forcefully into her fist. "A fine man."

All three Sharpe sisters paused in their activities to focus on their grandmother's terrible coughing fit. Panicked slightly, Hope sprung up and signaled to one of the servants. A footman returned with a pitcher of water and poured it into a glass that Hope handed to her grandmother. Grace came up to rub her back while a regretful Faith scooched down two chairs to sit by her side, taking her free hand.

Since coming to live with their grandmother, neither Hope, Faith, nor Grace had ever known her to take ill. Even at the death of their parents, she had remained strong and undaunted, barely even shedding a tear, much less taking to her bed as some might have done. She was a woman of robust constitution, and none of the girls had ever seen her sneeze, let alone cough.

"I'm sorry, Grandmother," Faith said earnestly. "I didn't mean to upset you."

But her grandmother shook her head as the coughing fit subsided.

"It wasn't your fault, dear," she said with a scratchy voice between coughs. "It's only a bit of tea I inhaled, I'm sure."

Hope shared a concerned look with her sisters, and as much as she wanted to believe that it had been a random choking fit, an unnatural chill went through her. She had experienced it only once before—the day her parents had left on their trip to the south of France seven years prior. They died of cholera only a few weeks later. Hope never saw them again.

Once her grandmother recovered, Hope motioned for all of them to take their seats. She tried to convince herself that they were overreacting, but over the next few hours, the coughing persisted. By week's end, their grandmother's constant coughing had become a permanent echo throughout their home.

The doctor couldn't find anything wrong with their grandmother and insisted that all she needed was rest. Over the next few weeks, Hope tried her best to believe the doctor's diagnosis, but by the time the soiree for Lady Natalie had arrived, she could no longer maintain her positive attitude. She refused to attend the ball, wanting rather to stay at home with her grandmother.

"You must go," her grandmother had ordered between coughs. Her pale eyes seemed dull and watery, though her raspy voice was insistent. "You must."

"But Grandmother—"

"Don't…" she said, coughing roughly into her clenched hand, "…argue. Mrs. Beesley will accompany you."

"Mrs. Beesley? But Grandmother, she is close to senile. She couldn't possibly escort us."

"Hope," Alice said sternly, causing all fight to go out of her.

Seeing that her quarreling only upset her grandmother, Hope nodded.

"Yes ma'am," she said, squeezing her grandmother's hand before leaving to get dressed.

Determined to appease her grandmother, Hope dressed in her best pale green gown, snaking a matching ribbon through her curly, raven hair. Their impromptu chaperone Mrs. Beesley, whose hearing had diminished drastically in recent months, arrived to escort them, and she ushered Hope and her younger sisters into the hired coach to take them to the ball.

Upon arriving at the Duchess of Spotsmore's home, Mrs. Beesley quickly found the sitting room, where she promptly sat down to nap. Hope was then abandoned immediately by Grace, who eagerly left to visit with her friends. Before Faith could wander off as well, Hope reached for her sister's elbow and leaned close to her ear as she spoke.

"It doesn't feel right being here, does it? What with Grandmother sick and all."

"She'll be fine, Hope. And you know she would want us to be sociable."

Hope gave her a pointed look, knowing very well her sister was trying to placate her. Faith was on her tippytoes, peering over the other guests, looking for someone in particular, prompting Hope to say something.

"You should be wary of dancing too much with your Mr. Delaney, Faith," she said as they moved out of the sitting room together. "He's garnering a reputation."

Faith rolled her eyes.

"From who?"

"It was in the gossip pages in the *Times* the day before last."

Faith gently pulled her arm out of her sister's grip.

"I assure you, Hope, that if Mr. Delaney is gaining a reputation, it's not from the likes of me," she said, scanning the ballroom. "Besides, he's been helping me with my watercolors."

Mr. Delaney was one of several artist friends that Faith had become close with over the past year. Faith had always loved the art of painting but had given it up a year ago after experiencing a heartbreak. She had fancied herself in love with an artist known singularly as Donovan, and when he'd disappeared months ago, Faith had lost all interest in painting. Thankfully, she had recently started to spend time with her friend, Renee, Mr. Delaney's sister, and once a week, Faith would attend a painting lesson at the Delaney home. Hope was happy that she had recently returned to her passion, but she worried that Mr. Delaney would break her sister's heart, just as Donovan had.

"Still, you shouldn't spend too much time in his company."

Faith was barely listening, focusing instead on scanning the crowd. Someone must have caught her attention, for her eyes lit up. She gave a little wave.

"There he is. And Renee is with him."

"Do be careful, Faith."

She turned to face Hope.

"Despite what you and grandmother believe, I'm quite capable of handling myself. Besides, it is not me that we have worry about."

Hope frowned slightly.

"Do you mean Grace? She rarely ever looks up from the pages of her books. Unless it's to consort with that reading group of hers."

"Exactly," Faith said. She began to walk away but added over her shoulder. "It's the quiet ones you have to worry about."

"Oh, but…"

She tried to continue their conversation, but Faith only drifted away, melting into the sea of guests moving about the grand ballroom. Hope sighed, fretting over the ever-present tension between her and her sisters.

There had been a time when the three of them had been very close. Before moving in with their grandmother, she and Faith particularly had been the dearest of companions. But in the years since their parents' death, each sister had come to different conclusions about life, and a wedge seemed to separate them, like the tendrils of ivy breaking through a brick wall.

Each of the sisters had dealt with the tragedy differently. Grace had withdrawn into an isolation that it seemed no one could breach, not even her sisters. Faith had become cynical, always expecting the worst. And while Hope had tried to lift their spirits, it seemed they found her relentless optimism as aggravating as she did their aloofness and pessimism.

Hope wandered across the edge of the ballroom, finding a large marble pillar to lean against at the edge of the ballroom where she could worry about her sisters and grandmother undisturbed—or so she had thought. Suddenly, a male voice spoke in her ear.

"My pearl." Jacob's voice shattered her concentration. "I was hoping to see you here."

Spinning around, she saw the mild, passive gaze of Jacob Pennington's brown eyes staring back at her. Jacob was a young man of average build and standard features. With wheat colored hair and a somewhat slanted forehead that caused his brow to appear heavier than it was, he gave the appearance of a great thinker, as he so often reminded Hope.

"Jacob, I'm so glad you're here. I've been having the worst few weeks," she said, her hand going up to the lapel of his jacket, but he quickly pushed it away.

Though the show of physical support would have buoyed her heart—and the rejection of it pained her—she refrained from telling him so. He would only reprimand her for being emotional.

"Now, now, we wouldn't want any gossip. I'm quite certain we can speak without touching," he chided as he glanced around. "We don't want people to think that the apple doesn't fall too far from the family tree."

Hope frowned. Jacob never wished to show affection, not even in private. But what was he talking about?

"My family tree?" Hope repeated, confused. "What does that mean?"

"My pearl, let's not make a scene," he said, ignoring her question.

"I am not making a scene," she said softly. "I am simply asking you a question. Why mention my family tree?"

"I don't think there's a need to delve into your family history here, is there?"

Hope was perplexed.

"What family history are you speaking of?" she asked, her voice dipping to a whisper as a couple passed them.

Jacob nodded at the couple, his own tone dropping.

"Let's not discuss it here. We don't want others gossiping about you sulking."

"I'm not sulking."

"You certainly sound as though you're sulking."

Hope exhaled and began to count in her mind. *One, two, three…*

"I'm not sulking," she said through gritted teeth, trying with all her might to hold on to her good nature. "I'm simply trying to have a conversation."

Jacob's brow lifted in surprise.

"My, I wonder what's gotten into you this evening. You seem peevish. Have you eaten?"

Hope inhaled slowly. She hated when Jacob spoke to her like a child. She counted to five again.

"I have eaten," she said slowly. "And if I seem out of sorts, I apologize, but it's only because my grandmother has taken ill, as I've explained in my letters, which have gone unanswered, and I'm somewhat worried—"

"My dear, we cannot act all excited simply because a family member is dealing with indigestion."

"It's not indigestion."

"Lady Alice is a healthy woman, my dear. I'm sure she will be fine."

Hope scowled at him.

"As you have not been by to see her—or me, for that matter—in nearly four weeks, I don't see how you can assume to know how she is faring."

A smug, knowing expression came over Jacob's face.

"Is that why you're so miffed? Because I haven't been by to see you? I told you I was working on a substantial case these past few months. If I'm successful in litigation, we might be able to bring our five-year plan forward six months."

"That is not why I'm upset," she said earnestly. "My grandmother is ill, and I'm worried about her."

He frowned.

"Didn't you hear me? Our plans may be happening sooner than later. I can propose to you next May instead of October next year. Isn't that wonderful?"

It was like having a conversation with a parrot. To an outsider, it might *look* like a conversation in that both participants were speaking, but one seemed totally incapable of listening to or understanding the other.

"Yes, that is good news. But I'm very concerned right now about my grandmother. Not to mention my sisters—"

"My dear, if you're more interested in going over the symptoms of some sniffles than in celebrating this good news, I think I'd much prefer to let you stew by yourself for some time until you get over whatever is bothering you."

Hope's. Resolve. Snapped.

"Sometimes I think you have all the empathy of a bee, Jacob. Except when a bee stings, it at least has the courtesy to die of shame or embarrassment. You, I fear, will never be so aware."

She knew she would regret her outburst, but in that moment, she couldn't help but take great satisfaction in his slack jawed face. Her grandmother always assured her that men of position chose to focus on themselves in order to allow them to provide as best they could for those who depended on them. Hope was set to marry Jacob, so she was expected to put his needs first. But really, how could he be so blind regarding his future fiancée's worries? Was he truly that indifferent to her distress?

Surely he could see she was upset. And yet all he had to offer were chiding remarks about her behavior and callous dismissal of her concerns. He seemed to expect her to fawn all over him, but heaven forbid they touch. It made Hope so angry at that moment that she couldn't stop herself.

Trudging through the grand house, hoping to find the powder room so she could take a moment to herself to settle her bubbling anger toward Jacob, Hope saw two ladies exit a brightly lit room. Though she barely recognized the two young ladies, she distinctly heard one of them say as they walked by, "That must be the one who was spotted kissing Lord Bartley."

"I guess *Hold-on Hope* finally let go," the other laughed.

Hope's feet stalled as she glanced at the young ladies who practically ran away down the hall when they saw her stop. Kissing Lord Bartley? Why would anyone assume that she had kissed him? She knew that gossip could spread quickly, and that something as simple as a lady tripping and a gentleman catching her arm to keep her from falling could be misconstrued as an embrace. But she didn't recall having laid eyes on Lord Bartley all evening. How on earth could such a rumor have started?

Frowning, she entered the powder room. Much to her surprise, she found Faith and Grace standing before her with pinched faces and strained mouths. Hope felt the inkling of dread.

"Faith? Grace?" Hope said, coming forward. "What is it? What's wrong?"

Both sisters twisted to face Hope. Grace's face was pale as a sheet, while Faith's eyes were red as poppies.

"Oh, Hope," Faith said, sniffling. "We're finished."

"Finished?" she said, her hands going to either of her sisters. "What do you mean?"

"I, well, I may have caused a situation," Grace began quietly. "But I swear, I had innocent intentions. Or…well, perhaps not *entirely* innocent, but I certainly meant no harm."

"I cannot believe this," Faith said, looking up at the ceiling.

"What's happened?" Hope insisted.

"Well…"

"Grace was spotted kissing Lord Bartley in the garden," Faith accused, rotating to her youngest sister. "Only the person who saw her assumed it was me."

Hope's mouth fell open.

"What?" she asked breathlessly. "Oh, Grace, you didn't."

"She did," Faith said, her voice quietly furious. "And the Delaneys have publicly cut me! Mr. Delaney says he will not allow his family to be tied to a woman who would behave so wantonly."

Hope turned toward her.

"You? But why would he assume you did it?"

"I'm guessing because it was some dark corner. How could they believe that it was me?"

Though their faces differed greatly, the Sharpes all shared the same dark, curly hair, and they were dressed similarly this evening. It would be easy to mistake one for the other in the shadows, especially when their backs were turned. But Hope frowned.

"That's odd. The two ladies who just left here said that *I* was the one who was caught. They don't know which one of us did it," she said. Then she shook her head. "Though in the end, I don't suppose it matters. Any scandal within the family will affect all of us."

"Will *ruin* all of us, you mean," Faith said, glowering at Grace.

"That's enough of that," Hope said firmly. "None of us can change what happened. All we can do is weather the storm."

"If I tell everyone it was me..." Grace began.

"It won't matter. One sister disgraced means a whole family disgraced," Faith pointed out, her voice heavy.

"But if you disown me, tell everyone how shocked you were at my behavior, maybe that will be enough to restore your reputations, at least partially—"

"No one is getting disowned," Hope interrupted. "We're a family, and we're staying that way, no matter what anyone says. Now, let's go out there and face them."

Faith seemed hesitant, but peering back and forth between her sisters, she groaned. Her hands came up to the sides of her head, and she shook out her hairstyle as well.

"This will be a disaster," she whined as Hope linked their arms together.

Hope held out her other arm to Grace, who looked at her sorrowfully.

"I'm so sorry, Hope," Grace said, shaking her head. "I promise I didn't do it simply to ruin us."

"Whatever your reasoning, my dear, this is our reality now. Come. We need to leave immediately."

Grace hesitated a moment before reaching for Hope's arm and clinging to her tightly. They would need to be each other's strength in the coming days.

They exited the powder room quickly, instantly observing the looks they received as they made their way down the hallway toward the foyer. It seemed everyone was eager to gawk at the trio as they hurried through the house to find the sleeping Mrs. Beesley. Before long, they were all out the door and in their carriage heading home.

Upon arriving home, Hope noticed the doctor's hackney outside, waiting in the street. Dread fell around her like a heavy cloak and she leapt from their carriage as soon as it stopped. She was through the front door and up the stairs before her sisters could catch up with her.

Reaching her grandmother's room, she found a line of servants all standing outside the matriarch's room. Every one of them was crying.

Hope's heart beat wildly when Faith called up from the bottom of the staircase.

"Hope! Mr. Pennington has arrived!"

Confused and unbalanced, Hope tried to still her shaking hands. She was torn between the need to rush to her grandmother's side and to see to Jacob. A maid, Ginger, came forward and curtsied, though her face was wet with tears.

"Begging your pardon, my lady," she started. "But there's no helping Lady Sharpe. She's passed."

The words didn't register at first. Passed? No. Surely not. Devastation rolled through Hope even as she tried to push the notion away. Why would she say that? She can't have passed.

"No," Hope said.

"Hope?"

She turned and saw her sisters at the top of the staircase. The silent sniffling and weeping of the staff seemed to be enough to inform her sisters of what had happened. Faith covered her mouth with her hand while Grace stood frozen in shock.

"Hope?" A man's voice, Jacob's, carried up through the house.

Numbly, Hope made her way to the staircase and descended, meeting Jacob at the bottom. She wanted to reach for him, but even in her fog-like misery, she kept her hands at her side.

"My God, Hope, you look terrible," he said, coming toward her. "Is your grandmother well?"

"No," she said softly, peering up at him. "No. She's passed."

Jacob's face fell.

"That is unfortunate. I had hoped she would be able to help rally her friends in society to quash an absurd rumor," he said. "As you were leaving Spotsmore House, I overheard that either you, Faith, or Grace was spotted kissing Lord Bartley."

Hope barely registered what he was saying. Her grandmother was no longer alive and a numbness seemed to be spreading throughout her body.

She moved past him, finding a hallway bench as she felt as if her legs would no longer hold her. Dropping to it, she leaned her back against the wall and stared into oblivion.

"Did you hear me?" he asked.

"Yes, Jacob. I did."

"Well?"

She turned her head to look at him.

"Well, what?"

"Well, how did such a rumor come to be?"

"I daresay it was because someone saw one of us kissing Lord Bartley."

For a moment, Jacob just gaped at her. "Do you mean to say it's true?"

"Yes." She saw no point in lying. She saw no point in anything, at the moment.

"Was it you?"

Hope blinked. The sting of his distrust was significantly dulled after the news about her grandmother, but it still hurt. That Jacob would believe her so unfaithful, well, it devastated her.

"No," she answered numbly. "It wasn't me."

"Well, that's something, at least," he said with a nod, shifting his stance. "However, I don't know how your sisters shall fare now that your grandmother has died. Not without you here to help clean up their mess."

Hope tilted her head, confused.

"Where am I going?"

"With me, of course," he said as he reached for her. His soft, smooth hand encircled her cold fingers as he pulled her to her feet. Hope swayed for a moment, unsure of what she was hearing.

"What do you mean?"

"We'll be married at once, and you won't have to suffer the scandal that your sisters will endure. We'll cut them off completely, of course. That's the only way our reputations will stay intact."

For a moment, Hope's heart swelled with appreciation. They were going to be married! But moments later, the meaning of his words trickled down her spine.

"Cut them off? I couldn't possibly. They're my sisters," she said softly, her eyes unfocused. "I can't abandon them, Jacob. Not now, not ever." Her brow pinched together. "Surely you know that, don't you?"

"I know nothing of the sort," he said stiffly. "Your sisters have proved to be nothing but trouble for you, and I don't see why you must suffer because of them. Let us leave this place right now. You will stay with my aunt while we secure a special license. We will marry as soon as possible and then you'll be free of their constant problems."

But even before Jacob had finished his words, Hope was shaking her head.

"No, Jacob. I … I can't leave them."

"You must."

Out of the corner of her eye, Hope saw Faith and Grace standing on the staircase, watching her and Jacob. She knew they had overheard everything. Ignoring the sting in her eyes, Hope slowly and purposefully pulled her hands from Jacob's.

This was the end.

"I'm sorry, Jacob," she said, her eyes downcast. "But I can't."

Thankfully, Jacob was too proud of a man to ask twice. After a few moments, the door opened and closed with a frightful slam. Hope jumped at the deafening noise. Her entire world had been upended in only a few hours.

Wiping away the tears that fell down her cheeks, she went to the coat rack and pulled down her cloak. She whirled the piece over her shoulders and made her way toward the door.

"Hope?" A small voice sounded from behind her and she turned. There, halfway down the stairs, stood both of her sisters, arms intertwined in a comforting grip. Grace took a step down, her arm dropping from Faith's. "Where are you going?"

"I need to think," Hope croaked, buttoning the cloak beneath her chin.

"At this hour?" Faith asked, her tone shaky. "Don't you think it's rather late?"

"I can't… I can't bear to stay still," she said and opened the door.

She closed the door behind her and made her way down the front steps, turning left and then right. She needed to walk, to be away from the unbearable weight of all that had happened that night and all the uncertainty she now faced.

What in the world were they going to do?

Chapter Two

Scottish Highlands, June 1855

GRAHAM MACKINNON STOOD perfectly still beneath the barrel-vaulted ceiling of the dining room in Lismore Hall. His gaze was transfixed on a massive portrait suspended on the wall, surrounded by fifty or so mounted deer antlers, an ode to the Scottish sense of decor. The painting had hung in this room for over a hundred years, and while Graham had often studied the faces portrayed in the piece of art, he always found himself a bit surprised to remember that these were his kin.

A dark-haired woman with a hint of a smile on her lips sat on a bench in front of a woodland scene beneath a towering beech tree. She was flanked by two young sons, both of whom resembled her, sitting on either side of her. A stern man with a square chin stood erect behind them, and his hand curled around the lapel of his jacket. He glared down at Graham. All of them were draped in the green and red plaid of the Clan MacKinnon, unaware that their family was only a few short months away from being destroyed.

Graham had never met his great-grandfather, as Fergus MacKinnon had died over eighty years before he was born, but he often found himself wondering about the old highlander. Would Fergus believe that he would be dead only six months after this portrait had been painted, one of the thousands who fell at the ill-fated battle of Culloden? What would he have done if he knew the Crown would seize all of MacKinnon's ancient clan lands, leaving his widow and two sons with nothing more of their once-vast estate but their beloved Lismore Hall?

And what would he do if he learned that his grandson, Graham's father, James, had lost Lismore Hall in a single hand of cards fifty years later?

Footsteps echoed from the hallway, jolting Graham away from his thoughts.

"MacKinnon!" an elderly, bejeweled woman said from behind him.

Dragging his attention away from the portrait, he bowed to greet her. Her blackwood cane tapped against the flagstone floor. She came toward him, followed by her butler, Andrews. "I didn't know you would be stopping by today."

He smirked, allowing himself to find the humor in the fact that an Englishwoman was living in his ancestorial home. MacKinnon had been visiting her the first Monday of every month for the past ten years, and every time, Lady Belle Smith acted surprised to see him.

"Lady Belle," he said, bowing over her outstretched hand. Taking it, he pressed his mouth to the back of her small, wrinkled knuckles covered in emerald rings. "Terrible weather we're having, no?"

A fierce roll of thunder echoed above them as the rain fell loudly against the ceiling. The storm had been raging since the night before. Inhaling deeply, Graham could smell the ancient, exposed timber above his head and the faint, musty scent that emanated through the red sandstone walls that always magnified during a rainstorm.

The storm was a blessing, dissipating the heatwave that had stifled the country for weeks. Graham felt as if he was finally able to breathe. He loathed the heat.

"It's dreadful, absolutely wretched," she replied, shuddering at the mention of it. Her eyes flickered to the windows along the far end of the dining room. "But," she said, perking up, pointing her index finger toward the ceiling, "I have no doubt it will stop storming by tomorrow."

"Is that so?"

"Yes," she said, pausing before addressing her butler. "Andrews, will you have some tea brought in?"

"Yes, my lady," the butler said with a nod, leaving the room at once.

Graham watched the man exit. He waited until they were alone to continue their conversation.

"And how can you be so certain that the weather will change?" he asked.

"The storm clouds have a purple tint to them," she said, lifting her cane and pointing it at the window. "Go and see for yourself."

Not sure what the color had to do with anything, but used to being ordered about by the older woman, he walked to the window. Pulling the gold damask curtain back, he looked toward the sky. As Lady Belle had reported, the angry, rolling clouds had a purplish hue.

"And purple signifies?"

Lady Belle gave him a reproachful glance. "Surely, you've heard the rhyme? If skies are purple, gather the kernel?"

Graham's brow furrowed. "Ack. That's a terrible rhyme," he said slowly. "And it doesn't make any sense."

"It does so," she insisted. "It means the next day is a good day to start sowing seeds."

He didn't believe a word of it. Lady Belle was a peculiar woman with a reputation for constantly expounding half-truths and fanciful ideas. The vast majority of them could have been easily disproven, except that no one ever really wanted to invalidate her. There was a strange appeal to Lady Belle that made the local people wish to indulge her.

It could have been her old age, sharp wit, or evergreen beauty. Even at seventy-five years old, Lady Belle was still a remarkably handsome woman. Her hooded blue eyes still shone with youthful mischief, and while wrinkles creased the corners of her eyes and mouth, they seemed to be caused by a lifetime of laughter in a way that enhanced the charm of her smile rather than diminishing it. Her once pale blonde hair had whitened, giving her a certain glow against the dark interior of Lismore Hall.

Yes, there were several reasons everyone who lived on the estate and the surrounding lands allowed Lady Belle a certain amount of grace. But mostly, it was because she had once, very publicly, made an English king beg for mercy.

"You're daft, and you know that, don't you?" Graham said.

Lady Belle barked with laughter and whacked her cane on the floor.

"Oh! You're a fresh man, MacKinnon!"

He smiled, enjoying the ease with which they spoke. Given the circumstances that had brought her to live here, he doubted Fergus MacKinnon would appreciate his descendant's strange friendship with the wily Englishwoman. Still, Lady Belle was the sort of saucy woman MacKinnon men had often been drawn to.

"The words don't even rhyme. Purple and Kernel."

"It's close enough."

"It's lazy language. And it's yours. You should try harder."

Lady Belle squinted at him.

"How do you say purple in your tongue?"

"Purpaidh," he said.

"Well, that's far too easy to rhyme. I prefer the correct way."

"The English way, you mean."

"Is there a difference?"

"Now, no starting that, Lady Belle," Graham said, coming back toward her as a footman pulled out her chair.

She winked at him and nodded to the seat next to hers at the long, oak table in the middle of the dining room. Three Paris Porcelain vases painted with cornflowers held an array of flowers cut from the walled garden that wrapped around Lismore Hall. It was widely regarded as one of the most splendid gardens in the

Highlands, and Lady Belle was always proud to display its blooms.

The oak table was long enough that it could easily seat sixty people. Graham sat next to her, ignoring the instinctive annoyance that he should sit at the side while she sat at the head of the table. It had bothered him greatly when he'd first started his visits ten years ago, but now it hardly fazed him.

Well, almost.

Andrews returned, followed by a slew of servants delivering platters of sandwiches, cakes, and tarts, along with piping hot tea and a small glass of brandy. Lady Belle always had her tea boiling with a brandy splash. She also liked to pour it herself, shooing away the servants as soon as they placed the items before them.

Once finished with her own cup of tea, she poured one for Graham and handed it to him, ignoring his grimace. Graham disliked tea and preferred coffee over anything, but Lady Belle had insisted years ago that if he wished to speak with her, he'd have to take tea with her. It was another thing that had grated him at the beginning of their friendship, but he'd reconciled himself to it. Now he added a dash of cream and drank it as fast as he could.

He held the dainty pink porcelain saucer in his large hand and lifted the teacup with the other. He was sure he appeared ridiculous. How clever that tea set manufacturers would build such a fragile, easily breakable product, guaranteeing a return customer. Knocking back his head, he swallowed the entire serving of Earl Grey swiftly, unaffected by the scorching temperature.

"How are your bees doing in this weather?" she asked. "Do they suffer much when it rains? I hope it won't affect business."

The reference to his business made Graham want to puff out his chest slightly. Since studying agriculture at university at his uncle's insistence, Graham had become relatively successful in life. Years prior, he had invented a seed drilling attachment that could be fitted on a threshing machine during the planting season.

It eliminated the need for two costly devices, combining the equipment for planting and harvesting into a single contraption. It had earned him a tidy sum of money that he had gone on to invest in a new venture: beekeeping. Lady Belle had allotted him the use of an old butterfly garden on the eastern side of the walled grounds at Lismore Hall.

"No, not at all. The bees love rain."

"Do they?" She stirred the brandy into her tea, took a tentative sip, and smiled. "Well, do you wish to ask me your question before or after my news?"

"You have news?"

"I do."

"Well then, let's get it over with so you can carry on as you like," Graham said, sitting up straight as he placed the saucer and teacup on the table. He reached past the delicate raspberry tarts and strawberry scones for a small, triangle-cut sandwich. Smoked salmon and dill—his favorite. Though, as always, he wished the kitchen would make the sandwiches substantially larger. He never came away satisfied from eating such tiny morsels.

"I do not carry on."

"Aye, you do, because you're always too invested in your story." He popped the sandwich into his mouth in one bite and practically swallowed without chewing. Lady Belle watched him with amused disapproval. "You never notice everyone else's eyes rolling in the back of their heads."

"You're a wicked, insolent man, MacKinnon." Lady Belle scowled at him though her eyes were twinkling at his teasing. "I should say yes to you today if only to finally put an end this friendship."

"Cor, you'll not be saying yes today."

"Then why do you still come to ask?"

Graham considered it, choosing his words carefully. Though he had become fond of the older woman, he didn't quite know how to explain to her that even though she would always refuse his request, it wasn't in him to stop trying.

"Well, I suppose it's because I enjoy your company, as annoying as you are. And because I would be lacking if I didn't at least ask. Once a month. For the rest of your life."

Lady Belle seemed pleased with his honest answer and leaned over the table.

"You're a sweet boy, Graham. If I was fifty years younger, I think I would have set my cap for you."

Graham smiled, moving his hand over the apricot tarts. Deciding instead on a petite raspberry pastry, he plucked it from the tray before replying.

"If you were fifty years younger, I'd be running in the other direction."

Lady Belle chortled with unrestrained joy.

Theirs was an odd relationship and Graham hadn't always liked her, but with fair reason. When he was ten, his uncle, Laird McTavish, explained to him how Lismore Hall had been lost. For years, Graham had disliked Lady Belle for being the victor of that card game, but there was an undeniable charm about her, and he could not help but be won over.

She wiped a tear away from her cheek as she laughed, trying to settle herself down.

"Andrews?" Lady Belle said, her brow creasing as she stared down at the slice of almond-topped Dundee cake on her plate. "Did the cook do something different with the recipe?"

"I don't believe so, my lady."

"Are you sure?"

"Would you like me to ask, my lady?"

"Yes," she said. Andrews left the room and she pointed her fork at Graham. "You know, I remember the first time I had Dundee cake. It was right here, the night you were born."

Graham had heard this story before.

"Oh?" he said, feigning interest.

"Your father insisted we have cake and champagne while we waited for word that you had been delivered."

An irrational bitterness settled in his gut. James should have been upstairs with Graham's mother, but instead he was in this very dining hall, gambling away Graham's future. His father had lost Lismore in an ill-fated hand of cards while his wife died in childbirth. The shame drove his father mad with guilt and he drank himself to an early death not a year later. Little wonder, then, that Graham had grown up feeling a lack of pride in his own name.

"Well, he did enjoy a drink or two, from what I've been told."

Belle gave him a piteous look just as Andrews returned.

"My lady, there has been no change to the Dundee cake recipe."

Lady Belle waved her hand absently at the butler as if she had half forgotten that she had even had him inquire about it.

"Tell me," she said, her bracelets jiggling together as she carved into another pastry with her fork. "How is my friend McTavish? You know, your uncle has not been to see me for some time."

"He's very well," Graham said, shifting in his seat. "Although he is cross with you."

"With me? Why so?"

"He said you ignored an invitation of his last month."

Lady Belle rolled her eyes.

"I was unwell," she said, putting her fork down. "I thought I sent my regards. Do apologize on my behalf. I hate to think that he's upset with me."

"Uncle has never managed to stay mad at you long."

Graham was very familiar with his uncle's temperament since the man had raised him, alongside a brood of his cousins. It had been a happy childhood. Though he knew he wasn't a McTavish, Graham had been grateful for the acceptance he'd found in his mother's kin. But the shame of his father's sins had weight heavily on Graham, even in his youth. He had made a promise that one day a MacKinnon would regain ownership of Lismore Hall, no matter what it took. But no amount of begging, threats, payment, or promises Graham had tried over the years could get the older woman to budge when it came to selling the property back to him. She had the deed and a clause written in the king's own will that she controlled Lismore Hall, and she would not relinquish it.

Graham leaned over the table. "Ready for my offer?" he asked.

"Yes," she said, smiling. "Yes, go ahead."

"Very well," he said, taking a deep breath.

Even though Graham knew the answer, a flutter of nerves always settled in his stomach before he started. "Lady Belle, it has been thirty years since you took the deed to Lismore Hall. This is my family's home. My ancestors built it. The rock we're standing on was placed here by their very hands. My own great-grandfather," he said, pointing to the portrait he had been staring at moments ago, "hangs from these walls."

Lady Belle nodded, smiling sweetly at him as though she were an understanding grandmother.

"Yes, I know, dear."

"Now I've grown fond of you, Lady Belle. I have, truly. I've no wish to take anything from you that you do not freely consent to give. But I'm more than willing to offer a fair price. Do you think you can ever find it in your heart to sell my home, a home I have never been permitted to fully know, back to me?"

There was a slight pause before she spoke.

"You know, MacKinnon, it's getting harder to say no to you," she said softly, a strange twinkle in her eye. "I think I should very much like to give this home of yours back to you."

He knocked over his teacup but quickly caught it. What had she just said?

"Excuse me?" he asked roughly, sure that he had misheard her.

Was she jesting with him? Or making him out to be some fool? She never said things like that. She always declined and they would resume their pleasant conversation.

"But I should like something in return."

Graham's ears began to buzz as if his bees were swarming around him. As he stumbled to his feet, a swell of hope and yearning exploded in his chest. He felt dizzy as emotion welled up within him.

"Are … are you serious?" he managed to croak out.

"I said I should like something in return," she repeated sternly, though he sensed she was pleased with herself for surprising him. "And you're not going to like it."

"Name it," he said quickly, hurrying to her side. "Any price, I promise." She knew he was more than prepared to be generous—but offers of money had never swayed her before. What had changed?

She smiled the same way that his aunt had when she demanded he and his cousins stop playing and take a bath when they were children.

"Well, this would be an exorbitant price, but not measured in gold. Her name is Hope. Hope Sharpe, and I'd like it very much if you marry her."

Graham gaped at Lady Belle for a moment before letting out a bark of laughter. But when she didn't move to join him in laughter at her joke, he frowned.

"Excuse me? Are you serious?"

"Oh, I'm quite serious."

"Who is she?" Graham demanded. And then, "I mean, I can't marry a lass I don't know."

"Well, *I* know her, and I'm an excellent judge of character," Lady Belle stated, waving her emerald clad hand as she refocused her attention on her tea, causing the carved jade bracelets to clang together. The varying gemstones rather clashed with each other, but Lady Belle was an eclectic woman, having become more so in her old age. It mattered little to her whether her jewelry matched or not. She wore her favorite pieces often and in defiance of complementing style.

She took a sip before acknowledging Graham's frozen stance. "Yes? Is there something wrong?"

"Aye, there is," he said slowly, his temper rising. "I just told you that I can't marry a woman I've never met before."

"Oh, I see," she said, setting down her cup. Taking up a linen napkin, she gently wiped the corners of her crinkled mouth. "Because you are in love with someone else?"

"No, I—"

"Well then, I see no obstacle in your way that would keep you from marrying my Hope."

"Look harder," he growled. "I'll not have my conjugal life managed by some ancient Englishwoman."

"It doesn't matter what you will or will not do," she said pointedly. "Because you do not understand what I'm saying."

"And what are you saying?"

"You have to marry Hope to get Lismore Hall."

"And why is that?"

"Because I'm leaving it to her," Lady Belle said.

For the first time in a long time, Graham's cheeks heated uncomfortably. He usually had better self-control, but he felt genuinely hurt at being deceived. He had assumed that after years of friendly banter and conversation, Lady Belle would eventually concede and leave Lismore Hall to him in her will. She had alluded to that once or twice, and now she was telling him it wouldn't happen. This Hope woman was going to inherit what should have been his.

"Mealladh nathair!" he bit out, both glad and disappointed she didn't speak Scottish.

"I know nathair means snake, so I can only imagine what mealladh means, but I won't hold it against you," she said, twirling one of her large emerald rings around her finger. "I know this has come as a bit of a shock."

"A shock?"

"She is a lovely girl, and I know you will suit very well to-gether."

"I'll not be match-made, so you can forget it."

"No, you'll be foolhardy instead. Very well," she said, focusing her attention back to the dish before her, though she didn't seem too interested in eating the tiny sandwich. "If you're so incensed about it, we won't discuss it further."

"Then I don't have to marry her?" Graham asked, his mood as foul as the weather.

"Of course not. No one is holding you hostage."

"Then you'll leave Lismore Hall to me?"

She did not face him, instead focusing on the branches from a Scotch broom whipping against the window. The snapping against the glass echoed between them.

"No."

"Ack! Bloody English!" he shouted, pivoting on his heel as a roll of thunder sounded from overhead. "You're all a bunch of backstabbing, unloyal bastards!"

"You Scottish are nothing but a roaming bunch of hotheads, unwilling to compromise."

"Aye, I'll not compromise my soul for you or any other damned English."

Lady Belle tapped her walking stick three times on the floor. Within seconds, Andrews appeared.

"Yes, my lady?"

"Andrews, could you see Mr. MacKinnon out? He's taken ill."

"Ack, I don't need to be tossed out of my own damn home," he said, furious. "This is treacherous, and you know it, Lady Belle."

"The girls arrive tomorrow around midday, I believe. If you wish to meet them—"

"What girls?"

She rolled her jade bracelets around her wrist and pursed her lips, visibly perturbed at his interruption.

"My nieces. The Sharpe sisters. Hope, Faith, and Grace."

Graham just stared at her.

"You are joking," he said. "Since when do you have nieces?"

"Well, Hope is twenty-six, so for about twenty-six years now," she said sarcastically before continuing. "They suffered a tragic loss several years back, and they have been under the protection of my sister, their grandmother, ever since. Unfortunately, my sister took ill a fortnight ago and has passed away. They are now under my care and are on their way to Lismore at this very moment."

Graham glared at her, unwilling to believe it. She had never said a word about family for as long as he knew her.

"Have you ever met them before?"

"Of course I have," she said, sticking her chin up in the air, offended. "I spend every winter with them in Cornwall."

"I thought you went to Italy in the winter."

"Whatever gave you that idea?"

He glared at her.

"*You did*," he said.

"Oh, well, it's no matter," she said hastily. "The girls arrive tomorrow, and I hope you will at least meet them—after your temper subsides, of course—before you make any rash decisions."

"You're out of your bloody mind if you think I'm going to marry one of your conniving kin. Curse James MacKinnon forever for playing whist with the devil herself."

"Scots," she breathed, bringing her index and middle finger up to rub at her temple as if she were fighting off a headache. "All of you are so dramatic." She stood slowly, driving her cane into the stone to steady herself. "I'm simply offering you a chance to reclaim your ancestorial home—a home, I might add, that you've claimed repeatedly you were willing to do anything and everything to get back into your possession."

"Aye, but—"

"And here I have a perfectly suitable offer, and you refuse it without even meeting the girl."

"Now, wait just one minute—"

"All I ask is that you meet Hope and see if you suit. If you do, then I don't know why a marriage wouldn't follow."

"Because I'll not have my fate dictated by the likes of you."

"Oh, MacKinnon, who better than me?" Lady Belle quipped.

"I've managed several generations of men in my lifetime. I held a king in the palm of my hand, MacKinnon. A king."

He scoffed.

"An *English* king," he countered with disgust, shaking his head. "And you've lost your mind if you think I'm going to play your games."

"I've not lost my mind. I'm merely hopeful."

He shook his head.

"I can't stand this. Good day."

"MacKinnon—"

"I said, good day."

Graham didn't look back. He couldn't. The sheer audacity of that woman floored him, and he would not give her the satisfaction of seeing him so unsettled—nor would he let her glimpse his heartbreak at the realization that he wouldn't inherit his ancestorial home. It was too much. He had put up with Lady Belle for years and while, yes, they had come to have a tentative friendship, he had always believed she knew that he had been wronged and that she was an honorable enough person to one day give him a chance to get the home back. It's what he deserved.

But an ultimatum? No, that was one thing he wouldn't stand for.

Graham burst through the front doors and into the pouring rain. A footman spotted him and hurried back to the stables to fetch his mount, but Graham wouldn't wait. He headed toward the stables himself, eventually meeting the footman as he brought around Graham's horse, a Clydesdale named Redcap. In an instant, he was on the horse's back and riding away from Lismore Hall. He tore off down the drive, eager to get away from this place.

How could Lady Belle have believed that he would agree to such an outrageous proposal? It was 1855, for God's sake, not the dark ages. He wouldn't be cowed into marrying some homely English bride to get what was rightfully his.

Riding as fast as he could through the storm, Graham ignored the hundreds of sharp stings as the raindrops slammed into his body. He rode along the crest of the rocky range that would take him back south to Loch Awe, where his uncle lived at Elk Manor. He needed to vent, to rage out loud at Lady Belle's audacity and swear never to deal with the likes of her again.

Because if there was one thing he knew for sure, it was that Graham MacKinnon would never marry Hope Sharpe.

Chapter Three

HOPE GAZED OUT the carriage window as it jostled forward, up through the stony hills and rough crags that had begun to crop up since leaving Cumbria. While the rolling hills to the south appeared like crushed, green velvet, these northern peaks of exposed rock and moss reminded Hope of a threadbare carpet laid over uneven ground.

She had imagined that Scotland would be a desolate place, composed of jagged cliffs and sharp rocks, but she had been mistaken. The vast countryside that seemed to go on forever was magnificent, and the farther they rode north, the more she felt a sense of calm. It was the strangest feeling, but it felt like she was coming home.

"How much longer?" Faith asked.

"It shouldn't be too much longer now," Hope answered, remembering her grandmother's words about patience.

She smiled sadly. At the end of the week after her grandmother's demise, Hope and her sisters received a letter from their aunt, Lady Belle. Upon learning about her sister's death, their aunt insisted that they come north for at least the remainder of the year to mourn in privacy. It was a lifeline and they had jumped at the chance, though Faith had been less pleased than both Hope and Grace to leave London behind.

Now, dressed in black, they traveled north through the Scottish Highlands. Hope was eager to finish their journey and find solace in the mountains.

"I wonder what it will be like, living with Aunt Belle," Grace said. "Grandmother never let us ask her many questions."

"Because she didn't like her for some reason," Faith said.

It was true. Alice had not liked Belle. Hope and her sisters didn't know much about their great aunt, except that she was exceedingly rich. They had lived for the last seven years in Belle's London home, but whenever Hope inquired about this enigmatic relative, her grandmother refused to share anything about her, except to say that they were sisters and not very close.

"I wonder why," Grace said, mostly to herself as she gazed out the window.

"At least we've spent time with her," Hope said. "It would be terribly awkward to go live with someone we've never laid eyes on before."

Five years prior, Hope had convinced her grandmother to invite Belle to London for Christmas so that they might show their appreciation for her generosity. It had been a tense meeting between the elderly sisters, but Belle had been courteous and kind. After that, she had spent every winter with them, much to Alice's ire.

"I think we've arrived," Grace said, her nose practically pressed against the glass.

All three sisters perked up and looked out their window.

A gate pulled open as their carriage approached Lismore Hall and closed behind them. As the carriage continued, the trees parted to reveal a breathtaking home.

It was like something out of a picture book.

A four-story tower, along with a cap house and several turrets, sprung up behind a twelve-foot-high wall that surrounded the exterior of the building. The walls were divided by pilasters into sections, and each compartment had a niche above, containing statues of saints—or so Hope guessed—as the carriage drove by. Those on the east wall had semi-circular pediments carved with scrolls, each ordained with the national symbol of the thistle.

Though the morning had been clean and bright, a thick mist hung over the grounds as they drew closer to the estate. Lismore seemed as if it were floating on a cloud.

A beaming Belle stood on a wide set of stone stairs, flanked by a slim young woman with frizzy blonde hair and freckles. She appeared serious for such a young lady, and Hope was curious about who she was.

A footman opened the door and helped Hope out, followed by her sisters. They came up the steps to meet Belle.

"My girls! My girls!" she hugged each of them as they reached her. It felt rather silly to be shown such affection, but then Belle always hugged them. "How was your voyage?"

"Long," Grace said as she embraced the elderly woman. "But worth it to be out of London."

"I can imagine," she said, peering at each of them. She had heard of the disastrous scandal. "London becomes dreadful when gossip starts."

Hope doubted Aunt Belle knew anything about living through London gossip. Grandmother always said her sister had been in Scotland for decades. She had married a wealthy man named George Smith, who had died shortly after their marriage. Apparently, she had been so devastated she had retired permanently after his death, apparently content to live in seclusion despite being rumored to have been left a vast fortune. She had once mentioned owning several homes throughout the United Kingdom, a set of apartments in Paris, and a vineyard in Italy, but Hope hadn't been sure if she was telling the truth.

"Let me introduce you to my personal secretary, Miss Rose Ryland," Belle said as she dug her knuckles into Rose's back, prompting her forward. "Go on, Rose."

"Yes, Lady Belle," the woman said, her voice low. She glanced at Hope and her sisters. "It's a pleasure to meet you."

"The pleasure is ours," Hope said. She and her sisters curtsied. "I did not realize Lady Belle needed a secretary."

"Well, I don't think she does," Rose said apprehensively,

giving her employer a pointed expression. "But she insists otherwise."

"I am a very rich woman, Rose, and rich women always need secretaries," Belle said, waving her free hand as if her statement was enough explanation.

"It's very forward-thinking of you to keep a woman as a secretary," Grace said before her cheeks became bright pink. "That's no offense to you, Miss Ryland."

"Oh, no, I quite agree. And it's Rose, please," she said with a smile. "But your aunt found out I had a head for numbers and insisted on hiring me to look after her finances after Mr. Gregory left her services."

"Yes, that was a shame, losing Mr. Gregory to a father-in-law who insisted he go work for his accounting firm." Belle sighed. "But I am blessed to have Rose now. Besides, what could a man do that Rose here could not?" she asked. "I've never conformed to the idea that men are better than women. I've only witnessed the opposite in all my years on this earth."

Hope smiled uneasily. She began to understand her grandmother's distrust of Belle. She was a reformist.

"It's beautiful here," Hope said.

"It is, isn't it?" Belle smirked. "I'm glad you like it, as it will be yours one day."

Hope gawked at her, as did her sisters.

"I beg your pardon?"

"Well, of course it will be. I've no direct descendants. You three are the last of my bloodline. Why shouldn't it go to you? The other properties will be distributed accordingly, but Lismore Hall will be yours, Hope."

Stunned by the revelation, Hope barely registered her sister tactfully changing the subject by talking about the garden.

"The blooms of these roses are massive," Faith said, admiring the garden. "It's completely walled in."

"Yes, it is," Belle said, walking back inside. "Lovely garden. Mr. Fitzpatrick is a master gardener. If you'd like, I'm sure he'd be more than happy to show you around."

"That would be nice, thank you," Faith said following her into the house.

The hall's interior was rather impressive, and though it was a stronghold, Hope had never been in a place that had exuded such warmth and comfort. The tall stone walls were covered with tapestries and paintings depicting Scottish clansmen and women dressed in red and green plaids, set against open landscapes.

Belle led them down the hallway into a room that Hope took to be a receiving parlor, though she wasn't sure if that was the original intent. It had large windows that overlooked the gardens and a massive fireplace as tall as her. In fact, she believed she and her sisters could stand shoulder to shoulder inside and still have room not to touch one another.

"Now, there are three perfectly suited bedrooms in the west wing I have had set up for you," Belle said, going around a large wooden desk to tug on a bell pull. "Hope, you'll be in the green room. It's the farthest room down and oversees a lovely part of the garden. Faith, you'll be in the bird room."

"Bird room?" she said, surprised. "I suppose the décor is responsible for the name?"

"It is, and it's just above the swan pond. Grace, you'll be in the blossom room," Belle said, pointing her ring clad finger at the youngest. "It's smaller than the others, but it was once used as an office for researching botany."

"Fascinating," she said. "Botany is not very far from anatomy."

"Grace," Hope said tentatively.

Grace's interest in anatomy had begun to worry Hope. Their grandmother had been adamant that young ladies shouldn't pursue such vulgar studies. While Hope had often privately balked at her grandmother's stringent ideas, she couldn't deny that Alice had been a smart, well-respected woman who only ever wanted her granddaughters to succeed. If she had been against the idea of such studies for her granddaughter, there must have been good reason for it, and Hope felt honor-bound to maintain the standards they'd been raised to follow. Since her grandmother's passing, the burden to keep her sisters on the straight and narrow now fell on her shoulders.

"Oh, don't quell her interests, dear," Belle said, twisting to face the youngest. "I know my sister didn't approve of your studies, Grace. But I assure you, anything goes at Lismore Hall."

Grace smiled widely, though Hope felt the need to defend her grandmother.

"Grandmother wasn't so rigid," she said as an army of maids entered the room. Hope watched as her sisters were unceremoniously pulled away, each by a pair of maids. "She was quite loving when the moment called for it."

"There's no need to explain, my dear," Belle said. "I knew my sister far longer than you did."

"Yes, but—"

"Go now and freshen up," Belle said as two maids came up on either side of Hope. "We'll talk more at dinner. And girls, I beg that you wear something other than these mourning clothes."

All three sisters stopped, stunned by the request.

"But we're in mourning," Hope said.

"For how long?"

"Propriety states three months," Grace began, reciting Hope's own words, only to be interrupted by Belle.

"Perhaps that made sense when you were in London. But there is no society here and I insist that you three try to cheer yourselves up. What better than to dress in pretty colors? Yes?"

"Um, yes?" Grace said, looking back and forth between her sisters.

Faith appeared somewhat confused, and while Hope didn't want to leave the conversation, she was already being dragged away by a pair of determined maids. They both had the same sleek, reddish-brown hair, and Hope had a distinct impression that they were sisters.

"Excuse me, but where are we going?" she asked as they led her to a large wooden staircase off the side of the main hallway.

"Lady Belle insisted that you each be bathed as soon as you arrived," one of the maids said, her brogue heavy. "You're to be settled and rested before tonight's dinner."

"Are we having guests?"

"Oh, no. Well, mayhap MacKinnon will come. Though after their last row, who knows?"

"Who? And what row?"

"Mr. Graham MacKinnon," the other maid said, smiling. "A fine man, but he and Lady Belle had a yelling match you wouldn't believe the other day."

"Oh goodness," Hope said, her brow puckering with worry. "You're awfully quick to share your lady's private business."

"Ack, 'tis only MacKinnon, and as you're part of this household now, I thought you should know. Especially considering, well ..."

The maid's words fell off as her gaze fell to her colleague. Neither seemed willing to elaborate as they continued down the hall.

"Considering what?" Hope asked.

Both maids remained silent, seeming to have just decided they had already said too much. Instead of speaking any further, one opened the door and led Hope into a beautiful room while the other added more wood to the fire.

Hope had a mind to continue her questioning, but the inquiring words were stolen right from her mouth as her eyes drank in the bedchamber. Her mouth fell open.

The room was vast and bright with papered walls depicting a delicate pink rose motif against a green background that encircled the room as if she were in her own secret garden. White crown molding topped the walls, and a pale blue sky with white clouds had been painted on the ceiling. Heavy dark furniture paired nicely with the pale green curtains and matching bed linens laid on a massive four-post bed square in the middle of the room. To the right of the bed was a set of windows opened onto a stone balcony. An abundant white climbing rose had crawled up the balcony, covered in dozens of blooms that grew all around the window.

It was gorgeous. So much so that Hope was taken aback.

"Oh my," she said, going to the window.

A garden, more beautiful than any she had ever seen, expanded out from beneath the shallow balcony. Her eyes went immediately to the white roses wrapped around the stonework. The tops of several blooming fruit trees peeped out from behind the balustrades. Hope had nearly made it to the open French doors when a maid crossed into her path, blocking her way.

"Ack, there's no time for that," the maid said, pointing to a large brass tub in front of the fireplace. Steam curled from the hot water that had been poured into it. "Bath first."

"May I ask your name?" Hope asked as the pushy woman turned her about and began undressing her.

"Una," she said as Hope's dress fell to the floor. Una nodded to the other maid. "This is my sister, Rebecca. Come now."

Hope was unceremoniously washed as her travel dress was taken away, and her other clothing was pulled from her valise to be aired out and then put away. She had wanted to dress immediately, but Una insisted she rest.

"But I'm not tired," she protested, far too interested in exploring her new home to sleep.

"Och, all ladies would be tired after journeying here, considering that last push from Cumbria," Una said. "Now rest, and we'll be up to ready you for dinner in two hours."

At the click of the door, Hope was left alone.

"Umph," she said as she wrapped a green silk robe around her night rail. Going to the window where the white roses hung, she stepped out on the balcony and glanced over the garden.

It was a lovely landscape. A prettier picture she had never seen. Her eyes drifted over the greenery below. The fog seemed unable to touch the ground here, seeing as the world beyond the stone wall was still draped in a thick mist.

To her left, a narrow set of stone steps was hidden behind the large rose bush that grew up to her window. She guessed it must be an ancient plant, considering how tall it had grown and how thick the branches were. She peered down to the grounds below. She wondered if it wasn't the best idea to go down dressed in only her robe and night clothes, but then it was a walled garden. It was meant to be enjoyed by the residents. Besides, the only people who would see her would be the servants and perhaps Lady Belle or her sisters.

She cautiously climbed down the staircase and came around the base of the rose bush. A swath of lavender, heather, and other tall grasses had been planted together, and Hope inhaled deeply, taking in the sweet scent. Tiny white flowers spread out from beneath the heather, and she fingered the tall, ornamental grasses as she strolled deeper into the garden.

A large pond fed by a stream carved beneath the wall was covered in lily pads and beautiful white and pink blooms. It was enchanting and yet, she had the oddest impression that she wasn't supposed to be here.

Suddenly, movement against the stone wall caught her attention. The overhanging ivy that covered the wall seemed to shake and what appeared to be a secret door, previously hidden behind the vines, was pushed open. In the next instant, a man of considerable size came into the garden.

Frightened, Hope leaped behind a tall, green topiary cut into a fleur-de-lis shape. She waited to see if the man would pass without seeing her, but for a long while, she could hear no movement at all. Confused, she peered over the branch and saw him, arms folded, staring up into the apple tree. He seemed deep in contemplation, and her fear that he was an intruder subsided. It was obvious that he knew this garden well.

His long arm reached over his head and plucked a nearly spent bud. Bringing it down, he twirled it between his fingers. Hope had never been one for spying, but this man was certainly interesting. He was tall and square-jawed, with auburn hair a touch longer than was fashionable. His tweed jacket and matching pants reminded Hope of the latest hunting styles that were quite popular with the aristocracy.

This man, whoever he was, was handsome in a rather brutal way, but the weight he seemed to hold on his shoulders spoke loudest to Hope. He seemed burdened, and she was pondering her urge to touch his shoulders and soothe his contemplativeness when the branch she was leaning on snapped.

Hope stumbled forward and elevated her gaze. The man was surprised, but also appeared rather confused as he tilted his head and came forward. Hope clasped her robe at the neck and took a step back.

"Stay away," she said, prompting him to stop. "Come no further."

Recognition flooded his face as he heard her speak. He looked her up and down with what seemed like disgust. She supposed he was one of those Scots who loathed the English. Still, she held her head up high.

"Ah," he began, sounding unimpressed. "One of Lady Belle's nieces, I presume."

"I am," she said, lifting her chin. "Miss Hope Sharpe. And you are?"

He didn't answer immediately, and a tingly sensation swept over her body. The hairs on the back of her neck stood up as his eyes swept over her once more. He took another step forward, and she took another step back.

"You're Miss Hope Sharpe?" he asked suspiciously.

"Yes, I am," she said, her tone slightly higher than usual. "And *you* are?"

But he still didn't answer. He observed her with a mixture of contempt and something else she couldn't identify. His face darkened and his brow furrowed, giving him a positively frightful appearance, as if he were some wronged man on his way to the gallows.

"You would be." One of his large hands pushed back the hair that fell over his forehead. "I suspect Lady Belle made a damn deal with the devil at some point in her life."

"I beg your pardon?" Hope asked, confused.

He glowered at her.

"Did she send you out here? Dressed in your night garments?" he asked, before tilting his head back. "I won't be tempted, Belle!" he shouted, as if Belle was hiding somewhere. "You're a bloody devil!"

Goodness. This man was obviously unhinged. She backed up a couple more feet.

"I don't know who you are or why you are in Belle's garden, sir, but I suggest you leave, as trespassing is a punishable crime."

"Trespassing?" He laughed bitterly, his accent doing strange things to her. The way his R's nearly rolled, but then didn't. Well, it made her shiver. "You think I'm trespassing?"

"I know you are," she said, squaring her shoulders. "Belle lives alone."

"Aye, that she does."

"Then you *are* trespassing. I insist you leave this place at once."

"Is that so?" he said, slowly coming toward her. Hope tried to back up again, but she bumped into a hedgerow of boxwood. He smelled like clover and honey. "And who is going to make me?"

Shaking with fear—and, heaven help her, some sort of arousal—Hope lifted her foot and kicked out, right between his legs.

"Ack!" he yelled, stumbling back long enough for her to whirl and race back toward the rose bush that camouflaged her secret staircase.

What a frightful brute. Hope hurried into her room, closing the opened doors behind her, and locking them with purpose. With any luck, he would realize his folly and leave the garden immediately, because she was going to immediately inform the staff that there had been a trespasser on the property.

Chapter Four

GRAHAM CURSED AS Hope scurried off and climbed the hidden staircase to a room that would have been his own while he was growing up had his father not lost Lismore Hall. He had become familiar with the house over the past ten years, since striking up a friendship with Lady Belle, but this was too much. To put this Trojan horse of a woman in that room was malicious as far as Graham was concerned.

He was already in a foul mood, given that he had been delegated by his uncle to inform Lady Belle that the McTavish clan would hold a ball in her nieces' honor a week from Friday as a welcome to the Highlands. Graham had never heard something so preposterous. It seemed his uncle had forgotten their lifelong hatred of the English. But when he'd said as much, his uncle had only smiled, apparently enjoying his discomfort. He wondered if his uncle and Lady Belle were conspiring against him.

Shaking out his bruised toes, he speculated what Miss Hope Sharpe would do when she saw him at the dinner table in an hour or so. She might scream, or try to kick him again. He wished she would. Anything to distract him from the unprecedented attraction he felt for her.

It had been immediate, like being on a horse that spooked. His heart dropped into his stomach the moment he laid eyes on her. She was fresh-faced and beautiful, with pale skin, dark eyes, and a set of lips the color of apple blossoms before they bloomed. With her curly, coffee colored hair tied back by only a single ribbon and draped over her shoulder, she resembled some medieval maiden.

Her soft, lush frame had been detailed by the cinching of her pale green robe, and for a moment, he had been stunned at the sight of her, looking like some fairy princess standing in her private kingdom. Only it wasn't her kingdom.

It was his.

That Lady Belle had chosen her made him particularly hostile. She was perfection, the picture of his every desire, and he had no doubt that Lady Belle had made a deal with the devil himself to lure Graham to do her bidding. Well, he wouldn't do it. He was his own man, and no amount of female meddling would control his fate.

He stalked across the garden as a voice within him reasoned that perhaps all was not lost. Why *shouldn't* he marry an attractive woman to gain his home back? It would hardly be a sacrifice to lay with a woman like Hope for the rest of his life. And if she were even-tempered and kind-natured, too, well, he just might be able to count himself a lucky man if he were her husband.

But it was the principle of the matter. Lady Belle had long implied that Lismore Hall would return to him one day, and while she had never outright promised it to him, it now felt as though she had snatched it away from him all the same. She was meddling in his life's affairs; it was a habit she had formed the very day he was born.

And as far as marriage went, Graham hadn't ever given the matter much thought. He always assumed it would happen after he gained ownership of Lismore Hall, and now that seemed highly unlikely. Hope Sharpe seemed prepared to kick him out, literally. He wondered if Belle had explained to Hope who he was and if she knew her aunt's plans.

Striding into the castle without preamble, Graham ran into Rose, who gave him a curious look. Why Lady Belle had hired this mouse of a woman to be her personal secretary, he did not know. Rose barely spoke above a whisper, and her intense stare made people uncomfortable. She would scurry away whenever she found herself in the presence of Graham and his cousins, particularly Jared McTavish.

She was an odd woman, to say the least.

"Mr. MacKinnon," Rose said softly, nodding to acknowledge his presence.

"Where is she?" he asked, ignoring pleasantries.

"The parlor," she said so quietly he had to strain to hear her. "But beware. She's in no mood for your antics today."

"My antics?"

"Yes. Her nieces have just arrived, and she's in high spirits. I doubt very much she wants you to spoil her jovial mood."

"So, you don't wish me to bother your mistress?"

"No, I do not."

"What a little traitor you are," he said, glowering at her. "You're a right loyalist when it comes to that Englishwoman."

"She pays me far too much money not to be," Rose said quietly as she continued walking, heading to do Lady Belle's bidding no doubt.

Graham smirked, unable to argue with that, even though he knew it wasn't the only reason Rose was loyal to Belle. In truth, everyone for twenty miles liked the unorthodox old woman. Any person who could disparage the King of England earned their trust, and while her popularity irked Graham, he couldn't deny it. If she didn't hold the ownership of Lismore Hall over his head, he wouldn't be able to find a single fault with her.

Stalking into the parlor, he found Lady Belle seated behind a large desk with her loyal butler, Andrews, standing beside her.

"Ah, MacKinnon," she said, scanning a paper in her hand. "You're punctual this evening."

"Did you send her out into the garden dressed in nothing but a night rail?"

"Send who into the garden?"

"Your niece, Hope Sharpe."

Genuine surprise lit the old woman's face as she handed the

paper back to Andrews.

"That'll be just fine," she said to the butler, who bowed and then left. She motioned to Graham. "Now tell me, you met Hope already?"

"You mean you didn't plant her in the garden for me to 'accidentally' find? Knowing full well I always enter the grounds from the east door."

"I didn't know you enter from the east door."

He rolled his eyes.

"The hives are outside the east door. Of course I always come in from there."

"Am I supposed to remember every detail concerning your honey enterprise?"

"It's on your own grounds. How can you not know about it?"

Belle waved her hand dismissively.

"I've far too many concerns to remember them all. And as radical as I may have been in my life, sending my innocent niece out in her undergarments to entice a foul-mouthed highlander is not on my to-do list." She paused for a moment; her mouth pursed together. "Did she seem impressed by you?"

"I knew it," he said, pointing at her. "You put her in the green room to agitate me."

"I did no such thing," she denied. "Aside from my room, the green room is the largest, and with the early summer flowers in bloom I thought she'd appreciate it the most. Besides, she is the oldest and deserves more space."

"You're lying."

"I've no intention of humoring your foul mood today, MacKinnon," she said, rising. "Why even come if you're going to be all brooding and miserable?"

"I came because you and my uncle conspire against me," he said, taking a seat as he dropped his body loudly into a leather club chair. He frowned, looking down at the seat. "This is uncomfortable. Where did it come from?"

"London, and it's not uncomfortable, it's fashionable," she

said, coming around slowly with her cane to face him. "What did your uncle wish to send you for?"

"He'll be holding a welcome ball for your nieces by week's end," he said suspiciously. "No doubt an attempt to undermine me and that unsuspecting lass of yours."

"Your uncle is merely being neighborly," she said. "Tell me, did you introduce yourself to Hope?"

"Nay."

"Well, then you'll have an opportunity to do so at dinner," Lady Belle said. "But really, MacKinnon, you should know I've never been mistaken in matters of the heart. I genuinely believe you and Hope would do very well together."

Graham snorted. Even if they did get along, it wouldn't matter. He wouldn't marry a woman simply to gain property, especially when it should already belong to him.

"It wouldn't be fair to her," he said. "Even if we did suit, Lismore Hall would always be between us. You've tainted it."

"So, I should have kept my mouth shut and hoped that you two would just naturally come together?"

He shrugged.

"Perhaps."

"Well, I haven't the time to wait around hoping for you and her to come together on your own. Especially since you seem so determined to not start a relationship with anyone until you possess this house. Aren't you lonely?"

"I have company enough," he said, knowing he was barely telling the truth.

Graham had cavorted with a number of women over the years, but they had been entirely casual affairs, focused on the physical rather than the emotional. He had never considered any of them a potential life partner—he had barely even considered any of them to be friends.

"You have bedmates," she corrected him.

"Same thing. And why don't you have the time?"

Lady Belle's face became shuttered and she pivoted around so that she no longer faced him.

"No one does, MacKinnon. Tomorrow is never promised. Now, if you'll excuse me, I have some correspondence to finish before attending dinner."

She left the room, leaving Graham to wonder what she had meant. She acted as though she knew for a certainty that time was running out. Possibly at her age, it could be. But as far as he could tell, she was perfectly healthy and only wanted to use him to make a match for one of her spinster nieces.

Although, spinster was hardly the word Graham would use to describe Hope. It was anybody's guess why the dark-haired beauty hadn't found a husband yet. She certainly stirred his curiosity, which irked him even more. Why was she unattached?

He stood up and walked toward the drink cabinet in the back of the room. Perhaps Hope was sharp-tongued or lacking in some inane talent that gentlemen of first society focused on. Or perhaps the Englishmen she had been accustomed to simply had terrible taste.

After withdrawing a bottle of scotch from the cabinet, he poured himself a draught and sank onto the settee positioned before the fireplace. Though the summer season had just begun, a fire blazed as Lismore Hall was often cold.

Taking a sip of the peaty scotch, Graham couldn't shed his curiosity when it came to Hope. A beauty like she should have been plucked from the marriage market years ago. Why was she still unattached? It was something he planned on learning, along with all the stipulations of Lady Belle's will.

Just then, footfalls and feminine chatter echoed throughout the outside hallway. Graham turned toward the doorway as two ladies entered, smiling, and talking to one another before they spotted Graham. They halted in their tracks.

A stilted silence followed before Graham raised his glass and nodded.

"Hello," he said, guessing these must be Hope's sisters.

They had the same dark hair as Hope, though their features

varied. One had blue eyes and wore a violet day gown with white stripes. She had a straight nose and did not smile at him. The other wore a rose-colored tiered dress. She had amber colored eyes, with a more defined brow than her sisters and a slimmer mouth. She gave him a cheerful grin.

They were both quite attractive, though Graham believed Hope was the most pleasing to look at. Her dark hair matched her eyes in a way that made her skin glow with a beauty that neither of her sisters could match. Still, he couldn't understand why none of them had been married.

The one in rose regarded Graham with a smile while the one in violet pinned him with a suspicious stare.

"Hello," the smiling one said, coming forward. "Are you a guest of Belle's?"

"A permanent pest, more like it," he said, standing. "You must be two of the three Sharpe sisters."

"We are," she said. "I'm Grace Sharpe. This is my sister, Faith."

The suspicious one nodded but made no attempt to come closer.

"How do you do?"

"Fine," he said, winking at the quiet one. Might as well have some fun with them before Hope arrived. "And you?"

Faith frowned while humor appeared in Grace's eyes as she looked back at her sister. Graham got the impression that Faith didn't appreciate teasing and that Grace was rather entertained by her discomfort.

"We're very well, thank you," Grace said, beaming at him. "Have you seen our Belle? We were told it was nearly time for supper."

"She's gone to finish some correspondence, but I'm sure she'll be done soon enough," he said, nodding toward the door. "The dining hall in just to the left, across the hallway. Her dining etiquette is quite casual, so if you wanted to meet her there, you should feel free to go ahead. She will not be offended."

"Are you attending dinner, Mr... ?" Grace let her last word linger so that he might introduce himself.

"Graham MacKinnon. And I'm still debating if I should subject Lady Belle and the rest of you to my presence."

Grace angled her chin, frowning. Just then, another set of footsteps sounded from behind them. Before Grace could inquire as to what he meant, Hope entered the parlor, dressed in a pale pink evening gown. Graham noticed her slight breathlessness, as if she had rushed there.

Upon seeing him, she stopped short, her dark eyes focusing on him and demanded, "What are you doing here?"

"Hope!" Grace chided, glancing between her and Graham. "Have you met Mr. MacKinnon?"

Graham watched to see if his name sparked any sort of recognition in her, but she showed no signs of being familiar with it.

"Who?"

"This is Mr. Graham MacKinnon. He's a friend of Belle's."

"A friend?"

"I wonder what sort," Faith said beneath her breath.

"I must apologize, Mr. MacKinnon," Grace began, glancing between Hope and Faith. "My sisters do not seem to be themselves."

"It's no trouble to me," he said, though his eyes remained on Hope.

It seemed to Graham that none of the Sharpes knew who he was. Grace glanced between him and Hope for a moment, as if waiting for something. Finally, when no one acted, she spoke again.

"Well, I suppose we should find that dining room," Grace said. "Mr. MacKinnon, have you decided whether you will be joining us for dinner?"

"I think I might," he said, having made up his mind to at least garner some information from the women. "Follow me."

He held out his arm. As they were all the same social rank,

the honor of his escort fell to the eldest. Hope hesitated for a moment, as if disbelieving that she was to be escorted by a man she had assumed was an intruder. Still, she gingerly placed her hand in the crook of his elbow.

The warmth of her small hand sent a warning throughout Graham's body. An image flashed in his mind of that same small hand moving over him, exploring, and learning the anatomy of his body. He cleared his throat and struggled to banish the image from his mind as they walked.

"So, you are not an intruder?" Hope asked softly enough that her sisters couldn't hear.

"No," he answered gruffly. "Far from it."

"Then who are you to my aunt?"

"A friend," he said, giving her a side glance. "For nigh ten years now."

"Ten years?" Hope repeated. "She's never mentioned you before."

Graham's brow lifted. Surely Lady Belle had informed her niece about him if she wanted them to marry.

"Hasn't she?" he replied.

"No," she answered. "Why would you believe otherwise? Should I know who you are?"

"I'd have presumed Lady Belle would have told you who I was. Considering…"

"Considering what?" she asked as they reached the dining room.

For a fleeting moment, he nearly told her about her aunt's heinous plan, but when they entered the room, they saw the old woman standing before them, leaning on her cane.

"Considering that it is rather uncouth to have a brutish Scotsman roaming about the castle," Belle interjected.

Hope's hand fell away from his arm, and he refused to acknowledge his regret at her release. The old woman winked at him in an infuriatingly knowing way, which only made him scowl.

He would not be managed.

"Considering your aunt—"

"—is more than ready to start supper," Lady Belle said, cutting him off as Faith and Grace came around from behind him. "Come. Hope, you'll sit to my right, and Grace can sit next to you. Graham? On my left, as with you, Faith."

All three sisters went toward their seats as Belle lifted her cane and pointed to the portrait of Graham's great-grandfather that hung on the wall behind them. "Do you see that painting, my dears?"

The ladies swung around while Graham stared at Belle. So, she hadn't told Hope anything about her matchmaking idea. Curious that she seemed to intend to hide it from her niece after being so frank with him.

"Is that who lived here before you, Aunt Belle?" Hope asked, her eyes scanning the painting.

"It is. That there is Old Fergus MacKinnon," Belle said as the girls all looked back at Graham. "Great-grandfather of our friend here."

"This castle belonged to your family, Mr. MacKinnon?" Hope asked, her eyes widening.

"I had no idea," Faith said.

"Neither did I," added Grace.

Graham opened his mouth to explain, but something stopped him. Whether it was shame at the story or the pointed glance Belle was giving him, he did not know, but a part of him wished to stay quiet, if only for a moment to see what Belle had in store for them.

He closed his mouth and shook his head.

"No," he said. "Lismore Hall never belonged to me."

"How did you come to live here then, Aunt Belle?" Faith asked as a footman came forward to pull out her seat.

Several other footmen came forward to seat the rest of the party. Faith and Grace observed Belle while Hope kept her eyes on Graham.

"Well, let's just say I had a bout of good luck the day Lismore Hall came into my possession. But that was a lifetime ago," Lady Belle said as the ladies reached for their napkins, only to have them taken from their hands as the footmen opened them with a flare and placed them on their laps. Graham noted the surprise on the sisters' faces at being treated so delicately by the staff and he wondered what their life had been like in London. "Long before any of you were born."

"A lucky day indeed," Graham said sarcastically.

"Mr. MacKinnon said that you and he have been friends for ten years," Hope said as a footman came up and ladled potato leek soup into her dish. "Is that true?"

"It is," Belle said. "Although we weren't great friends in the beginning."

Graham watched her as she spoke, wondering how far she would go with her story.

"You weren't?" Hope asked, peering at Graham.

"No. As you can imagine, Mr. MacKinnon was quite annoyed with me."

"Whatever for?" Faith asked.

Belle leaned toward her great-niece.

"Why do you suppose, dear?"

None of the sisters seemed able to come up with a reason why Graham would be upset, prompting him to speak.

"Because she didn't come into ownership of Lismore by buying it from my family," he said slowly. "She won it."

"Won it?" Hope repeated. The small line between her brows appeared again and Graham had the sudden urge to press his thumb against it to soothe it away. "How?"

Graham was still for a moment, surprised that he was uncomfortable with Hope's concerned tone. Clearing his throat, he leaned back in his chair and waited for Lady Belle to continue. She only nodded at him, prompting him to continue.

"In a card game. If rumors are to be believed, they played at this very table." Graham's hand moved across the well-worn wood. The table was nearly two-hundred years old and seemed more fitting for a Viking banquet hall than in the home of a member of the modern English aristocracy. It didn't matter that his family had eaten off this oak table for two centuries. It belonged to her now.

Graham pressed his thumbnail into the corner of the table, unconsciously trying to leave a mark. The Paris Porcelain vases from the other day had been replaced with crystal vases, now filled with white roses. "Isn't that right, Lady Belle?"

"It is," she said.

"Who were *they* exactly?" Hope asked.

"Well, who was it now? Your aunt here, obviously. My father and King William IV, before he was king, and his brother."

Each Sharpe sister froze with their mouths open. An uncomfortable heat began to crawl up Graham's neck as their watchful gazes glided back and forth between him and Lady Belle.

"King William?" Faith said incredulously.

"Yes. I suppose your grandmother never told you. Hardly surprising, actually, as she wasn't particularly proud of it," Belle said, and for the first time since they had met, Graham saw a flicker of discontent pass over her eyes before disappearing. When she spoke again, however, she held her head up. Graham wondered if she wasn't as sure of herself in front of these three innocent misses. "But the king and I were very much in love."

"In love?" Hope repeated, her hands coming up to either side of her head, as if she were trying to comprehend this baffling piece of information. "But how?"

"My dear, if I have to explain how, I don't—"

"No, no," Hope said, shaking her head. A bright blush bloomed on her cheeks. "I don't mean how were you in love. I mean, how did you ever come to know the king?"

Lady Belle took a deep breath.

"Your grandmother and I grew up in London. We lived in a very fine house and were well-received by the most prominent families. Alice and I were all set to make prosperous matches, but

I couldn't stand the idea of marriage. I was an arrogant child and assumed I knew everything. Refusing to be cowed into a life I had no desire to be a part of, I ran away."

Graham had heard about her escapades before, but the reaction of the sisters was interesting to watch. Grace's forehead was crinkled as a hand covered her mouth, while Faith appeared much too interested as she leaned closer, eager to hear more. Hope, on the other hand, remained perfectly still, her eyes locked on the old woman.

"At the tender age of sixteen, I decided to become an actress. My parents disowned me, and Alice never forgave me for leaving, but I would not be shamed. I was wildly successful on the stage, if I do say so myself. After spending nearly five years on Drury Lane, one evening during a particularly moving performance of *Pizzaro*, I was spotted by none other than the Duke of Clarence, which was his title at the time." Lady Belle smiled, seemingly lost in the long-ago memory. "He found me afterwards and claimed to have fallen instantly in love with me. I told him he was a fool and shooed him away."

"You told the king he was a fool?" Grace asked, shocked.

"Well, as I said, he wasn't the king yet—merely a duke. And yes, I did, and I continued to tell him so for months. Of course, he eventually wore me down. He asked me to quit the stage and while I didn't want to necessarily, I knew the reality of my situation. Old actresses never ended up with much. So, I rented my own private apartments and became his mistress."

The silence that followed was piercing.

"But … but Grandmother said you had a rich husband who died early in your marriage," Grace said.

"I've never been married a day in my life," Belle said, her nose in the air.

"A mistress …" Hope repeated.

"So that's why Lord Bartley always asked if the apple fell farm from the tree!" Faith said, her small fist hitting the table. Seeing the surprise on everyone's face for her outburst, she smiled apologetically and uncurled her fingers, her nails tapping against the wood. "It never made any sense to me."

"He asked you that?" Grace asked.

"More than once." Faith said, the corners of her mouth pulled up in a sneer. "I never understood why. Only now it makes sense."

"So, you didn't buy this house with money left to you by your husband?" Hope asked.

"No, I did not," Belle said. "You see, Willie and I travelled quite extensively together. Thirty years ago, we decided to come to Scotland to visit with his friend, Mr. James MacKinnon. It was a grand time, filled with dancing and merrymaking and a slew of other things that young ladies need not know about. On the last night of our visit, we decided to play a game of whist."

Familiar heat crawled over Graham's skin. He hated this part of the story.

"Willie and his brother were very poor players, but then, Mr. MacKinnon was rather good. We played back and forth for several hours. I put up as collateral all of my jewelry, a stable of royal horses, and even a vineyard in Italy that Willie had bought me as a gift. He wasn't very pleased about that, but he dared not stop me." She bobbed her head at Graham. "Mr. MacKinnon was eager to win that vineyard. So, he put up Lismore Hall. We laid our cards down and I won."

"And your father lost," Hope said quietly as she turned to face Graham.

Graham remained still as he listened. Hope's genuine reaction unnerved him, and while he told himself he didn't need her sympathies, he felt rather grateful for them.

"Did you remove the MacKinnons?" Faith asked.

"Heavens no," Lady Belle said. "I clean forgot about my winnings until a year or so later, when I received the deed by post. His solicitor had found the deed, which had been signed over to me, while going through Mr. MacKinnon's papers after his death. You see, darlings, the very night of the card game, our friend Graham here was born. Unfortunately, his mother died in childbirth and his father, so ashamed at having lost the only thing left to his family, drank himself to death only months afterward."

"Oh, goodness no," Hope said, her hands flying over her mouth.

Graham didn't appreciate the pity he heard in her voice. All three sisters were observing him with various amounts of commiseration, and he hated it. He had long made peace with the fact that his father hadn't been strong enough to hold himself accountable, but Graham wouldn't be subjected to their pity.

"That's enough, Lady Belle," he said, his tone rougher than he would have liked. "They don't want to be bored to death about histories long since passed."

"But you became friends?" Faith asked, swiveling her head between her aunt and Graham. "So, there is a happy ending, isn't there?"

"Well, that depends on when you believe the story ends," Belle said. "But Mr. MacKinnon is right. It's been a rather boring friendship since he came back to Scotland ten years ago."

"Where did you go?" Grace asked. "Or were you not raised in the area after the deaths of your parents?"

"My uncle—my mother's brother—took me in, and I was raised not at all far from here. But I never had reason to return when I was a child, and once I was grown, school took me away and then business," he said. "I returned ten years ago."

"Where do you live now?" Faith asked.

"When he's not in Glasgow to see to his business affairs, Mr. MacKinnon occupies the estate's old hunting lodge, some miles north of here," Belle said just as Hope stood up unexpectedly.

"If you'll excuse me," Hope said, obviously distracted as she left the room in a hurry.

Concern tugged at Graham's chest as she left. He thought he had seen her wipe at her cheek. He faced Belle, who only shrugged, and then back to the others who were giving each other a knowing look.

"What is it?" he asked them. "What's wrong with her?"

An unspoken conversation seemed to transpire between the sisters. Grace nodded and Faith twisted to face Graham.

"Mr. Pennington dropped Hope a little under a month ago," Faith said, uttering the man's name with disgust. "I believe she's just realized why it was so easy for him to do so."

"But what could my father's story have to do with her courtship troubles?"

"Nothing," Grace assured him. "But Mr. Pennington was very concerned with what was proper. He must have known something about our…" she shot Belle an apologetic look, "…colorful family history," she continued, "which would explain why he stalled so much when it came to making Hope a proper offer. And then I suppose the latest scandal was the final straw that made him wash his hands of her for good."

"Men," Belle huffed, clicking her tongue against her teeth. "Fools, the lot of them."

Graham ignored her and continued his questioning.

"What scandal? Did Miss Sharpe do something?"

"No, it wasn't Hope," Grace said quickly.

"Grace," Faith warned.

Some secret was being kept from Graham and though he hardly wanted to be involved with these women, he evidently didn't have much of a choice.

"What happened?" he asked with authority.

Grace and Faith faced one another. Grace swallowed hard and shook her head while Faith rolled her eyes and sighed heavily.

"One of us was caught in a rather compromised position at a ball in London, over a month ago," Faith said.

"But because we all look quite similar from behind, no one could identify which one of us it was," Grace added.

"And your Mr. Pennington believed it was Hope?" Graham asked.

"He's hardly *my* Mr. Pennington," Faith said with a scoff,

wrinkling her nose. "I wouldn't take him as a gift. And no, Hope told him it wasn't her. But he wished to take her away. He proposed to marry her and leave the two of us behind to bear the consequences of our supposed shame without her. She refused."

Graham stared at the two before glancing at Belle, whose brows lifted with delight.

"Blood of my blood!" Belle said joyously. "I had heard there was some sort of scandal, but I didn't know to what extent. No wonder you were all so eager to come north."

"So?" Graham said. "Which one was it?"

Both sisters stared at him.

"We won't tell," they said in unison.

"We decided that since we'd all be considered in disgrace regardless, we shouldn't give the gossips the satisfaction of knowing who it was," Grace added.

Graham was dumbfounded when Belle yelped with laughter.

"What a fine set of sisters, indeed!" she said happily. "Oh, you truly are my kin. You know your grandmother and I had a very similar pact years ago, before my acting days."

As Belle went into a story about her youth, Graham observed the doorway Hope had exited. He was under no obligation to go after her, and he certainly wasn't interested in involving himself any more than he already was, but where the other Sharpe sisters appeared content to leave Hope alone, he couldn't quite accept it. She'd seemed decidedly upset—surely someone should check on her.

Pushing his chair back and standing up, he mumbled his excuses and left the dining room. Searching up and down the hallway, he noted the closest doors she could have escaped through would have been either the parlor door or the front door. When he found the parlor empty, he exited the castle.

Far to the left, on a stone bench beneath a lilac tree, sat a slump-shouldered Hope. She seemed unaware of his approach at first. Her head only swiveled toward him when she heard a twig snap beneath his foot.

"Oh, Mr. MacKinnon," she said, wiping her tear-streaked cheek. Her eyes were red. "I'm so sorry."

"For what?" he asked as he came to a stop before her.

They were only a few feet apart.

"For having to see me like this," she said, head bowed as if she were ashamed. "I must look a fright."

"You look fine," he said, ignoring the uncomfortable tightness in his chest. There was something about seeing women cry that unnerved him. He shifted his weight from one foot to the other. "Are you well?"

"I am," she said, appearing to force a smile. "It's just that, I had been rather confused about something that was said to me in London, and Belle's story filled in a blank spot." A hand came up to her forehead and pressed her index and middle fingers against the small wrinkle in between her brows. "I'm sorry that your home was gambled away."

Graham hadn't ever believed anyone who said they were sorry for his misfortune. Until now.

"It's not your fault," he said.

"But I am appalled by it. Belle shouldn't have taken this place away from you. Not when you'd been orphaned already."

"It was my father's property. He had every right to do what he did."

"It wasn't just his though. It was the family's home," she said. "He did not have a right to gamble away that."

Graham stared at her, hesitant. She had put into words the very thought that plagued him during his most volatile moods. It moved him that she recognized the unfairness of it all.

For whatever reason, the bitterness he had often tasted when he thought of Lismore Hall diminished as the silence stretched between them.

"Thank you for saying that," he said, ashamed for being so brash toward her earlier in the garden. "And I don't know what was said to you in London that would make you cry, but I know who ever said it is a damned fool."

She stared at him as another small, sad smile appeared on her face.

"That's kind of you to say—"

"No," he said, taking a step toward her. "You don't understand me. Whoever would make someone like you cry deserves far more pain than they could survive."

Although Graham had decided not to like her before even meeting her, whether out of spite or principle, he now found himself wanting to comfort her. She sniffled again as her gaze fell, apparently unsure how to respond, and before he could stop himself, Graham lifted his hand and touched her cheek. She froze, as did he. Surprisingly, neither one pulled away.

"Mr. MacKinnon," she breathed after a moment, her eyes lifting to meet his. "What are you doing?"

Damned if he knew, except that he was overcome with a desire to banish whatever bad memories haunted her that made her cry. A shiver went through her body and he wondered if she was cold. For the barest of moments, he speculated what it might be like to pull her into his arms—and perhaps even warm her lips with the press of his own. What might she taste like if he were to lean down and kiss her? And would it be effective for making her forget all the things that plagued her?

He dropped his hand immediately. Clearing his throat, he turned, scraping his thumb nail against the pads of his fingerprints, as if to rid himself of any evidence of touching her.

What was wrong with him? And why was he so suddenly bewitched by a woman he had already decided had no business in his life? Even if she wasn't aware of her aunt's plot, he needed to remember and repeat it as often as possible.

Hope was not for him.

"My apologies," he said roughly, hating his own voice. "I should go."

"Oh," she said as he turned his back on her. "Good-bye?"

But he didn't answer her. Instead, he focused on long, deep breaths as he made his way to the stables, repeating his newfound mantra.

Hope is not for me. Hope is not for me.

Chapter Five

HOPE HAD GONE straight to her room after Graham left, carefully avoiding the dining hall as she made her way through the stronghold. She wasn't sure what to make of the ill-tempered highlander, but one thing was for certain.

She had never been more attracted to a person in her entire life.

It was embarrassing, really, to be bombarded with thoughts and feelings that she had never experienced before. Her mouth had gone dry the moment he touched her and all she could think about walking up to her room was how much she'd wanted his hand to move down around her neck before pulling her into a searing, soul-shattering kiss.

Goodness. What would Jacob think of her if he could see her now? He'd be appalled by what Mr. MacKinnon had said and done—and likely disgusted with her for being so aroused by it. Where gentlemen like Jacob had always been respectful and courteous, Graham appeared annoyed and somewhat charged, as if he had never learned or never cared about the propriety of social normality. It shouldn't have made her blood heat—but it did.

He was big, but not only in stature. His presence, his personality seemed to draw the attention of everyone around him and Hope had certainly been caught up in his magnetism. And there was no denying the man was handsome, with his dark, reddish hair that had a slight wave to it. The squareness of his chin was terribly appealing and Hope hadn't been able to take her eyes off his mouth when he spoke.

Hope had always wanted a more physical relationship with Jacob, albeit, a proper one. A few dozen kisses would have been plenty, but he had always told her that such behavior was unattractive. There *had* been a kiss once—a kiss she had initiated and that Jacob had allowed for a moment before pushing her away. It had been, up until tonight, the most stirring event of her life. But it paled in comparison to what she and Graham had just shared. Even though Graham had pulled his hand away quickly, there was something different about his touch. It had scorched her, electrified her and she was rather ashamed at how much more she'd wanted to explore it further.

Her entire being had convulsed beneath his gentle brush of fingertips. She had never even shivered from Jacob's kiss, let alone quivered.

Had Graham felt it? The shake in her body? Oh, what a humiliating thing to experience. Surely she would never be able to face Graham again.

Bringing her thumb up to her lip as she walked down the hallway, she unwittily traced over the skin, as if she could conjure up what it would have been like to kiss him. She had only her imagination to draw on, since her experience with Jacob had been so limited. After that first kiss, he had persistently rebuked her advances, calling them 'feminine wiles.' He had explained that her attempts to lead him into temptation were evidence of the weak, sinful nature of women, and that once they were married, he could rein in her more sensual disposition.

Hope had spent many an hour wondering why, if it was the nature of women to be seductresses, Jacob was so very resistant to being seduced. She had stared at herself in the glass again and again, wondering if she lacked the face or figure to attract a man's attention and desire. She had heard stories of aristocratic men who seemingly couldn't help themselves when it came to the fairer sex. And while she knew she should be pleased that Jacob was too moral and upstanding to behave in such a manner, the truth was that she'd felt frustration at her own wants and wishes that she was forced to suppress.

Hope had wanted to kiss him, but her desire to kiss Graham now? Well, there was no comparison. Graham's sheer presence had been nearly overwhelming and oh, how she enjoyed it.

Hope leaned her back against the heavy wood door in her bedroom. This day was proving too stimulating for her.

What if he had actually kissed her? Heat began to prickle at her skin as she recalled her sister's foolishness that night at the Spotsmore ball. Had she felt like this? And was this feeling worth the sacrifice that they had all endured since? Hope knew the correct answer of course, but it was very strange that the correct answer and the true answer were not one and the same.

Because if she could feel this way from Graham doing nothing more than touching her, she might have sacrificed her entire life for a kiss. *His* kiss.

Her shoulders slumped as her desires turned to shame. What a dreadful thing to admit. But she couldn't fault Grace if she had felt something similar that night. No wonder Jacob had been so worried about Hope's concupiscence. Her family was one of scandal and wantonness, and everyone in London knew it ran in her blood.

Hope sighed as she began to pull out the pins in her hair. She placed them in a little porcelain dish, painted with purple roses, that sat on the vanity table.

She couldn't believe her aunt had been the mistress to the late king. Moreover, that Belle had won Lismore Hall in a card game. A card game! How could she ever look Mr. MacKinnon in the eye? No wonder he'd seemed so ill-tempered when they first met. He probably secretly hated Belle—and, by connection, Hope as well.

Trying to ignore the pit of guilt that was growing in her stomach, Hope opened the wardrobe and crouched to rummage through the built-in drawers, reaching for her night rail. But when she pulled, it snagged. Stretching her arm further into the drawer, she groped along the wooden interior for the displaced nail or splintered wood that her nightgown must have caught on.

The pointed object grazed her fingertips. Gritting her teeth, she wrapped her hand around the fabric just beneath the snag and yanked it hard. When the garment came loose, she fell slightly backwards, only to frown at the fabric in her grip.

A dull, square piece of cloth sat above the crisp white fabric of her night rail. It was dingy and for a moment Hope thought to throw it away. But then her eyes caught on the pattern. Hope carried it over to the oil lamp on the edge of her vanity table. Squinting at the fabric as she held it next to the light, she distinguished a green and red plaid. It was the tartan worn by Fergus MacKinnon in the dining room portrait.

How very odd.

Inspecting the small piece of fabric, Hope wondered how long it had been lost in the back of the armoire's drawers. Whose bedchambers had these once been? Glancing around the room, she searched for clues, but nothing grabbed her attention.

Setting the piece of plaid on her nightstand, she decided to ask her aunt about it tomorrow. Hope was assisted by Una as she changed into her night shift. Once the maid dimmed the oil lamp, she left, and Hope climbed beneath the green satin brocade bedding that had been stitched with gold thread. It was far more luxurious than she had ever been accustomed to.

Closing her eyes, she tried to make her mind blank. But peace did not come.

Despite her exhaustion from the day, Hope was restless all night, unable to find a restful sleep. Her dreams were vague, with visions of doors slamming in her face while a thick gray fog surrounded her. She couldn't see anything and the harder she strained her eyes, the darker it became. Her breath became shallow as she sensed a presence drawing closer to her. Then, a single cello string echoed around her. Her heart pounded and a voice sounded close to her ear, deep and heavily accented.

"Hope."

Her eyes snapped open as she sat up in bed, pressing her hand to her beating heart. It hadn't precisely been a nightmare and yet she couldn't shake the sensation of having been stalked. For several seconds she breathed heavily until her heartbeat settled. The gray light of dawn gave her room an unnatural glow. Though she was weary at still such an early hour, she pushed back the covers. Hope had no intention of returning to that unsettling dream.

Pulling out her most cheerful gown, colored bright yellow and crème, she began to dress. Thankfully, it had a set of buttons going down the front, making it easier for her to dress alone. After braiding her hair and pinning it up in simple hoop, she rotated her body toward the mirror above the vanity. Agitation showed all over her face as she pressed the pad of her forefinger against the small crease between her brows. She would have a face full of wrinkles soon enough if she didn't stop displaying every emotion she experienced on her face. Sighing, she decided to head downstairs, though she was already yawning and longing to return to her room by the time she reached the dining room.

Breakfast was a quiet affair. While her sisters seemed unbothered by all the revelations from yesterday, Hope couldn't quite come to terms with it. She pushed her porridge from one side to the other of the blue and white china bowl, preoccupied with her thoughts. On the one hand, Belle's behavior as a young woman shocked her. But on the other, how could Hope stand in judgment against the person who had been their saving grace for years? Grandmother had certainly not approved of her sister's lifestyle, and yet she had not quibbled about staying in Belle's London home for all these years. Wouldn't gratitude be a more appropriate response than condemnation? And yet, if Hope accepted it, it was as though she were betraying her grandmother in doing so. She had always told Hope and her sisters the importance of being a proper young lady, and Hope had agreed most of the time.

But maybe she wasn't cut out for being a proper young lady.

"Are you feeling well, my dear?" Belle asked, stirring her tea.

Hope straightened her shoulders.

"Sorry," she said, remembering that her grandmother had often corrected her when she would get lost in her thoughts.

"There's no need to apologize," Belle said.

Faith and Grace both stopped eating their toast and tarts.

"You do seem rather quiet," Faith said, concerned. "What's wrong?"

She didn't wish to discuss her tumultuous feelings at the moment, especially when she was wrestling with what she felt versus how she thought she should feel. She wanted to know more about Belle's history, but she worried that any questions she asked would sound critical.

"Nothing," Hope said, forcing her tone to sound light.

Silence followed.

"Very well," Belle said before addressing the other two. "I thought we would go to the village this morning so that you girls could explore your new surroundings."

"That would be wonderful," Grace said, leaning over the table slightly. "I was hoping to visit the bookshop."

"Bookshop?" Belle repeated, a single silver brow arching upward. "Well, I wouldn't call it a bookshop, but I'm sure you'll find Haggarty's an amusing shop."

Grace's smile faltered as Faith leaned forward.

"Might there be an art supply shop? I've managed to bring my watercolors, but I'm afraid I don't have any canvases."

"Oh, I believe there is. Right next to Rory's blacksmith," Belle said, turning back to Hope. "Will you come, Hope?"

"Yes, of course," she said, spooning some porridge into her mouth so she wouldn't have to speak any further.

Thankfully, Belle nor Hope's sisters pressed her. As soon as breakfast finished, they began to get ready. Her sisters wore similar brightly colored gowns, as did Belle, though hers was slightly old fashioned, with a more flowing cut at the waist. Rose also joined them, though she was wearing a rather plain, faded brown dress with small, yellow flowers stitched into the hem.

All five of them quickly clambered into the same large carriage that had delivered Hope and her sisters to Lismore the day before. Thankfully, it was large enough to fit all five of them comfortably, since the village of Glencoe was over an hour away.

"Why is town so far?" Grace asked, surprised when Rose mentioned the time that it would take to get there.

"Well, there are a few establishments between here and Glencoe Village. Some homes as well." Rose slipped on a pair of lace gloves as she spoke. "The Cock and Sparrow Inn is just about halfway, but I don't recommend any of you ladies go there."

"Why not?" Hope asked.

"The owner isn't fond of the English. To be honest, he isn't fond of anyone. I wouldn't go there myself unless it was absolutely necessary."

"But why is the village so far?" Faith asked, peering out the carriage window as they rode. "I should think town would only be a few miles away. Something walkable."

"I believe the MacKinnons who built Lismore Hall preferred solitude," Belle said, clutching the cane planted before her. "Besides, the landscape of the mountains provides the castle with a good deal of protection."

"The location was chosen so other clans couldn't attack?" Grace asked.

"Precisely," Rose said.

Hope eyed her aunt curiously.

"May I ask you a question, Aunt Belle?"

"Of course, my dear."

"Why did you take that bet, with Mr. MacKinnon's father? Surely you knew it was made by a desperate man. It wasn't right."

Belle shrugged; her clear eyes settled on a focal point.

"It's how kingdoms rise and fall, my dear. Desperate acts by desperate men have always molded the world we live in. I was simply a player. James MacKinnon didn't have to make that bet, but he did."

"But he couldn't have been in the right state of mind," Hope argued. "He had to be drunk or foolish, or—"

"My dear, you're putting too much blame at my feet. He was a grown man, responsible for his own decisions. It was not my fault that he gambled away his home. Why blame me for that man's mistake?"

Hope's mouth pulled sideways in contemplation as she digested her words. It was true. Graham's father had made his choices, and Belle was not to blame for them—even if allowing a man to gamble away his family home wasn't the Good Samaritan thing to do.

"I think she was very clever to win Lismore Hall," Faith said, her chin high. "Men have always been incompetent creatures. Why should Belle carry the burden for a fool?"

"But Mr. MacKinnon didn't deserve to have his birthright taken from him," Hope said.

"No, but then his father should have had the foresight to take care of his offspring."

"That's true," Grace said. "If James MacKinnon cared about his family, he would have never put the hall up as collateral."

"That's unfair to assume he didn't care," Hope said, unsure why she was defending a dead man. "We cannot know what he was thinking. Perhaps he was ill or might have even been impaired in some way. Isn't it, well, unneighborly to take advantage of those less fortunate? It isn't honorable."

A shuttered expression passed over Belle's stony face. The fine lines at the corners of her mouth and eyes deepened and she appeared much older than she ever had.

"My dear, I'm not the person to discuss honor and virtue. I've done things in my lifetime that would make most men blush. Now, I am certain your parents and grandmother raised each one of you to be good, kindhearted ladies, and I applaud that. Truly I do. But I am not, nor have I ever claimed to be a good lady. I've witnessed a humanity that would congratulate a monster and condemn a saint, all because society called for it. The hypocrisy was not for me, and so I chose to live outside of the strictures of society, on my own terms. However, I won't be made to into a villain because of my past. I am who I am, and I hold no guilt because of it. Do I make myself clear?"

Hope's wide eyes were locked on the old woman's face. She nodded slowly. The way Belle saw things was completely foreign to Hope. Yet, even as she tried to rationalize it with her strict upbringing, Hope couldn't help but find truth in her aunt's words.

After a moment of silence, Faith leaned forward.

"Aunt Belle, how come grandmother never told us about your past?"

"I suppose she was embarrassed." Belle shrugged, her hands tightening around the top of her walking stick. "And I know your parents weren't too fond of me, and even less when poor Willie passed away."

"What was he like?" Faith asked, inching closer to Belle. "The king, I mean."

A hush fell over the carriage at Faith's question. All the ladies, including Rose, leaned a little closer to hear Belle's response.

"He was exuberant," Belle said, the hint of a smile appearing on her powdered face. "Lavish and relentless, but always very sweet to me. I remember the first time he asked me to marry him—"

"Marry him?" Grace exclaimed, sitting back. "You were going to be queen?"

"Heavens no, child. It was not meant to be," Belle said. "He would have had to seek permission from the courts, as well as his father at the time. They would have never approved, not with all the political advantages a royal wedding was supposed to create—and that was back when no one expected Willie to ever become king, given that he had two elder brothers. But it didn't matter anyway. I would not be tamed by a marriage contract, even by a duke."

"I hardly think becoming a member of the royal family would have restricted you," Faith said with a calculating expression.

"Oh, no?" Belle quipped, brows raising. "You forget Queen Caroline then."

King William's elder brother, King George IV, had a terrible marriage, as was well documented. He had restricted Queen Caroline's access to her family and friends early in their marriage and sought a divorce immediately after the birth of their daughter, Princess Charlotte. While Caroline had some support from the reformers, her banishment from his coronation had lasting effects on her popularity.

"But you cannot deny you interfered in King William and Queen Adelaide's marriage," Rose said. "You were his mistress after all."

"I was *one* of his mistresses. Willie did enjoy his women. But I refuse to acknowledge any wrongdoing. He was a prince of the realm, and I held no sway over him." Hope's brow quirked up and Belle smirked. "Well, perhaps a little sway."

"There were other mistresses?" Faith asked. Her mouth hung open and Hope watched her face twitch as though she were doing some advanced math problem in her head. "Can a man have more than one?"

"Perhaps that's a story for another day, Belle," Hope said quickly, extending her hands up in an attempt to stop her from speaking. "As fascinating as your life has been, I'm afraid we are still rather innocent."

"Innocent," Belle repeated with a soft chuckle. Hope held her breath waiting for their aunt to say something cutting about the scandal they had all survived in London, but she only chuckled softly. "More than you know, my dears. More than you know."

They rode the rest of the way in silence. While it was highly unusual to speak to unwed ladies about scandal, the incidents had taken place many years prior and therefore seemed more like history than current events.

Still, how sad that Belle had been sequestered for so long away from her family. Hope understood her grandmother's reasons, as she probably didn't wish to corrupt Hope or her sisters, but she doubted Belle would ever do anything to harm or hinder them.

Grateful when the carriage finally arrived at Glencoe Village, Hope emerged to find a bustling town filled with people. There were all sorts of shopkeepers and other townspeople who seemed as though they were setting up some sort of event. All manners of people seemed to line the street. Most of the men were wearing green and blue tartan kilts.

"Look, Hope. Kilts," Faith said, wiggling her eyebrows.

Hope rolled her eyes. She had once made the comment saying that she thought kilts were dashing and Faith would never let her forget it.

"Yes, I see."

"What's going on?" Grace asked Rose as they strolled down the lane. "There seems to be a great many people here."

"Festival preparations for the games," Rose answered, the hint of a smile hovering on her lips. "It's grown a bit over the past few years, but the McTavish clan loves to celebrate."

"McTavish?" Hope repeated.

"Yes. These are McTavish lands."

"I thought they were MacKinnon?"

"No, the MacKinnons lost their lands during the Tragedies. The McTavish clan had been a wee bit cleverer at hiding their involvement during the uprisings and were never officially declared an enemy of the Crown." She glanced around. "Laird McTavish is one of the few highland lairds to still retain much of his ancestors' lands." Rose looked back to Hope. "He's a bit of a relic."

"How so?"

"Well, the clan system fell out of practice about a hundred years ago, but he still thinks that as the laird, he needs to take care of his people. Even though many of the other lairds are clearing their lands for sheep and deer parks. Some are even paying their kin to emigrate to the Americas. Laird McTavish has tried to avoid having to do so. He's held on, but … the changing times are a force beyond his control."

"That's so sad."

"Aye, it is, but everyone does their best. Mr. MacKinnon's business, for example, has been able to employ several dozen people, and as he keeps his operations on McTavish lands, it's a benefit to the locals."

"His business?" Hope asked.

"Aye, the beekeeping and whatnot. He's managed to create quite a success, what with all the honey, wax, and venom."

"Venom?"

Rose smiled knowingly.

"I thought that might catch your attention. I thought he was quite mad when he was explaining it, but apparently Lady Belle's physician, Dr. Hall, has a use for it."

"That would make sense," Grace said. "There are dozens of primeval civilizations that used bee stings for medicinal purposes. I once read a book that mentioned an ancient text from China—"

"Ah!" Belle said, interrupting Grace as she flicked up her cane and pointed it through the crowd. "I see Douglas McTavish now. And Jared is with him."

Belle waved her cane at a striking older man, with a short reddish white beard. He was wearing a cap on his head and the McTavish green and blue tartan. His eyes lit up with recognition as soon as Belle's cane caught his attention. A younger man who had the same squarish build followed him, and Hope knew instantly that they were related.

"Lady Belle!" the older man said through the crowd as he came to greet her. Douglas McTavish clasped her hand and kissed her knuckles. "I didn't expect to see you today."

"My nieces wished to come to town to discover their new surroundings, as did Rose," she said happily. "May I introduce Hope, Faith, and Grace Sharpe? Girls, this is Laird Douglas

McTavish and his son, Mr. Jared McTavish."

The sisters all curtsied. Hope was certain the eyes of an elderly man eyes lingered on her, as did those of his son, who bowed.

"A pleasure to meet you all," Jared said.

"And to see you again, Miss Rose," his father added.

Hope smiled at Rose, but she was surprised to see the young woman's face had gone pale and void of emotion as she stared at Jared McTavish.

"Lady Belle has proven a dear friend of the McTavish Clan," Laird McTavish said, pulling Hope's attention away from Rose. "Any kin of hers is full welcome here. We'd be honored to throw a party for you by the week's end, to celebrate your arrival."

"That would be very kind of you, Laird McTavish," Hope said, turning back to face him. "But we wouldn't want to be any trouble."

"No trouble at all! Any excuse to have a ball," he said, winking, which caused Belle to laugh.

Hope looked between the two and saw a bit of a connection between them. She wondered if they had ever acted on their obvious mutual attraction. Then, remembering who her aunt was, she blushed.

"Might I ask you where the ribbon shop is, Laird McTavish?" Hope asked.

"Just down the lane, to your left, right next to the kilt hire shop."

"I'd be happy to escort you," Jared said, coming forward.

"Ah, I'm actually in need of your assistance." Belle lifted her hand, taking the young man's arm as if he had offered it to her. "I've an appointment with Dr. Hall."

Though he looked slightly deflated, Jared bowed courteously.

"Of course, Lady Belle."

"Perhaps next time, Mr. McTavish," Hope said as the young man escorted Belle in the opposite direction. She twisted back to her sisters and Rose. "Shall we?"

"I've an appointment with the butcher," Rose said quickly,

not making eye contact with any of them. "If you'll excuse me."

All three watched Rose hurry off. What had that been about?

"That was strange," Grace said, careful not to bump into anyone in the crowded street. "Did Rose seem upset to anyone else just now?"

"I didn't notice," Faith said with a shrug.

"I did."

"I wonder why," Grace said quietly as they walked.

Hope wondered too, but as they reached the ribbon shop, she chose to shuffle her concern away as they browsed. There was a fine assortment of ribbons and Hope was rather surprised to see the varying displays, surprised to discover that Scotland had far more fine silks than she would have expected to find outside of London.

After several purchases, Hope and her sisters exited the shop. She saw the swinging wooden sign that spelt out Kilt Hire. She was curious about the piece of cloth she had found in her room. Knowing it belonged to the MacKinnon clan, she wanted to see if it could be restored.

"Shall we try a piece of gingerbread from that vendor over there?" Grace asked hopefully.

"Let's go find the paint shop first," Faith suggested.

"I'll meet you over there," Hope said, walking toward the store.

"Where are you going?" Faith asked.

"I've a question that wants answering," Hope said as she entered the shop.

A short little man with a lengthy mustache stood behind a table where a long piece of plaid was laid out. He seemed to be measuring the fabric when he glanced up. As soon as he spotted her, his eyes nearly popped out of his head.

"Hello!" he said enthusiastically, dropping his measuring tape as he came around the table. "How may I help you?"

"Hello," she said. "I was just wondering if—"

"Oh, I don't have any ribbons. That's next door, lassie," he interrupted, seeming almost offended.

"Yes, but I was wondering if you could—"

"Did ye no hear me?"

"Sir," Hope said firmly as she reached into her reticule. She extracted the square of plaid and handed it to the little man. "I was wondering if you could repair this."

He barely gave it a passing glance.

"It's a rag," he said after a moment. "What do you want with it?"

"I would just like to see it restored and I didn't wish to harm it by cleaning it myself.

The man made a face and took it in hand to inspect it. After a long moment, his forehead puckered as he held it up.

"This is MacKinnon plaid," he said, peering around it at her. "What do you want with MacKinnon plaid?"

"I simply wish for it to be cleaned, that's all," she said, attempting to grab it. "If you are unable to do so, simply say as much."

"No, that's not it. I can restore it easily enough, though it's such a small piece it wouldn't be fit to wear. Unless …"

The little man moved around his table and opened a drawer. Hope heard the tinging and clashing of metal when he drew out a sizable locket. He held it up to her, smiling as if she should be happy to see it.

"What is it?" she asked.

The man frowned.

"It's a pin brooch locket," he said, circling the table to show her. "Usually worn with the fly plaid. But this one is particularly interesting."

The man held out his hand to show a sizeable silver brooch that fit in his palm. It was in the shape of an intricate knot surrounded by a thistle. With a small tap of his thumb, the brooch popped open, revealing a secret compartment—one large enough to hold the plaid she had brought, if it was folded carefully. Was that what this man had in mind? She'd never heard of a plaid being kept in a brooch, but perhaps that was a common custom here?

"Oh," Hope said.

He snapped it closed, and Hope glanced up at him.

"Come back in an hour, I'll have it cleaned up for you and put in here."

"Oh, but that's not necessary," she said as the front door opened.

"What isn't necessary?" a deep, masculine voice sounded behind her.

Hope whipped around to see Graham standing before her, his tall frame barely fitting in the little shop. He gave her an inquisitive stare beneath the auburn locks that fell over his forehead. Suddenly frantic, she twisted back to the shop owner.

"That's fine," she said in a soft tone. "I'll be back in an hour for it."

"But—"

Hope's brow lifted and, with wide eyes, she shook her head slightly. She didn't wish to be caught with a piece of MacKinnon plaid in front of Graham. Understanding seemed to dawn on the man and he winked.

"Very good, my lady."

"Back for what?" Graham asked.

"Belle wished for me to get her a swath of McTavish plaid, so that she might wear it during the ball," Hope said quickly.

Graham eyed her suspiciously. "She never has before."

Hope shrugged.

"You know Belle. She's a bit of a wild one, isn't she?" Hope said with a smile, hoping to distract him from the shopkeeper.

It seemed to have worked because in a moment, Graham's gaze became heated. Hope flushed in response. She nodded and edged past him.

"If you'll excuse me," she said to the shopkeeper before exiting the building. "Thank you!"

"Yes, my lady," he said back as she hurried out the door.

"Not so fast," Graham said, following her out into the crowded street. Hope did not wait. "Where are you going so quickly?"

Away from you, she thought.

"It's of no concern of yours, Mr. MacKinnon."

"Aye, but it could be."

She observed him as he fell into an easy stride alongside her. Her eyes dropped to his legs as they walked, and she couldn't contain her curiosity.

"Why were you in the kilt shop?"

He gave her a sideways glance.

"I was in need of a new kilt pin," he said, though she wasn't sure if she should believe him.

Once more, she peered down at his trouser covered legs.

"You're not wearing a kilt."

"No, I'm not."

"Then why would you need a kilt pin?"

The corner of his mouth pulled up.

"For when I do wear one."

"And when would that be?"

"You're a somewhat forward thing, aren't you?" he asked but before she could answer, he continued. "Do you think every Scotsman must wear a kilt at all times?"

"No. It's just that the McTavishes wear them. It looks as though most of the men here in the village do. I was just curious as to why you don't."

"It's not practical to wear every day, particularly when I'm in Glasgow. I prefer trousers."

Graham's words sounded practiced as if he had recited them often. What a strange thing to notice.

"Oh."

"You sound disappointed."

"Excuse me?" she asked, having lost her train of thought. "Oh no. It's just that, well, I think I had assumed everyone here wore kilts and plaids all the time." Her cheeks warmed. "I supposed that's a bit foolish."

"No," he said, his tone low. "I don't think that's foolish at all."

She gave him a self-deprecating grin.

"There's no need to tiptoe around me, Mr. MacKinnon. I'm quite aware of how ridiculous I can be sometimes. My imagination is extensive. My grandmother always told me that I should remain firmly in the present, as I tend to drift away in one of my daydreams."

His green eyes glanced at her.

"I don't think a healthy imagination is ridiculous. It's natural to be curious. You had a dream and it was a Scottish dream, so I certainly can't fault you for that."

She tried to smother her smile as she twisted away from him. It was amazing how nervous he made her, yet she felt equally excited.

Just then a young boy, no more than ten, came running by. Hoping to avoid returning to the kilt shop with Graham in tow, she stopped the boy.

"Excuse me?" she said, waving her hand a bit to catch the lad's attention.

"Who? Me?" he asked.

"Yes," she said bending slightly at the waist. Turning, she pointed to the gingerbread cart. "Would you be a dear and go tell those two ladies that their sister wishes for them to pick up her pin brooch locket from the kilt shop?" The boy made a face, as if to convey that he had far more important things to tend to. Reaching into her reticule, Hope pulled out a half crown coin. "Please?"

The youth's bright eyes lit up as he took her offering.

"Yes, my lady!" he said with a quick nod, before bounding toward Hope's sisters.

As she straightened up, she saw Graham giving her the strangest of looks.

"What?" she asked, tilting her head.

"Nothing. It's just that you're awfully trusting."

"Why shouldn't I be?"

He shrugged and continued watching her.

"It's just not something one sees often. Especially from a Londoner."

"Well, as I'm originally from Cornwall, I'll forgive you that statement, but I assure you, I've rarely been given a reason not to trust people."

"Which means you've been kept sheltered."

Hope frowned slightly as they continued their walk.

"Not completely. It's just that I've a strong belief that if people are given the benefit of the doubt, they'll prove themselves worthy of it. For the most part, people do the right thing."

"But not always?"

"No, but often enough to secure my view on humanity."

"And what a view it must be," he said, his deep tone tinged with sarcasm.

She glanced at him, eager to explain that an optimistic point of view, particularly in defiance of constant poor circumstances, was exactly the thing that had given her the strength to carry on—but the teasing in his eyes made her forget her words.

The memory of his gentle touch flashed in her mind as she stepped into a shallow dirt hole, tripping. Instantly, the solid, muscular form of Graham caught her arm.

"Careful," he said. She tried to pull her arm back, but he held her steadily. She peered over her shoulder to see who might be watching them, but he smirked at her worry. "Were you expecting people to gawk? Why would they? It's the gentlemanly thing to do, isn't it? Helping a lady walk."

"I don't need help walking."

"Your feet say otherwise."

"I'm merely unaccustomed to walking on dirt roads."

"Ah, yes, because London cobblestone is so even." Hope tried to scowl, but couldn't help but smile. "Well, you needn't worry about me accosting you in broad daylight."

"I wasn't worried about that. I'm just... not used to being escorted."

"No?" he said, his brow furring. "Not even by your gentleman friend back in London?"

Hope found it a little forward for him to bring up Jacob, considering the last time they spoke she was crying over being thrown over by him, but surprisingly she didn't mind it.

"No, actually. Mr. Pennington was very strict about touching. He avoided it as much as possible."

Hope swallowed as Graham frowned.

"Why?"

"Well, because he was concerned for me, I suppose. He never wanted to overstep, lest someone get the wrong idea, sullying my reputation as a result."

"So, he never escorted you? In a park, or museum?"

Hope opened her mouth and then closed it. It had seemed a perfectly respectable thing for Jacob to always keep his distance back when it was happening, but now, holding onto Graham's arm, she found she wasn't scandalized at all. Why *had* she let Jacob convince her that it was so wrong? Nothing about this felt wrong at all.

"No, he didn't," she said. "He told me that he didn't want to appear as a Casanova."

The corner of his mouth twitched.

"A Casanova? From holding your hand?" he repeated humorously. The word sounded delightful with his accent. "He'd have to be a true lady-killer if he thought hand holding would make you swoon. And did he call himself that? A Casanova?"

Hope opened her mouth to explain when the sudden yelps and shouts of young men caught her attention. Graham shifted his head and leaned over the side of the bridge. Hope leaned over the side as well and beheld several young men swimming in their underclothes. Shirtsleeves, plaids, and trousers were strewn across the rocky edge of the stream which pooled into a good-size swimming hole at the base of the bridge. Hope turned around quickly, her blush deepening.

"'Tis only a swim," Graham said, noticing how fast she rotated from the scene below. "Surely, you've gone swimming before?"

"As a child, but not as an adult," she said over her shoulder.

"You should try it."

"No, thank you."

"Och!" he yelled down at the young men. Hope snuck a peek at them. "Put some clothes on! There are ladies present."

Some lads hooted and hollered while others sank deeper into the water in an attempt to hide their bodies. Graham laughed, and Hope's attention landed on him. His relaxed grin seemed to melt away slightly as he regarded her. A warm, fuzzy feeling settled in her stomach and she swallowed, nodding back toward the waters below.

"Who are they?"

"My cousins actually," he said leaning his back against the stone bridge. "You'll meet them at the ball."

"Oh no," she said. "But you've embarrassed them."

"That? No," he said, shaking his head. "They shan't be embarrassed by that. But if they are, they have only themselves to blame. They shouldn't have been so in a position of being caught near naked."

"You are never caught in such compromising positions?"

"No," he answered, his tone surprisingly solemn. "I wouldn't allow it."

"You wouldn't allow it?" she repeated. "Are you afraid of being embarrassed?"

"Afraid? No, but I don't know anyone who enjoys it," he said.

Hope wondered if he was ashamed of his father's loss of Lismore Hall. She wished she could ask about it, but it seemed too private, too personal a matter to broach with him. Deciding to keep their conversation light, she walked away from him, knowing he'd follow.

"I don't like being embarrassed either," Hope said, her eyes dropping down. "But I don't consider vulnerability a weakness."

"Vulnerability is a synonym for weakness."

"It is not," she countered. "Why, I know of a story about a musical conductor whose vulnerability saved his life."

Graham gave her a skeptical look.

"I don't believe it."

"It's true. You see, the conductor was so in love with his wife that he wrote her a melody that was meant for only her to hear."

"If this is a story—"

"It would be if you didn't interrupt," she quipped before continuing. "Now unfortunately, some years later, the conductor found himself on hard times and had to sell his composition. Though he thought he would be mortified to release to the public this deeply personal piece of music, he was rather regaled as one of the great musicians of his time." She glanced around, watching a pair of squirrels chasing each other around the base of a tree. "All because he had decided to be vulnerable."

He was quiet for a long time before he spoke.

"That's a load of hogwash," Graham said.

Hope frowned. It had been a story that Jacob had told her during their courtship.

"It is not; it's true."

"That sounds like some romantic swill a man would tell to a lady he's trying to…" He broke off as he saw her face. "Och. I didn't mean to say that."

"Yes, you did," she said, her gaze on the ground before them.

"Well, perhaps. You're not mad about it, though, are you?"

"No."

A pause followed. When she glanced up, she saw a rather infuriating smirk tugging at his lips.

"You are. Why? Because I called you a romantic?"

"I must be going, Mr. MacKinnon. Thank you for escorting me."

"Wait—"

"I really must be off."

And with that, she faded into the crowd, eager to be out of his presence. What did he know about romance? It was obvious that

Graham had never been in love. Therefore, he had no idea what he was talking about. He had obviously never desired anyone, never yearned to be held and cherished, and…

Shame slammed into Hope. Her insides crumbled as her shoulders slumped. Perhaps Jacob had been correct. Perhaps she really was as wanton as her family.

Chapter Six

BELLE HAD INSISTED that Hope and her sisters treat Lismore Hall as their home, and over the next several days, that was exactly what they did. While Faith had set up her easel and watercolors in the east hall gallery, Grace happily explored the library where a vast number of medical books had been gathering dust for years.

Hope, on the other hand, felt restless. While the castle certainly provided a great deal of entertaining opportunities for exploration, what with its hidden passageways and ancient history, she felt rather confined. Deciding that she needed to walk—far, wide, and aimlessly—to quiet her ever growing thoughts, Hope made her way to the walled garden one afternoon.

The scent of late springtime flowers filled her nostrils as she climbed down the hidden stone staircase that led out of her bedroom. The gardener, Mr. Fitzpatrick, had his back to her, tending to a holly hedge at the south side of the garden. Not wishing to disturb him, Hope moved with a quickened pace toward the little wooden door that led into the bee yard. As gently as possible, she unlocked the little metal latch and pushed open the rough-cut door, closing it quietly behind her.

Turning around, Hope saw several dozen egg shaped wicker domes, each sitting on a wooden table on an upward sloping field, edged on three sides by a forest. Frowning, she had just taken a cautious step forward when the faintest of buzzing sound hit her ear and she froze. She had quite forgotten all about the bees.

She was frightened at first, until she realized that the bees wouldn't attack her simply for being there. Still, she kept to the left of the field, avoiding them until she found a path leading through a pine tree grove.

The sun filtered through the tall branches, dappling the dirt path with fragments of light. Hope inhaled deeply. The scent of earth and pine resin settled over her in the most comforting way. London had never been a joy to smell, but the air around Lismore was somehow sweet.

Before long, the trees thinned somewhat and the horizon shone in the distance. Hope could see several massive mountains, surrounded by a mist that seemed to be rolling up the sides of the foothills, sitting behind a large expanse of water. The puffy white clouds and blue sky reflected brightly in the loch and hundreds of tall, pointy purple flowers, swayed gently in the breeze.

Hope let out a little huff of amused breath, stunned at the beauty of this place. It was strange to feel so comforted in such a vast landscape, but she had never felt so at home in her entire life, not even in her own bedroom back in London. Heading down to the water's edge, she found a large, flat rock to climb up on.

Sighing, she stretched out her legs beneath her blue-and-cream-colored skirts, and looked out over the water, enjoying the solitude of the highland wildlife. Laying down, she folded her arms behind her head and closed her eyes. The warmth of the stone radiated against her back as the sun kissed her face. This place was truly lovely and she wondered how long she could stay before her aunt would send someone to look for her.

By the sounds of the cursing Scotsman, not long at all.

"Bloody bowfin trout!" An unfamiliar, masculine voice yelled. "I've not had a bite all damn day."

Hope lifted herself onto her elbow and looked behind her where she believed the voice had come from, but she didn't see anyone.

"What are you doing on this side of the loch anyway?" another voice said and to Hope's surprise, she recognized it.

It was Graham.

"I rowed clean across it and I still couldn't find one boggin fish," the other man said, just as she finally spotted them.

A tall, somewhat fair-haired man came out from around a group of trees, dressed in a kilt, shirtsleeves and what looked like a gansey. Hope had heard about the knitted fishing sweaters from some gentleman or other, bragging about their sporting skills during a ball in London. Supposedly it was so tightly knit that water couldn't sink into it. Two wicker baskets bounced against his kilt-clad hips as he walked, with two straps crossed diagonally across his chest. He was carrying a long wooden pole as he made his way toward the edge of the water some several yards away, where a little boat sat. He was completely unaware of Hope.

A few steps behind him was Graham, dressed in his usual dark gray trousers, shirtsleeves and a partially buttoned gray striped vest. He looked rather charming in a devil-may-care, natural sort of way, causing a faint fluttering feeling in Hope's stomach.

"You know, fishing is supposed to be a peaceful pursuit," Graham said, stepping around a large rock on the shore.

"So, everyone keeps telling me," the slightly fair-haired man said, throwing his things into the small row boat. "It's a delusional sport. I'm not doing it again."

"Och, you don't mean it."

"Yes I do."

"I'll come with you next time, eh? Show you how it's done."

"It'd be a waste of time," the man said, as he bent down at the front of the boat. With apparent ease, he lifted and pushed it into the water, jumping onto it as it freed itself from the muddy shore. He turned back. "I'll see you at your uncle's then?"

"Aye," Graham said with a nod, lifting up his hand as the man sat, rowing away.

Hope was sure that Graham was going to turn back but just

as he did, he paused and she felt a sudden trail of gooseflesh flare up the back of her neck, causing her to shiver. Slowly, he turned around and—without searching, almost as if he knew instinctively where to look—his eyes pinned her to right where she sat.

She inhaled sharply as he tilted his head, staring at her as if he couldn't quite believe that she was there. Embarrassed that she had been caught eavesdropping, she shifted her body, bringing her legs over the edge of the rock as he came forward.

"Hope?" he said, confused. "What are you doing out here?"

"I was thinking," she said, before shaking her head. "I mean, I went for a walk, to think and ended up here." She turned her head, gazing out over the water to the rowboat, before looking back at Graham. "I didn't mean to eavesdrop."

"You're out here alone?" he asked, ignoring her apology.

"Yes."

"Don't you think that's a bit unwise?"

"Why would it be unwise?"

"It's dangerous wandering about by yourself. You could get hurt or lost."

"Oh, no," she said, leaning her body forward to slide off the rock.

Graham's hands were up on her waist before she could stop him. He lifted her down to the ground, and though he let go, she was sure his hands had lingered for a moment longer than was necessary. She swallowed.

"'Oh, no,' what?"

"Hmm? Oh," she said, remembering her thoughts. "I just meant, no, it isn't dangerous." He made a face as if she didn't know what she was talking about. "I often go for walks alone. Nothing has ever happened to me."

His frown deepened.

"You mean, you'd go on walks through London, unaccompanied?"

"Yes."

"And no one ever said anything?"

"Well, no. My sisters never could keep up as I tend to walk rather quickly, and my grandmother would usually be asleep when I went out—"

"You went at night?" he asked incredulously, cutting her off. She gave him a perplexed look.

"Yes."

He let out a quiet curse, though Hope still heard and she tilted her head. Why was he so put out by this information? Yes, it wasn't the most proper thing to do, but it was something she hadn't been able to help. Sometimes a woman just needs to walk alone, to sort out her own mind.

"And you don't see any issue with that?"

"No, I don't."

"How have you survived this long?" he asked, shaking his head. "Don't you know what could've happened? What could *still* happen if you go off alone around these parts? Even if no one bothers you, you could still fall into a river, crack your head on a rock, be attacked by a stag, trip off a craig—"

"Well, you're making me miss London."

"But that's even worse! Pickpockets, cutthroats, thieves, murderers, all lurking about your doorstep, waiting to make a mark."

"I lived in a perfectly safe neighborhood in London, thank you very much."

"Oh?" he said, unbelieving. "And I suppose if anyone did cross your path, you'd give them the benefit of the doubt?"

Hope squinted at him.

"What is your aversion to believing in people?"

"Reality."

"Excuse me?"

"I have an aversion to believing in people because I live in the real world. Where no one does anything for anyone for nothing."

Hope lifted her chin.

"Well, that's a very cynical outlook to have."

"It's the only sensible outlook to have," he countered, taking a step toward her. "And the fact that you somehow have managed to go through life unscraped just makes you the exception. Not the rule."

That was an unfair assumption on his part. Hope had delt with a great deal of tragedy in her life and she wasn't going to let him minimize it simply because he had decided to let his obstacles defeat him.

"I have not gone through life unscraped," she said somewhat forcefully. "I've had my fair share of misery. But I don't let my bad fortune dictate my life, like some people."

He glared down at her.

"Like me?"

"You said it," she said, ignoring the heightened speed of her pulse. "Now, if you'll excuse me, I think I'll return home, of which I'm certainly capable."

Pushing past him, Hope was faintly aware of the scent of clover that seemed to cling to him. Of course, he didn't let her get very far without falling into an easy stride next to her, even though she was trying to walk purposefully fast.

"I didn't mean to imply that you weren't capable," he said as they entered the copse of pine trees. "But you can't truly believe that traipsing alone through the wilderness is wise, can you?"

It was cooler here than it had been out in the sunlight, and the air was heavy with moisture and the scent of sap. A delightful shiver went through Hope, though she wasn't sure if it was from the temperature change or the fact that Graham's shoulder brushed against hers.

"Nothing bad has happened so far."

"But that doesn't mean it can't."

"So, I should spend all my time worrying about things that may or may not happen?" she asked. "It seems rather trite if you ask me."

"You never know what could happen."

"Well, perhaps one day I'll find out," she said smartly, smirking to herself when a large hand suddenly wrapped around her wrist, pulling her round as the wind escaped her.

With her back pressed up against the rough bark of a pine tree, Graham towered over her, gazing down at her darkly. The shock of being touched and held in his grip made her heart skip. She knew she should be offended, furious even, but her mouth fell open as she stared into his green eyes.

"Perhaps you will," he said, his tone oddly soft despite his words sounding like a threat.

"W-what are you doing?"

But he didn't speak. Instead, he looked down at her with a heated stare that made her skin tingle. The flutter in her stomach grew and when he bent his head down toward her ear, her eyes closed as her breath caught.

"You should be wary of people, Hope. Not everyone is trustworthy," he whispered, his breath warm against the sensitive skin.

She wanted to tell him he was wrong, to push him away—and she nearly did. Bringing up her hands, she landed them on his chest. She had every intention to push him, but the strong, solid form of him was too interesting, too new.

At first, she didn't move. She just held her hands to his chest, but then slowly, her fingers moved up as her mouth hung open. She had never touched a man like this and to her humiliation, she couldn't stop herself from enjoying it.

He pulled back only a fraction and she saw his eyelids flutter down as he watched her. She could feel his heart beating erratically and she was nervously glad, for hers was equally irregular.

Slowly his gaze lifted, and she was sure he was going to touch her hands and press them down. But then his hands were in her hair, and he was kissing her as if he were trying to teach her something he couldn't quite understand himself.

Hope's entire body was immediately consumed in a wash of unmitigated need. Her fingers curled into his shirtsleeves, pulling him further into their kiss. His tongue searched her mouth, lapping and tasting every bit of her as he pulled her toward him, crushing her body against his firm frame.

This was what Hope had always dreamed of. To be kissed, held, touched with such possessiveness that her toes curled. She moaned into his mouth. Never had she expected that the unknown desires that plagued her in the middle of the night could be managed, celebrated even, for that's what this felt like. It was as if she had finally found what she had always been looking for, and she never wanted it to end. When he tore away from her, she nearly fell over trying to follow him, to keep their bodies joined.

But Graham's long arms held her steady while he kept her at bay. They were both struggling to regain their breathing and eventually he shook his head.

"Hope, I—"

"Please don't apologize," she said quickly, worried that he might, but he only looked confused.

"What?"

"I... Please don't say you're sorry."

"I'm not sorry."

Pleasure bloomed in her chest.

"Oh. Good."

"But I, this... We can't do this."

"Oh," she said, nodding, though she didn't understand. "Yes, of course," she swallowed. Then added, "Why?"

But he didn't answer. Instead, he groaned.

"It's just... It's not happening."

She nodded again, unable to understand why he was so determined. Perhaps he didn't find her attractive? Or maybe she hadn't been good at it.

Heat spread across her cheeks, but to her confusion, Graham took her arm and tucked it into his as he pressed her to walk again. She did so on unsteady feet, all while her mind was reeling. What had that all been about? Thankfully, he didn't speak and by the time they reached the bee yard, he seemed perfectly put together, save the concerned look in his green eyes.

He opened the little wooden door that led into the walled garden. She wanted to say something, anything, but her words failed her and when he didn't speak either, she hurried away.

Chapter Seven

ELK MANOR, THE MacTavish stronghold, had looked over this part of the highlands for hundreds of years. It had always been a place of comfort to Graham, but as he stood in the middle of his uncle's crowded ballroom, awaiting the arrival of Lady Belle and her nieces, he was troubled. For days, his thoughts had been consumed by memories of his afternoon with Hope. As much as he tried to reason away his attraction to Hope, he couldn't ignore his genuine, visceral response to her.

He hadn't meant to kiss her, hadn't wanted to, considering who Hope was and what it would mean, but then Graham hadn't been able to help himself. He'd half expected her to push him away, but after that initial hesitation, her hands had come up to his chest, her fingers had curled into his vest, and she had moaned ever so softly into his mouth. That alone had nearly undone him, and he'd fallen deeper into the kiss.

She had tasted like honey, and the mere memory of holding her was difficult to push aside. For days he thought of nothing else. They had fit so perfectly together, so bloody perfectly, that it was as though he had suddenly come under a spell. A spell that seemed to break the moment he remembered that he wasn't supposed to be kissing her.

Hope is not for me.

He needed to keep his mind clear of her so that he could think straight.

He had gone back and forth about Belle's offer a dozen times since hearing it and a dozen more since kissing Hope. He could marry her and have Lismore Hall back in his possession, but something about the idea rubbed him the wrong way. Perhaps if he was honest with Hope, Graham could convince her to sell it back to him once she inherited it.

Yes, that's what he would do. He would simply tell Hope the truth and buy it back from her later. She had been sympathetic to his story and morally offended when she'd learned how her aunt came to own Lismore Hall. It would probably be easy to convince her to sell it to him, but he was surprised to note that a significant part of him disliked the idea. Gaining Lismore with or without marrying Hope was equally unattractive. He was damned if he did, damned if he didn't. What was he going to do?

A buzz erupted from the group of people surrounding the entrance hall and he took a sip of wine as he nodded at a tall, fair-haired man approaching him. Logan Harris was Graham's oldest friend and had been the fisherman Hope had spied on the other day. He had recently returned home from the Second Burma War and had earned a parcel of land upon his return for saving an entire brigade.

"Logan," Graham said with a nod.

"Graham," Logan said, peering over the crowd. "Tell me, have the English invaded yet?"

"Just about," he said, nodding toward the entrance hall, where several McTavish ladies were making the Sharpes' acquaintance. "That's them."

"You'll forgive me if I don't rush to greet them," Logan said, taking a wine glass from a passing servant. He seemed just as displeased with the prospect of entertaining the Sharpes as him, though Graham knew he had different reasons. "I'm not fond of the English."

His dislike of the English wasn't merely because he was Scottish. His mother had been from London and had abandoned him, his sister, and their father when he was young.

"Who is?" A McTavish cousin said, coming up to join them.

"But these Sassenachs are easy to look at."

"Aye, particularly the oldest one," another cousin said. "Hope, isn't it?"

"It is." Graham said as an odd sensation rolled within him. Jealousy? No, it couldn't be. Or rather, it *shouldn't* be. But he had known envy his whole life and this touch of jealousy was familiar to him.

"Beauties or not, they're still English," Logan said, as the footman across the room stepped forward.

"Lady Belle Smith and her nieces, Miss Hope Sharpe, Miss Faith Sharpe, and Miss Grace Sharpe."

The crowd parted ways, and Belle entered the hall smiling widely as Laird McTavish approached her to welcome them. The three Sharpe sisters, dressed in the latest London fashions, followed after her, appearing slightly nervous beneath the curious gazes of the other guests.

Graham's eyes were immediately on Hope. She wore an ice-blue silk gown, with short sleeves and long gloves. A sizeable silver brooch had been pinned to the center of her bodice and Graham's insides clenched. Her dress was too revealing, too perfectly fitted for her body and he was both eager and angry at the sight of her.

He didn't want to want her.

Why was she wearing something so revealing anyway? The damn neckline was pinned in such a way to accentuate her breasts and make nearly every man in the room stare at her. Jealousy tore through him as he glared around. He felt murderous toward anyone who even glanced at her as he fought to keep his composure.

"Huh," Logan said as he stared in their direction, seeming rather mesmerized. "Who is the tall one?"

"Faith," Graham said, hating that his voice sounded brittle. "Why?"

But Logan didn't answer. Graham noticed him staring at the middle sister, though he wasn't sure why Faith would catch his attention with Hope standing right next to her.

Logan quickly finished his wine.

"Excuse me."

He disappeared somewhere into the crowd, heading in the opposite direction. Graham didn't quite understand his reaction, but he didn't really care. All he was interested in was Hope.

Her dark curls bounced slightly as she walked and he found himself mesmerized. Not only by her beauty, but by a deep appreciation of her character. She was straightforward in an unconsciously charming way, and he found that he only wished to be near her again, even if she ignored him or scolded him again for his cynicism.

He made his way through the crowd, befuddled by his own feelings. Belle had gone to speak with someone toward the edge of the room, leaving her nieces to answer dozens of questions from his inquisitive family members. Graham navigated through the sea of cousins, friends, and extended family to follow Belle.

It had been strange the way the McTavish clan had all but adopted the old woman into their family. For a king's mistress, she had blended in seamlessly with the McTavishes.

She certainly acted like a dowager lady of the stronghold. An elderly woman who had been speaking with her turned away, leaving Belle alone. Graham came up to where she stood, leaning heavily on her blackwood cane. She smiled at him.

"Ah, MacKinnon. How nice to see you."

"Is it?" he asked, not bothering with pleasantries.

"Well, I think so. Have you thought any more about my offer?"

"The one where you trade your own flesh and blood for nothing?" he asked under his breath. "Yes, and the answer is still no."

"Because you think she is too plain? Or too dull?"

"No," he said, annoyed. "Because I can't wrap my head around why you want this. What's in it for you?"

"In it for me?" she repeated, incredulous. "I'm seventy-five years old, MacKinnon. There's nothing I want and nothing I need."

"Then why push this match?"

"Because *you* need it, as much as she does," she said earnestly. "I've watched you for years, seen the way you obsess about Lismore Hall, striving above all to get it back. It's not healthy to obsess about something like a building. And yet, now I give you a perfect opportunity and you are throwing it away."

"By forcing me to marry for it?"

She rolled her eyes. "Such language. No one is forcing you to do anything."

"You *are* though."

"I simply don't understand your aversion to her," Belle said, peering past him. He twisted to follow her gaze, landing on Hope. "What's wrong with her? She's as good as any young lady."

"It's not that."

"Then what is it?"

Graham opened his mouth to speak, but he couldn't. The words would not come. He had long held private beliefs about himself and if he spoke about them out loud, it would only solidify them.

"It's none of your concern," he said finally.

Lady Belle's mouth flattened into a thin line.

"You're being terribly stubborn, MacKinnon, even for you," she said, gazing over the crowd. "Lismore Hall would be yours if only you married her."

"Why are you so invested in this?"

Belle's eyes shifted and Graham got the distinct impression that she was hiding something from him. She drifted away from him, refusing to answer his question.

"Do whatever you wish, MacKinnon. But don't blame me when your dream is taken away. Permanently."

She raised her cane in greeting at someone across the room and left him alone against the far wall of the hall. Belle was behaving suspiciously, and he was determined to figure out what she was up to and why she was so eager for this match between him and Hope.

Scanning the room as he walked, Graham saw Hope standing a little way away from everyone else. Knowing he wouldn't be able to avoid her all night, Graham advanced toward her quickly. When she caught sight of him approaching her, he could have sworn her eyes brightened.

Chapter Eight

HOPE SWALLOWED HARD as Graham neared. No man had ever looked at her the way he was watching her now, and though she couldn't explain why, her entire body felt hot. He wore a green and blue plaid, shirtsleeves, and a formal jacket, and Hope was convinced she had never seen a more handsome man.

Hope's eyes drifted down as his bare shins kicked out from beneath his tartan and she had to steel herself to keep from shivering. The crowd seemed to part as he moved, and she held her breath. Though she had seen plenty of kilt-wearing gentlemen that evening, the thought of touching Graham's muscular legs…

Oh no. Not touching. She could never do that.

"What?" she squawked as he halted before her.

"Excuse me?" His brow furrowed. "I didn't say anything."

"Oh no, not you," she said, shaking her head.

He smirked at her.

"Then who?"

She shook her head again.

"I'm sorry, I'm… I'm just a little overwhelmed by this soiree," she said, surveying the ancient room. "It's very beautiful here."

"Aye," Graham agreed, glancing around. "This was my mother's childhood home."

"She was the laird's daughter?"

"Aye, the chieftain of the Clan McTavish. It was once one of the largest clans in the highlands."

"But not anymore?"

"Not for a long time," he said, focusing back at her. "But McTavish kept his people as close as he could, and while others fell away, this one stayed. Diminished, but still strong."

"And from what I understand, you help employ quite a few people from the clan, correct?" she remembered what Rose had told her at the market.

"Who told you that?"

"Rose."

"Did she now?" He glanced around.

Hope followed his gaze, but she couldn't quite see over everyone's heads with the ease that he could. Instead, her eyes fastened on the tartan sash that he wore diagonally over his shoulder. "You're wearing a kilt."

Graham gazed back at Hope, and one of his brows arched slowly.

"Aye."

Heat crawled up Hope's neck.

"I thought you didn't like kilts."

"I ne'er said that. I said it was impractical to wear them year-round. I wear it when it's appropriate."

"Like at balls?"

"Aye, and formal occasions."

The green and blue was different from the MacKinnon plaid, and she frowned.

"I thought you were to wear your father's tartan?"

He nodded.

"That is the general rule."

"But you wear the McTavish plaid. Not MacKinnon." She gestured toward his sash. "You're supposed to be wearing red and green."

His eyes narrowed as her hand drifted absentmindedly to the brooch at the center of her neckline.

"And how would you know about the MacKinnon plaid?"

She fumbled slightly with the brooch and gently popped the hidden latch on the side. The locket opened up in her hand, but she did not reveal its contents. Instead, she looked into his eyes and saw an ocean of emotions that she couldn't decipher. It occurred to her that he might be offended by what she'd done. Perhaps it was poor etiquette to have a piece of his family's tartan made into jewelry.

Hope snapped the locket back together, suddenly unsure. She didn't want to upset Graham, and she worried for a moment that he might try and take it from her. He would be well within his rights, she supposed, but she wouldn't let him.

Her hand dropped from the brooch.

"Oh, I made the mistake of asking a shopkeeper in the village about tartans and how they worked. He was very well informed," she said. "Besides, the painting of your grandfather is rather, well, menacing. I'm afraid the MacKinnon plaid has been burned into my mind."

His eyes lingered at the spot her hand had been, and there was a new emotion on his face that made Hope's cheeks flush.

Just then Faith, Grace, and Rose appeared on either side of Hope. Faith handed Hope a glass of lemonade while Grace nodded along with the music, smiling. Rose wasn't smiling. Her attention seemed focused on a group of boisterous lads not too far away, listening to Jared McTavish speak.

"It's terribly exciting, isn't it?" Grace said as she watched. "I never dreamed we would be invited to a clan banquet. It's wonderful."

"I'm glad you're enjoying yourself," Graham said.

"It is rather interesting," Faith said, sounding more apprehensive than enthusiastic. "I've never seen so many kilts in one place. It's a fascinating piece of fashion. Don't you think, Hope?"

"Faith," Hope said under her breath as she took a sip of lemonade, praying silently that her sister would stop teasing her.

"Do you like kilts, Miss Sharpe?" Graham asked Faith.

Faith smirked.

"Well, not as much my sister here, but—"

"So, this is your uncle's home?" Hope interrupted quickly, taking a step forward, so that Faith was partially blocked from Graham's view. He raised his brows, but he didn't pursue the topic.

"Yes. It was built in the tenth century, originally. Actually, there's a bit of a romantic origins story. And considering how much you enjoy romance, I suppose I should tell you about it."

Hope's cheeks warmed. He was teasing her, but not in a cruel manner. Rather, it was like he was inviting her to be in on the joke.

"How did you know Hope likes romantic stories?" Grace asked.

Graham shrugged.

"All women do, don't they? Besides, I owe your sister a story," he said and to Hope's utter embarrassment and delight, he winked.

"Not all women," Faith muttered, taking a sip of her beverage.

Faith had often proclaimed that romance was nothing more than fanciful fluff. Hope couldn't understand why her sister was so determined never to fall in love.

"We would be very happy to hear your story, Mr. MacKinnon," Hope said, elbowing Faith ever so gently.

"Yes, please," Grace added, coming forward.

Graham smirked at Grace's eagerness, and Hope's heart fluttered. The stubble that the men wore on their faces this far north had seemed unkempt to her at first, but when standing in the middle of a Scottish stronghold, surrounded by men and women dressed in traditional Scottish wear, it seemed charming, in a rough sort of way.

As he began to tell his story, Hope relished the chance to stare at him, noting the gentle creases at the corners of his green eyes. His nose was average in size, and his hair had been combed back to reveal a slight widow's peak. It fell to the side of his head in a decidedly roguish fashion. His mouth was full and Hope had to fight to ignore the way her stomach seemed to flip when he spoke.

"Legend tells of a lass who fell in love with a man deep in these woods, long ago," Graham said. "The man loved the lass very much, but he had been captured by the fae people and the fae queen would not let him free."

"Fae?" Grace repeated. "Like little people?"

"Aye," Graham said, as a few others overheard his story and came to stand with them. "The fae are a mischievous and tricky bunch."

"Excuse me," Faith said. "I think you mean to say they're *supposed* to be a mischievous and tricky bunch."

His brow creased.

"No, I mean they *are*."

"Mr. MacKinnon, you cannot expect us to believe that you believe in fairy creatures."

Everybody that had been listening to Graham's tale craned their necks to stare at the middle Sharpe sister. She blinked back at them, utterly confused by their reaction.

"Faith, it isn't polite to interrupt," Hope said hastily, hoping to avoid offending anyone. Though fairy tales were commonly believed to be fiction, it wasn't unheard of for country folk to believe in the old stories, especially those that had been passed down from generation to generation. It wasn't courteous to disregard their beliefs, even if she didn't share them herself. "Please, Mr. MacKinnon, continue."

"Well, this man who had been captured by the fae queen needed to be rescued."

"Aye, and only a bonny lass could do it," said a handsome, stout man with copper-colored hair. He looked rather similar to the McTavish men. "Tam Lin!"

"Tam Lin!" others said, smiling and nodding at the mention of a beloved folk heroine.

"Who is Tam Lin?" Hope asked.

"Tam Lin was the brave lass who outsmarted the fae queen and won her true love's freedom," Jared said as he elbowed his way into the group.

"You mean a woman was the rescuer?" Grace asked, bobbing slightly up and down on her heels. "That's brilliant."

"Och, who is this smart lass?" a woman with fiery red hair asked, coming up.

"Grace Sharpe," Grace said with a quick curtsy. "And these are my sisters, Hope and Faith."

"A pleasure to meet you. I'm Mrs. Jeanne Carlyle," she said. "So, you lot are living in Lismore Hall?"

"Yes," Grace replied.

Hope watched Jeanne's gaze land on Graham and she could have sworn a tension was growing in him.

"Well, go on, Graham," Jeanne said after a stilted pause. "Finish the story."

"Is there more?" Hope asked him. "What else is there to say other than that Tam Lin saved her love?"

"Aye, she did," he said slowly, tearing his eyes away from Jeanne to focus on Hope. "But it was how she did it that makes the tale truly grand. See, the fae queen insisted that Tam Lin wasn't strong of heart and couldn't manage her tasks. She told Tam Lin that if she could hold onto her love, she would set them free. Then the queen used her magic to change the man's form.

"He turned into all manners of beasts, but he warned Tam Lin that no matter his form, he would do her no harm and she was to hold on tight. He also warned her that when he changed into a burning coal, she was to toss him into a stream and he would appear."

"Naked," an older woman said saucily, causing everyone to laugh.

"Aye, naked," Graham said, smiling, his green eyes twinkling with mischief. "And Tam Lin was to hide him from the fae. Well, she did, and though the fae queen was furious at her loss, she accepted defeat and they lived happily ever after."

Several people cheered while some lifted their glasses in honor of Tam Lin.

"That was a delightful story," Grace said with a clap.

"But how does it relate to this stronghold?" Hope asked.

"Well, Tam Lin and her beau decided to leave the enchanted forest where the fae lived. They travelled far and wide until they came upon the mouth of the river. They followed it up into the highlands and came to a grove in the pines where a red calf grazed. Taking it as a sign, they built their own home and a stable for their calf. The rocks they pulled from the earth were all red sandstone, which," he said, stretching his hand out toward the closest wall, "is the very stone that made this stronghold."

A slow smile pulled at the corner of Hope's mouth. *What an enchanting man*, she thought as everyone clapped.

"That really was a wonderful story," Hope said, taking a step toward Graham. "Thank you for sharing it."

He stared at her for a moment and was just about to speak when Jared spoke, his eyes on Hope.

"It's grand to have you and your sisters at Elk Manor, Miss Sharpe," Jared said with a deep bow. "May I introduce you to the rest of my family?"

"Yes, please," Hope said.

"You already know cousin Graham," he said before he pivoted toward the red-heady woman. "This is my sister Jeanne, and those two," he nodded his head toward two identical copper-haired men, "are Michael and Jamie." Jeanne smiled and the other two grinned. "This is Miss Hope Sharpe and her sisters, Miss Faith and Miss Grace Sharpe."

Hope's cheeks warmed. She was glad to make everyone's acquaintance, but the scowl that appeared on Graham's face made her curious. Why did he look so cantankerous?

Just then, two sharp whacks caught everyone's attention. The group that had been listening to Graham's story spun around and saw Belle waving her cane from several yards away. Apparently, the noise had been her banging it on the floor to get everyone's attention. She pointed it at Graham. Though he appeared peeved to be summoned so, he took a deep breath.

"If you'll excuse me," he said to everyone as he left.

"Of course."

When he was out of earshot, Jared spoke.

"It amazes me that he lets the old bat order him around," he said as he leaned closer to Hope.

Her smile faltered, displeased with the moniker he had used for Belle. She was about to defend her aunt when Rose spoke up. Hope had nearly forgotten she was with them.

"You'll watch your tongue regarding Lady Belle, Jared McTavish," Rose said, a slight tremor to her voice. Her cheeks were bright red and while her words were loud and clear, she couldn't quite seem to face Jared as she spoke. "She's a right decent woman and you've no business calling her such names."

Jared stared at Rose, giving her his full attention for the first time that evening.

"Aye, Miss Rose, I didn't mean anything by it," he tried. "Lady Belle wouldn't be offended if she'd heard me, I promise. I call her much worse to her face during her visits when she insists on playing cards with me and the lads."

"She plays cards with you, Mr. McTavish?" Hope asked.

"Aye, sometimes. She's a shark, that one, and I've told her as much." He winked. "She's not your average sort of lady, you know."

"Yes, I do know that," Hope said, making yet another personal note about her aunt. Rose, however, didn't seem pleased with Jared's explanation.

"Call her anything you'd like, but not behind her back," Rose said stiffly.

"Don't be angry," Jared continued. "I only meant that say that she's too heavy-handed with ordering Graham about."

"Are they not friends?" Hope asked. "From what Belle says, I was under the impression that she and Mr. MacKinnon have a very close friendship."

"They are, but he gives that woman too much rein." Jared said. "It's not healthy for a man to take orders from a woman."

Hope tilted her head. That sounded like exactly what a man would think.

"Is that so? And I suppose your wife agrees with such sentiment?"

"I'm not married."

"Nor will you be with that attitude," she countered, much to the glee and giggles of the others who had overheard. Everyone except Rose.

"I've never known such intelligent Englishwomen," Jeanne said, smiling widely. Her green eyes sparkled with delight. "Tell me, were you all this entertaining in London?"

Though none of the Sharpes moved, Hope knew each of her sisters had the same false smile plastered on their faces.

"London was a dreadful bore compared to this," Faith said. "But we did not receive dance cards. How do we know when a gentleman wishes to dance?"

"Like this," said the redhead Jamie, who dragged a protesting Faith onto the dance floor.

Grace squealed as Michael seized her hand, and before she knew it, Hope was being tapped on the shoulder by a smiling Jared.

"May I have this dance? So that you might teach me more of your radical ways that I might find a proper lass?"

Hope laughed and took his hand. "Absolutely."

Chapter Nine

B ELLE STOOD ALONG the side of the dance floor, appearing both worried and annoyed. Graham approached her quickly and dipped his voice.

"Yes?"

"Your uncle has informed me of some news," she said softly, looking around to make sure no one overheard. "One of your cousins has asked to court Hope."

"Court her?" he repeated. The fine hairs on the back of his neck stood up in warning. "She's barely met anyone. Who in their right mind is trying to court her already?"

"Now, as I am the only guardian she has, I must tell you I am considering giving my consent—"

"You bloody well will not," he said.

"Well, she won't be available forever, MacKinnon," Belle said. "And Jared McTavish would make a fine husband."

"Jared?" Graham said loudly, causing several people to stare in their direction.

"He's your uncle's heir and in a better position than any other man here. Besides, he's stated he's quite taken with her—"

"He's met her once."

"That was enough to be charmed by her."

For heaven's sake, had everyone lost their bloody minds? The woman had hardly been here two weeks. Was he the only person who thought it was an insufficient amount of time to get to know someone? And what was Jared playing at? He had never expressed interest in marriage before. Now all of a sudden he was keen on the idea?

Something suspicious was afoot, but Graham wasn't sure what. All he knew was that the idea of Hope being tied to his cousin didn't sit right with him.

"Over my dead body," he said as he searched the crowd.

"MacKinnon, you will not interfere in Hope's personal business. If you don't want her, she will certainly have to marry someone else."

"Och, so now you don't want me to marry her?"

"I don't care much what you do anymore if you don't want her."

"I don't know why you're so damned set on this plot of yours. I'll not be bullied and threatened by you or anyone about my future," he said through gritted teeth.

"No one is making you do anything. I'm simply pointing out that if you won't have her, Jared will."

He gazed across the sea of people and Graham saw Jared, dancing with a smiling Hope.

His jaw clenched.

"Why are you so desperate to marry her off?"

"I'm simply trying to secure her future, as well as her sisters'. They're not as worldly as you or me and they'll need someone trustworthy to protect them and help them through life when I'm gone."

"And are you planning on dying anytime soon?" Graham said sarcastically. Silence followed.

Graham turned his attention back to her. The crease in Belle's brow was deeper, her wrinkled face twisted into a worried expression he had never witnessed before. Realization began to dawn on him, and he wondered if he had said the wrong thing.

"Lady Belle—"

Her hand flew up and he stopped speaking.

"So be it. Let Lismore go to your cousin. Stubborn fool."

She swung around dramatically, her skirts puffing out as she did. He was dismissed and, apparently, freed from her meddling. But her failure to respond to his question irritated him. Was she unwell?

Glancing back across the ballroom, it took only seconds for him to find Hope again. Graham had never seen a woman so set on being happy. Almost as if she were determined to find joy in every situation. Even now, as the music played and she twirled faster and faster, the largest smile was plastered on her face. It made him inscrutably happy and oddly irritated that she should be smiling while being held in another man's arms. He reminded himself firmly that she didn't belong to him. But as he walked along the edge of the dance floor, watching her twirl across the dance floor, a new sensation sprung up within him.

Unwanted desire. Physically, he had craved her since he first laid eyes on her. But he had been able to chalk that up to mere animalistic instinct. What he hadn't expected was to be enthralled by her and he couldn't bear it. He refused to want her, if only to spite Belle.

Graham knew he should turn his back on the entire affair, make a clean break, but that prospect was equally unsatisfying. If he decided to wash his hands of the ordeal, he had no doubt that she would eventually marry someone else, possibly Jared, and he couldn't allow that either.

He had never experienced such a sensation before. No person had ever stirred a possessiveness that seemed to swallow him up like when he saw Hope dancing with Jared. He had no claim to her, no reason to become incensed. Hell, he barely knew her. Jared was one of his greatest confidants, and yet it didn't matter. All he saw was Hope, her body pressed against someone who wasn't him, and his resolve snapped.

He crossed the dance floor and reached them in seconds.

"Ah, cousin, you should find yourself a dance partner," Jared said with a friendly smile as he and Hope nearly bumped into him.

Graham didn't reply. He only held out his hand, his complete attention on Hope.

"Oh," she said, visibly startled by his actions. She seemed unsure of what to do as she glanced between Jared and Graham. "Um." Swallowing, she slowly retracted her hand from Jared's. "A-all right."

"Och, no," Jared said, annoyed. "Go find your own."

But Graham didn't listen. He steered Hope away, and they glided swiftly and effortlessly through the masses, edging closer and closer to the outside of the circle. Hope kept her eyes steadily on Graham, obviously waiting for him to speak, but he didn't know what he wanted to say. He only wanted to be away from the crowd to give himself some time to think.

"That was rather impolite," she said as they danced.

Graham tried to ignore the softness of her body beneath his hands. Instead, he focused on her words.

"So?"

Hope frowned.

"Is that all you have to say?"

He wasn't sure what he wanted to say. Hope let out a huff of disapproval and tried to wriggle away from him, but Graham couldn't let her go.

"Wait. Come with me," he commanded.

He didn't know what propelled him to hold onto her, but he wouldn't release her, and by the expression on her face, he wondered if she perhaps wasn't at least a little curious herself.

On the third go about the room, he slipped out the back door, pulling her along.

His hand went through his hair as he tried to sort out his emotions, all the while with Hope standing before him. Perhaps it was because of what she represented. She was his chance to regain ownership of his heritage. Surely that was why he had dragged her out of the castle, fighting off the urge to snarl at anyone who got in his way. Surely it was just the idea of what he could have that made him feel so desperate.

They stood on the slate stacked terrace that overlooked a

winding stream that cut through the forest. She was breathing deeply, arms crossed and visibly agitated.

"Why did you bring me out here?" she asked, with a shiver.

"Are you cold?" he asked.

"No. Actually I rather prefer the cold."

"Aye, so do I."

She looked at him for a long moment with a puzzled expression.

"Why are we out here? What everyone must think we are doing?"

"Ack, tis only the McTavish Clan. They probably think we're having a row."

"And they would be correct," she said quickly. "You had no right to pull me away from that gentleman."

"Save your praises for a better man. Jared isn't a saint."

"He's a sight more well-behaved than you."

Graham took a step toward her. "I'll have you know, I'm the most levelheaded Scot for a hundred miles."

"Ha," Hope said boldly. "If you're the most levelheaded, I should return to England at once."

"Aye, perhaps you should," he snapped. "You being here is causing far too much trouble for me already."

His annoyance, desire and agitation seemed to reverberate between them. She tilted her head, as if it were hard to understand him.

"What do you mean? I've not done anything."

"You have," Graham said, crowding her in a way that demanded she crane her neck back to see him. "Since before you got here. Never have I known a woman to cause such trouble before I even met her."

"That's hardly fair. You didn't know me before I arrived."

"Aye, and now I do." His voice dropped slightly as he glared down at her. "And I was right. You're nothing but trouble."

His words seemed to have an odd effect. Hope stared at him, pain crossing her face, and Graham hated himself. He hadn't wanted to hurt her, but Lord above, he couldn't be conned into marriage just for a house.

His fingers moved through his hair. It was hard to focus with her so close.

"I'm sorry you feel that way," she said softly as her hand rose to her chest. Toying with the brooch, she appeared unaware of the fact that she was fidgeting. A click sounded, followed by a small snapping noise. "But it isn't my fault that you find me so terrible."

Damn it. Graham groaned.

"I don't find you terrible," he said, feeling compelled to apologize. She clicked her brooch. "What I meant to say was—" *Click. Click.* He frowned. "I just find you—" *Click. Click.* He couldn't finish his thoughts with that constant clicking, and the placement of her hand was rather distracting. "What is that?"

"What's what?"

"That." Graham nodded toward her chest. "What's that noise you're making?"

Her hand dropped instantly.

"It's nothing," Hope said quickly.

Too quickly.

"It's something. Show it to me."

"No."

He stared at her for a moment and, without thinking, without breathing, he took another step toward her, eliminating what little space was between them. She didn't retreat. With their bodies only inches away from one another, he peered into her deep brown eyes.

"Let me see it," he said huskily.

She seemed slightly dazed by his words and how close he was. Hope shook her head, but Graham was already lifting his hand to her chest.

With his eyes locked on hers, his large, calloused hand covered her smooth, elegant one. His fingers rolled her tiny treasure away and though he couldn't remove it from her gown without undoing the pins that held it in place, he thumbed to the edge of the brass ornament until he found a latch.

Graham pressed on it and with a soft click it opened, like a little book in his hand. Her pink cheeks flushed and while he initially supposed she was embarrassed by how close he stood, as his eyes drifted down to the locket, he understood the real reason.

There in his palm, no larger than a skipping stone, showed the MacKinnon family plaid. He hadn't been expecting that. To see the red and green tartan, held in place on her dress, very near her heart… well, it did something to him.

"I'm sorry," she whispered after a long time, sounding worried. "I didn't mean to offend you by wearing it."

"You haven't offended me," he said, his tone rough. "You've surprised me, 'tis all. Where did you find it?"

"There was a torn piece in one of the wardrobes at Lismore Hall. I wouldn't have taken it, but it was so small a piece that I thought it would be a sort of tribute to your family, in a way. I thought it would signify our appreciation, mine and my sisters', for how kind you've been to our aunt over the years."

What stories had Belle told her nieces about their friendship?

"What did Lady Belle say about me exactly?"

One of her slender shoulders shrugged as she lowered her head.

"She said that you've been a dear and loyal friend since she came to live here permanently, ten years ago. That you've always been kind and patient and that there was no better man she's ever met."

The crest of Graham's cheeks burned at the praise Lady Belle had bestowed on him. It was an outright lie, of course. They had butted heads since the beginning and he had been a hellion to her in the beginning of their acquaintance.

"Did she really say that?"

"Yes." Hope nodded. "Anyway, I thought it was a fitting thing to wear here, but now I think I was mistaken."

"It's not your fault. I was just surprised to see it. I don't wear the MacKinnon plaid." His gaze dropped back down to the locket. "I never have."

"Never?" she asked, surprised. "Is it because of what happened with your father?"

He was quiet for a moment, unwilling to share such a private matter with her, and yet, unable to stop himself, he spoke at last.

"Aye," he said slowly, eyes on his plaid. "Losing the house was my father's biggest regret in life, or so my uncle told me. He was never able to recover from it. I was ashamed of him for a long time. There was never any amount of pride for being a MacKinnon. I wear the McTavish tartan out of respect for the uncle who took me in, but also, because I was ashamed of my own family's legacy."

He had never said the words out loud, and though Graham knew it was a dreadful thing to admit, it was true. Maybe he was a traitor, but he had always been ashamed of his father's choices and thus had little pride in the plaid he was supposed to wear.

"I swore as a boy that I would not wear the MacKinnon tartan until I recovered what my father lost."

She looked down at his hand. Her cool fingers wrapped around his. Suddenly, heat and desire shot through his veins. "I'm sorry. I didn't mean to hurt you by wearing it."

"You didn't," he said.

"No?" she replied, skeptically. "Then perhaps I shocked you. You don't have a very pleased expression about you."

Graham took a deep breath as he stared into her eyes.

"Don't I?"

"No."

"Then I suppose you did shock me. Not any more then my own feelings though."

"How so?"

"Honestly?" he asked, and she nodded. "It would only frighten you if I explained it."

"Please?" she said softly. "I won't be afraid." He found he couldn't deny her.

Leaning forward, he bent his head so that his mouth found the edge of her ear. Hope shivered as his bottom lip gently grazed the soft cartilage.

"The truth is, that up until this moment, MacKinnon plaid has never made me feel anything except shame. But seeing it on you, as small as that piece of it is, well… I didn't expect to be so moved at the sight of it…"

The gentle intake of breath reminded Graham of that soft moan that had escaped her lips when they first kissed. As he bent his head, his mouth found hers with a captivated urgency. He didn't know what divine power had forced those words from his lips, but then, he didn't care. Kissing her was the single most important thing he had ever done in his life.

His arms wrapped around her, drawing her against his chest as a dozen sensations ran through his mind. She tasted like sugar and smelled like the glen after a rain. She was tender and curious as her hands came up to his chest, tentatively touching him as though he might vanish. Graham kissed her harder, eager to demonstrate that he wasn't going anywhere.

What had come over him? Never in his life had he allowed himself to be so at the mercy of his own desire. Since the moment he saw Hope in the walled garden, she had fascinated him, even though the mere idea of her should have made him wary. But her authenticity had confused him. Hope was far too forthcoming. She was clever and optimistic and he found himself wanting to protect her, even though he was the exact person she should be most cautious around.

Did she realize what her aunt was doing? He needed to come clean and tell her the truth, but the more he kissed her, the less he wished to talk and the more he wanted to touch every inch of her.

His hands grazed over her arms, tugging at the short sleeves to expose her perfect shoulders that he kissed and licked and nipped at. His mouth roamed back up her neck as she gripped his head to her. She seemed just as affected as he, and he was filled with a fierce desire to carry her away to some secret place.

Only he wouldn't be so lucky.

A soft feminine cough sounded from far away. They both froze, and he slowly lifted his head to see Rose, who appeared very torn indeed.

"Oh!" Hope said, backing away from Graham, who let her go immediately.

Rose came forward with determined steps, peering over her shoulder as she did.

"I'm sorry to interrupt," she said, her eyes darting between Graham and Hope. "But you mustn't be doing that. Not here anyway."

"Oh goodness," Hope said, a blush coming over her face. She tried to cover her embarrassment with her hands as she pressed her fingers against her cheeks. "I am mortified."

"Was your plan to shame her?" Graham said accusingly, coming up to Rose. "You've some nerve, Miss Rose."

"Of course, it wasn't. I didn't come to shame anyone," Rose said in a harsh whisper. "I'm trying to save you."

"Save us?"

Just then, Belle, Laird McTavish, Jared, Faith, and Grace rounded the corner.

"MacKinnon! Alone with my niece?" Belle said in mock shock, followed by genuine surprise. "Uh-oh. Wait. Miss Rose?"

"Yes, ma'am," Rose said, stretching her arm out over Hope's shoulders. "We've all come to take a bit of fresh air. Terribly stifling inside, it is."

"Yes, that's why Lady Belle suggested a tour of the grounds," Laird McTavish said, his brow knitted together as he stared at Hope.

Graham looked between Lady Belle and her secretary. As he saw a stilted glare exchanged between the two, he realized what had nearly happened. Belle had tried to trap him in a compromising position—and Rose, for whatever reason, had stopped it.

Unbridled fury bubbled up inside his chest as his angry eyes landed on the old meddler. He was very close to wringing her neck and if there wasn't an audience surrounding them at the moment, he'd certainly have given her a piece of his mind.

"You," he snapped at Belle, his tone furious.

"Ah, Mr. MacKinnon," Hope said, coming up. Her voice stilled him for a moment. "Thank you so much for showing Miss Rose and me the grounds. They were quite beautiful to see in the moonlight."

He knew she was trying to defuse the situation, but he couldn't help but feel hostile.

"If you appreciate the moonlight," Jared said, coming forward, "I'd be honored if you and your sisters would join us at the games. Of course, the majority of the events take place during the day, but we do have a bonfire of sorts afterwards. It's in about two weeks' time."

"The games?" Grace asked, her head tilting.

"Aye, the highland games," Jared said, smirking at Graham. "You all are more than welcome to attend."

"Oh, that would be lovely."

Lord above, Graham thought as his gaze traveled from person to person. The whole damn clan was becoming smitten with these Sharpes, and they were becoming equally invested, seemingly unaware that they were each merely pawns on Lady Belle's chess board. Well, the McTavishes could have the lot of them. Graham stalked away, right through the middle of the group.

"MacKinnon," someone called after him, but he didn't stop.

Chapter Ten

HOPE WASN'T SURE what she expected when Jared McTavish invited her and her sisters to the games, but this was not it. Several white tents dotted the valley below the pyramidal mountain ridge known as Carn Eige. The ridge broke out of the green ground like a rock had been pressed through torn suede, and the shadows of the clouds above danced across the various shades of heather, grass, and moss.

The sheer size of the mountain had made Hope gawk when the carriage transporting her, her sisters, and Rose came out of the glen. All sorts of carts and camps lined the road, set up for the games that would take place during the day before the bonfire that evening. Hope found herself once more wondering if she would see Graham.

When he had left the ball at Elk Manor, he had been furious and Hope couldn't quite understand it. She was sure he had been upset by something she had done, but he did not give her the opportunity to clear things up. She had seen him the day before yesterday from her bedroom window at Lismore Hall and had gone down to speak with him, but by the time she had reached the apple tree, he had gone.

Hope glanced up to the sky. Massive white clouds that looked like kingdoms all their own rolled against a blanket of blue, blocking out the sun. She began to worry about tilting over as the carriage climbed the base of the mountain up the steep slope, and she was grateful when the vehicle stopped.

"The day could not be finer," Rose said, peering out of her window as the carriage stopped. "It's a great day for a race."

"It's a shame Aunt Belle couldn't make it," Faith said.

Belle insisted Rose accompany Hope and her sisters since she could not attend. Belle had an appointment with Dr. James Hall, a doctor who was currently working as a police surgeon. He had grown up in the area but had moved his offices to Glasgow. Since his visits north were few and far between, Belle had few opportunities to see him, and thus she had explained that she couldn't possibly attend the race. She all but forced her reluctant secretary to accompany her nieces in her place.

"Be careful where you step," Rose said as the coachman opened the door. "These slopes are filled with holes and rocks. You will turn an ankle if you aren't careful."

The terrain this far north was rougher than the clean walking paths in London, and Rose had advised Hope and her sisters to wear their riding habits and sturdy boots. Hope was wearing a new Basque-style outfit she had bought for that year's season. Instead of a gown, the Basque was two separate pieces, a dark, emerald jacket paired with a black skirt trimmed with the same emerald hue. Each sister wore wide-brim hats instead of bonnets, tilted forward as was the fashion.

"About that, Rose," Hope said. "I didn't see any sort of track or downs path. Where will this race take place?"

"Right there," Rose said, pointing into the distance as she came up to stand next to Hope. Hope turned to see the expanse of land before them. "The men will start from that pole, a little away from the tents. Do you see it? They start by running a foot race down the slope, although they don't always complete it on foot."

"What do you mean?" Hope asked.

"Well, it's a bit steep, and there are rabbit holes all over. They're likely to trip and roll down if they can't keep their footing."

"Isn't that dangerous?" Grace asked.

"Foolish is more like it," Rose said, her tone one of displeasure. "Jared McTavish nearly broke his leg last year."

"Goodness," Grace said. "Then why do it?"

"Because they're men," Rose said, as if that explained everything. Hope smiled despite herself. "Once they reach the bottom of the slope, they'll cross that river and get on their horses. Then they'll ride to the tree line down there." Rose pointed down the valley.

"That far?" Faith said, gazing off into the distance.

"Aye. Then they'll race around that first lone oak tree before heading back over the river. Whoever makes it back first wins."

"And what do they win?" Hope asked.

"A favor from a fair maiden," a deep masculine voice said behind her. Hope whipped around and found herself face to face with Graham.

The sun shone behind him, outlining him in a way that made Hope's eyes water and her heart skip a beat. She hadn't spoken to Graham in nearly two weeks, and her strong reaction to his presence surprised her. He towered above her, dressed in his kilt again, like some ancient knight in a painting, and she had to bite the inside of her mouth to stop it from dropping open.

Good heavens, what was wrong with her?

"S-surely not," she stuttered while Rose and her sisters had the oddest expressions on their faces.

"Well, not in the last two hundred years, but once upon a time ..."

Hope let out a tittering laugh but quickly stifled it, worried she was coming off like some sort of fool in front of him. She needed to say something intelligent and witty to regain the upper hand again.

"I hope you don't break your neck," she blurted out and then swallowed. "Running, I mean. Well, I mean, falling off your horse, too. Really, there are so many ways you could break your neck. Either way, I hope you don't."

Silence followed. Panicked, she turned to her companions.

Rose and Grace were covering their mouths, presumably to hide their smiles, while Faith mouthed 'what is wrong with you?' For the life of her, Hope did not know.

Graham smirked, though his brow knit together and he tilted his head.

"Thank you for those words of encouragement," he said just as Jared and Jeanne joined them. Jeanne wore a cream and emerald striped gown and her red hair was pinned back in a smart, practical hairstyle, though several strands seemed to be falling out of place already.

"Fine day for a race, innt?" Jeanne asked.

"Aye, fine a day as ever there was," Jared said, grinning at Hope. "How do you do, Miss Sharpe?"

"Very well, thank you," Hope said, trying not to blush at his pointed interest in her when he should have addressed all the ladies present. "Are you competing in the race, Mr. McTavish?"

"Aye, I am."

"Rose was just explaining to us how it was done."

Jared's gaze flickered to Rose for a moment.

"Miss Rose would be the best to explain it. She has been coming to see us race for nigh five years now, haven't you?" Jared asked, but before he let Rose answer, he continued. "Who will you champion, Miss Sharpe?"

"Champion?" she asked, confused. "What do you mean?"

"Well, each competitor has a lady who he races for," Jared explained, smiling at Graham. "Innit true, Graham?"

"Aye," Graham said, seeming a bit stiffer than he had been a moment ago. "The McTavishes are prone to romantic gestures."

"Ack, it's not romantic. It's historic."

"Like the knights of old." Hope's heart beat faster as she observed Graham. The expression he gave her was not sweet or romantic. It was scorching. To avoid it, she quickly turned to face Jared. "It is a bit romantic, Mr. McTavish."

"Aye, and Miss Sharpe is quite a romantic herself," Graham said. "Aren't you?"

Hope's cheeks burned with embarrassment. She wasn't sure what Graham was playing at, but she felt annoyed as she wondered if Graham was mocking her.

"Is that so?" Jared asked, smiling.

"Leave Hope alone, you two," Jeanne said, coming up to hook her arm into Hope's. Her green eyes seemed to match the emerald color of her dress. "They're both teasing you. None of the men take favors from anyone. They race for no motive other than their own desire to be the biggest jackass of the highlands."

Hope's mouth fell open at the curse while Faith snickered and Grace slapped her hand to her mouth. Jeanne led Hope and the rest of the ladies away toward a pointed pavilion.

Chairs had been set up to support the eldest attendees, who sat surrounding several tables. Two gigantic oriental rugs had been laid out, overlapping one another. Massive cushions, pillows and the like had been strewn in a way that reminded Hope of an illustrated book of the *Rubiyat* by Omar Kyaamann. Guessing that they would be expected to sit on the ground, she let Jeanne pull her down to the spot with the most oversized pillows.

"We'll be able to see just about everything from here." Jeanne nodded to the others to sit. "You know, Jared nearly broke his leg last year."

"That's what Rose was saying," Hope said, looking back at Rose.

"Aye, she would know," Jeanne said with a sly glance at the freckled blonde. "She's been in love with Jared ever since she first laid eyes on him."

"I have not, Jeanne!" Rose said hotly but quietly, ensuring no one overheard. She leaned forward and continued in a low voice. "Do not say such things."

"Why not? It's true."

"It isn't. I'm not in love with him," Rose insisted, though her cheeks shone bright red.

"Fine, have it your way," Jeanne said, clearly not believing her. She leaned closer to Hope and added quietly, "Don't let her fool you. She'd travel to hell and back just to please my brother."

"And he doesn't feel the same?"

"He doesn't even know Rose is alive, the laggard-head. Here he has a perfectly sweet, smart lass hanging on his every word, but because everyone hangs on his word, he doesn't realize that she's in love with him. I was going to fix that, you know, until you showed up."

Hope shifted slightly to face Jeanne.

"What do I have to do with it?"

"Well, Jared's not stopped talking about you since the ball. I think he's set his sights on you."

Hope shifted her weight slightly from one foot to the other. She wasn't sure what to say.

"Oh, no, surely not. We've barely spoken."

"He says you're as fine a lass as any. There's a rumor he may ask your aunt for her blessing so that he can court you."

Hope's mouth dropped open as the rest of her body became still.

"Court me? But we hardly know one another," Hope said, unsure. Though she had enjoyed Jared McTavish's company, she wasn't sure there was the potential for much more than friendship between them, even if he was rather flirtatious at times.

"Well, such is the point of courting. For now, what Jared knows is that he thinks you're fine, and so does Father, and so do I."

Hope smiled at Jeanne. She glanced over the field to the line where the men lined up to start the race. Jared McTavish was a good-looking man, who seemed to have a sweet temperament and a mischievous glint in his eye, but Hope couldn't help but admire the man standing next to him.

Graham wasn't nearly as quick to smile, nor was he mischievous. Something about him made Hope sad, and it unnerved her as she watched him bend to pull up his kilt hose and strap it to his leg. He was severe and unfathomable, unlike his easygoing cousin. Despite everything, though, there was just something about Graham that fit her.

As if he could sense her gaze upon him, Graham stilled, his eyes catching hers. Hope immediately whipped around, not wanting to be caught ogling him.

"Of course, I told him it dinna matter," Jeanne said as she watched Hope. "Not when you were already spoken for."

"Spoken for?" She swallowed, ignoring the warmth crawling up her back. Was Graham still looking at her? She cleared her throat. "Spoken for by whom?"

"Graham MacKinnon, of course."

"Oh goodness, no," Hope said, shaking her head, though her heart began to beat faster at the mere suggestion. Were people really gossiping about her and Graham? She didn't want to be connected with him like that, but she couldn't ignore the thrill that went through her at the idea of being spoken for by him. "Mr. MacKinnon and I are barely friends. Acquaintances, really. Nothing more."

"Believe what you like, Miss Sharpe, but I was a lady in love once," Jeanne said as a far-off happiness shone in her green eyes. A passing breeze caused a few strands of auburn hair to dance across Jeanne's face. "I know what it's like to be caught by a man's gaze—and it's what I've seen when Graham looks at you. I'd sooner lose me right arm than not believe that he's about you."

Hope opened her mouth to argue, but then she caught sight of Graham again with his cousins at the starting line, smiling and patting Jared on the back as they prepared to begin. He appeared so happy in that moment, and she wondered what he must have been like in his youth. Had he been bitter from the beginning about what happened to him? Obviously, the love he shared with his cousins had buoyed him in life. Yet another stab of guilt sliced through her that she was related to Belle, who had robbed him of so much, even as a small voice in her mind seemed to whisper that perhaps she could give it back one day.

She wasn't sure how, or even if it was possible, but as the

men lined up for the race, she promised herself that one day she'd be instrumental in helping Graham achieve his goal of reclaiming his ancestral home.

Jeanne sighed, grabbing Hope's attention.

"It's a foolish race, this is. But my Duncan did love it."

Hope wasn't sure what to say. She had learned that Jeanne's husband, Duncan, had perished in the Burmese war, but this was the first time Jeanne had actually mentioned him.

"My aunt told me she only met your husband a handful of times before he left for war," Hope said quietly. "She said he was a fine man."

"Aye. Duncan was very fine," Jeanne said, her tone light yet heavy simultaneously. "He and Logan Harris went off together. We were young, babes really when we married, but he was determined to fight, and I was quite taken with the idea of being married to a soldier." Though her words were gently spoken, Hope noted a deep sadness. "It's been three years, but sometimes I swear he still… Well…" She laced her hands together, unable to finish the thought.

Instinctively, Hope squeezed Jeanne's fingers.

"I'm sorry."

Jeanne smiled sadly, shaking her head as if she could shake off the sudden melancholy that had come over them.

Just then, an elderly man with a long white hair and beard to match came hobbling with a cane toward the center of the starting line. One of the twins, possibly Michael McTavish, attempted to help the old man, but was hit in the shin with the old man's cane and shooed away. A ripple of laughter tore through the competitors, and a smirking Michael hurried back to the starting line. The aged man held up his hands and everyone quieted.

"Greetings!" he shouted as everyone in the crowd yelled a greeting back. "Ach, settle down, settle down!" He waved a hand over to the competitors. "The Casan Laidir race has been held in these past hundred years to demonstrate the strength and speed of the McTavish clan. It is a Scottish tradition that goes as far back as King Malcolm's race and one we proudly still uphold today." Cheers erupted around Hope as she and her sisters clapped along. "All right, all right! Now, gentlemen. Are ye ready?"

"Aye!" a collection of masculine voices said in unison from the group gathered between the tree trunks that were designated as the starting point. From what Hope could see, fourteen men lined up, with Graham and his cousins at the righthand side.

"Good." The old man fumbled with his pistol. It seemed he was unsure how to use it. "Now, at the sound of my pistol—"

CRACK.

Several ladies screamed while Hope and her sisters flinched as the gun went off, the bullet landing in a puff of dirt on the ground before the old man. The men were off instantaneously. Laird McTavish came up to escort the elderly man back to the chairs, carefully taking the firearm away.

Hope covered her mouth in surprise as the men ran down the slope at full speed. She was sure the momentum from running downhill would trip them, particularly on the uneven terrain, but only one or two men fell, rolling down the hill like cut lumber pushed off a cliff.

Her hands moved up the sides of her head and she held her face in dread.

"Oh goodness," Hope said, her brow crinkling beneath her fingertips. "Are they going to be all right?"

"Well, no one's ever died from participating in the Casan Laidir, if that's what you're asking," Rose replied.

"It's not," Hope said, straining her neck to see over the shoulders of the rest of the crowd, keeping her eyes on an ever-shrinking Graham as he ran ahead of the rest.

"What does Casan Laidir mean, Rose?" Faith asked, peering down the hill.

"Strong legs," Rose answered. "The McTavish claim to have the strongest legs in the highlands. It's an odd thing to claim, to be sure, but then there are the games to consider."

"Games?" Faith repeated.

"Aye. Some twenty years ago, the Lonach Highland and Friendly Society had the idea of holding a series of competitions, like they did in the olden days. Laird McTavish is a fan of those ancient stories and insisted on competing." Rose stood on her tippy toes to see better. "They've gone every year and always win all the foot races."

"Do they?" Hope asked. "That's quite impressive."

"It is," Rose agreed, watching the race. "Oh, I hate this part."

"What part?" Hope asked, seeing the men fast approaching a rushing river.

"It's not deep, but the water is quite fast and the rocks are slippery. Some years ago, Logan Harris cracked his head on a rock. I was just a girl then, but I'll not forget his bloody head as they carried him out."

"Mr. Harris participated?" Faith asked, interested.

"Yes," she replied. "Have you met him?"

"Briefly, at Elk Manor," Faith said, her face unreadable. "He doesn't seem the type to participate in this sort of thing."

"It was before he left for the war. He was a gangly young lad then, always eager to prove himself. He was winning by a long stretch that day, I remember. But he was too quick and lost his footing."

"Oh," Faith said.

"Every single one of them has nearly killed themselves in one way or another growing up here," Rose continued. "It's what makes them who they are."

Hope focused back on the race. Jared had been keeping pace with Graham as they came out of the river, but Graham was pulling slightly ahead as they reached the horses. A silly desire to see Graham win bubbled within her and she had to swallow back a cheer as he climbed up on the horse's back and vaulted off toward the cabers.

Hope's hands came together, bouncing slightly with excitement as he tore back across the river, farther away from those just finishing crossing on foot. Graham came hurtling back toward the slope as Jared followed close behind. A thrill went through her at the thought that Graham might win, when he suddenly pulled back, rearing the horse to a stop yards away from the finish line.

"What … what is he doing?" Hope asked, trying to keep the whine out of her voice. He was going to lose the race.

Graham slid off his steed and took several steps toward a man lying on the grass, clutching his shin. One of the men who had fallen at the beginning had stayed on the ground. Graham knelt down just as Jared crossed the finish line, and while a loud burst of cheers and congratulations erupted around Hope, she kept her eyes on Graham.

After a moment of assessment, he helped the young man rise and walked him up the hill. Within moments, Michael and Jamie crossed the finish line, followed by a burly man with a black beard. Graham was next, half carrying the injured contestant, whom he handed off to an older gentleman providing medical assistance.

"He lost, to help that man," Hope said.

It seemed Graham hadn't cared about winning at all. A warmth began to spread throughout her heart. Graham was a gentleman.

"Aye, that's MacKinnon," Jeanne said, sighing as if it were commonplace knowledge.

Jeanne went forward to congratulate her brother as the crowd encircled Jared. Hope tried to keep her gaze on Graham, but he was already moving toward the tents and fanfare of the festival further down the mountain.

Hope watched him walk away for a few moments before joining the others as the rest of the competitors came across the finish line. After the last man had come back, an informal garden tea commenced. Everyone ate, drank, and laughed as stories were told. While Hope enjoyed the laissez-faire atmosphere of the party, she couldn't help but glimpse over her shoulder from time to time, wondering where Graham had gone.

Once the meal was finished, Hope and her sisters, along with Jeanne and Rose, accompanied Jared and his brothers down the hill toward the makeshift tent town. As they approached the festival, Hope noticed a large stone circle in the center with massive amounts of dry wood, leaning together in a triangle.

"When will the bonfire begin?" she asked.

"Aye, we'll light it just at sunset," Jared said, pointing to the horizon. "Not too long now."

He offered her his arm as they came to a rocky stream and Hope took it. Jared was gentle and had a good temperament, but Hope felt no draw toward him. Not like she did for his cousin. Hope removed her hand from his arm after she was back on solid ground.

"Thank you," she said as she traipsed forward, hoping to match the pace with her sisters, as Rose hurried ahead.

Oh, dear. Hope debated going after her, to explain that she had no designs on Jared, but Jeanne caught up with her.

"There's no point in saying anything about Jared to her," she whispered as she leaned toward Hope. "She'll just deny having any feelings for him."

"But I don't want her to think I have designs on your brother."

"It doesn't matter."

"But why?" Hope asked as they walked. "If she feels a certain way, she should be honest. If not with him, then at least with herself."

Jeanne shrugged.

"She's an odd bird. I've told her many times that the only way to get Jared to notice her is to approach him head-on, and tell him exactly how she feels. He's a bit of a dolt in these sorts of matters."

"Jeanne, he's your brother."

"Exactly, which is why I can talk about him like this. He may not be a fool in some areas, but Jared is only aware of things in his direct line of vision and if Rose insists on living on the edge of his view, then nothing with ever come from her feelings for him." Jeanne climbed nimbly over a relatively large boulder before continuing. "I offered a dozen times to help her, but she always refuses."

"Perhaps she's too shy?" Hope offered as they came to the edge of the tent town. "Or maybe she's afraid he'll reject her?"

"That could be," Jeanne said, though she didn't sound convinced. "You see, I think she likes a bit of pining, but too much isn't good for your health."

"Well, perhaps we can help," Hope said, as the wheels of her mind began to turn. She frowned. "But what can we do? We need to get Jared's attention and somehow make sure that Rose is at the center of it." She bit the inside of her lip as she thought. "Maybe we can force Jared to see her, to actually take notice of her."

Jeanne eyed her suspiciously.

"How would we do that?"

"I'm not sure. Does she have any talents? Can she sing?"

"I'm not sure."

"Can she play an instrument? The pianoforte perhaps?" Jeanne shook her head and Hope's shoulders dropped. "If only there was some way to put her front and center."

After a moment, Jeanne's fingers slapped against Hope's forearm.

"She can dance."

Hope gave her a pained smile. Jeanne didn't seem to understand.

"Well, of course she can. All ladies can dance."

"No, not the kind of dancing you're picturing. Here, I have an idea," she said and leaned close to her ear. "Rose can sword dance."

"Sword dance?"

"Yes. Her brothers were well known for it and she's mentioned before how she learned along with them when they were children. We can do a sword dance. Tonight."

"We?"

"Well, of course. She wouldn't do it otherwise. Your sisters will have to help us."

"But we don't know how to sword dance."

"You don't need to. I have a plan," she said, winking as she pulled away from Hope's arm. "Let me talk to my father."

"All right."

Jeanne hurried off as Hope ambled past the tents and carts, enjoying the smells of delicious foods and spiced wine. Seeing Faith and Grace a few feet away, she moved through the crowd. She wasn't sure if Jeanne's plan would work, but she was hopeful, and she would need her sisters' help.

After Hope spoke with her sisters in whispers, Faith seemed less than pleased while Grace was nearly jumping up and down with excitement.

"Oh, this will be so much fun!" Grace exclaimed.

"I don't see how making fools of ourselves is going to help matters," Faith said.

"We won't be on anyone's mind when they see Rose," Hope said, peering over their heads. "Come, let's find Jeanne."

As the sun set, Hope, her sisters, Jeanne, and Rose come together in a circle. As several men lit the fire, to the cheers and claps of everyone, Jeanne helped tie up the girls' bustles.

"I don't see why we have to do this," Rose said, fixing her hair so it wouldn't come loose. "It seems awfully silly to me."

"My father's a silly man," Jeanne said as she tightened Grace's skirts. "But you know how he is. He loves revelry."

"Aye, but why cannot the men do this? It's a sword dance, after all."

"My father insists that I'm the best dancer in the family and I won't do it alone. Now hurry up," Jeanne said.

"And you all know what to do?" Rose asked Hope and her sisters, who nodded emphatically. "When did anyone have time to teach you?"

"Oh, well, Belle did when she would come visit us during Christmas," Hope lied.

"Lady Belle?" Rose said with suspicion. "With her cane and all?"

"Oh, well no, she taught us by telling us where our feet were to go, but I think we've become quite proficient in it. Don't you think so, Faith? Grace?"

"Very proficient," Grace agreed, nodding.

"Yes," Faith said, without conviction. "Very."

Hope glared at Faith from over Rose's shoulder.

"Very well, let's get it over with," Rose said as she led the way to face the crowd.

The rest followed her in a single line. Hope usually became quite nervous before performing, whenever she was requested to play the pianoforte or heaven forbid, sing, but this was different.

"Ladies and gentlemen!" Laird McTavish spoke, getting everyone's attention. "My daughter and her friends have asked to put on a performance and I canne say no. They've decided to start tonight's festivities with a dance, one that I know you'll all recognize." The smiling laird looked back at them and winked. "Ready?"

"Aye," Jeanne said.

He turned back.

"Very well. Music?"

As the first notes of the bagpipes chimed through the early evening air, Jeanne, Hope, and her sisters fell back to form a line behind Rose, who bent forward at the waist, and bounced on the tips of her toes. With her legs fully extended, she kicked straight out, her skirts tied high to avoid getting in the way. Turning to her right, she repeated the bouncing and kicking, now raising her hands as she did so.

Hope and her sisters watched with glee as Jeanne cheered Rose on. It really was a beautiful dance, and Hope wondered if she might truly learn it one day.

Gazing around Rose's dancing body, she spotted Jared in the

center of the crowd, observing Rose with the strangest expression on his face. He had been smiling like the rest of the group before the dance began, but it seemed something had come over him, and his gaze was now locked on Rose's face.

Hope tried to get around her sisters to see if Rose was watching Jared when a strange shiver went through her. Glancing around the bonfire, she caught sight of Graham, arms folded, watching her. He had a calculating expression on his face as he stood by the side of a food cart, a towering figure next to the small crowd that surrounded him.

Why should he look so serious, she wondered. Turning back to the others and finding that everyone was preoccupied with watching Rose, Hope decided to sneak away.

Slipping away, she placed her hands on several shoulders to excuse herself as she squeezed through the crowd. By the time she reached Graham, he was practically glaring at her.

"What's the matter?" she asked when she finally reached him. "You're scowling."

"I am not."

"You are," she said, folding her own arms across her chest to mimic him. She furred her brow. "See? You look like this."

Though Graham's face didn't change, a hint of amusement shone in his eyes. He turned his head, surveying the crowd around them before nodding his head backwards, silently asking her to follow him. She did. Past the tents, and people, toward the other side of a line of carriages that had been parked around the camp.

Once they were alone, he turned to face her, visible through slashes of firelight that danced between the shadows. Though they had been seen by several people, Hope wasn't overly worried about being caught in any sort of situation like they nearly had at Elk Manor. The feeling of these games was decidedly more relaxed than the atmosphere of a proper ballroom.

"You've played a nasty trick on Rose, not dancing with her," he accused quietly, much to Hope's surprise.

Did he really think she would do something that would purposely harm Rose? Annoyed, she folded her arms across her chest.

"You know nothing about it," she countered. "We have a plan, you see. Jeanne and my sisters."

"To make a fool out of her?"

"No, of course not. It's to make your cousin take notice of her. She's rather shy when it comes to him, as I'm sure you know, and we wanted to give him a bit of a push to make him notice her. We thought this was a clever idea," Hope said, tilting her chin up. "Besides, I would never harm Rose."

Graham's stare was scrutinizing but Hope remained unmoved. Then, after a moment he sighed.

"No. I suppose you wouldn't. Jeanne certainly wouldn't either." Hope smiled. "But it still isn't any of your concern whether or not Jared notices her. You should have left them to find their own way."

Her smile faltered.

"I'm surprised you're even talking to me."

He bent his head.

"Why is that?"

"Aren't you ignoring me?"

"Ignoring you?"

"Yes. You've barely spoken to me since the ball at Elk Manor."

He frowned.

"I had business in Glasgow, but I was at Lismore the day before last."

"Yes, I saw you in the garden. But when I went to join you, you took off."

"I had work to do," he said, peering over her shoulder back to the fire. Hope turned as well. At that moment, the music ended and a great cheer broke out over the crowd. Facing Graham again, she saw his suspicious gaze once more. "Rather like your aunt, after all, aren't you? Meddling in people's lives."

"What does my aunt have to do with this? And I hardly think getting your cousin to notice a woman is meddling."

"Well, it's not *not* interfering."

Hope squinted at him.

"I'm sorry, do you not like Rose?"

He blinked.

"What?"

"Or maybe you don't like your cousin."

"Ack, what are you going on about?"

"Only that you seem rather put out that someone should try to bring them together, but where's the harm in that?"

"If they were going to come together, it should be of their own volition. You lot are always meddling. Jared need not be led by any woman—"

"Ha," Hope said sarcastically. "If the world waited for men to do as they ought, we'd still be waiting for, well …" She paused, trying to think of something clever.

Graham stepped toward her and she glanced up at him, utterly unable to think up a clever quip. Through the carts, moving bodies and tents, the light from the bonfire flickered against him as he approached her.

"Aye?" he said, his tone rather rough. "What would we be waiting for?"

"Um," she said, staring into his heated gaze. She swallowed. "Well, something, I'm sure. Never you mind."

Graham's shadow-covered face smirked down at her and a shiver went through her.

"I would have thought *you* would want to get Jared's attention."

Hope let out a small laugh.

"Me? Oh goodness, no. Mr. McTavish seems a very fine man, but I've had my fair share of men," she said. Graham's mouth tightened, and she suddenly realized how sordid that had sounded. "Oh! No, that's not what I meant. I only mean to say that I've rather had my fill of, well, men's courtesy. I'm quite happy to be left alone."

"Is that so?" As he took another step forward, eliminating the remaining space between them, Hope's heart raced. "Because of your Mr. Pennyton?"

"Pennington," she corrected him. "And yes. That was enough experience for me, I'm afraid. I've quite had enough of masculine attention."

Graham didn't speak right away. They watched each other, the shadows of the distant bonfire dancing across his face. He appeared like he could be a pagan and her heart thudded, heaving against her chest, as if it were trying to break free.

Slowly, he raised his hand to her face. His fingers grazed her cheek, pushing back a loose strand of hair and tucking it behind her ear.

"I don't think you've ever really had masculine attention, Hope," he said, his accent curling around her name like smoke around an ember. Hope opened her mouth to argue, but hesitated when he leaned forward. Her breath caught in her throat as his lips grazed the edge of her ear. "Not the kind you deserve, at least."

"D-deserve?" she stuttered slightly.

He breathed against her skin, his breath hot.

"Aye."

Hope's eyes closed as she swayed slightly, trying to fight off the growing desire to touch him. For years, Jacob had shamed her for her cravings to be held. He, along with her grandmother, had told her repeatedly that such longings were improper, but she never succeeded in quelling them. She certainly couldn't now. Graham was so close; the heat radiating off him was too tempting. Her resolve to keep her hands to herself broke.

Opening her eyes, she dragged her oval-shaped fingernails against the fabric of his sleeves as his hands came up to rest on her hips. She could have sworn she heard his breath catch as she bent her head and whispered into his ear.

"What, what sort of attention do I deserve, Mr. MacKinnon?"

Chapter Eleven

A TREMOR SHOOK Graham's body at the gentle scratching of her nails trailing over his arms. She was restrained, hesitant almost, and he wondered if it was because she was truly unsure or whether it was just that she had been brought up that way.

God, she was tempting. Tilting his head until their temples met, he inhaled deeply. His fingers flexed against the softness of her hips. The scent of apple blossoms filled his senses as he breathed her in. It was dangerous being with her like this. He had avoided Belle's plot thus far, and while he had no desire to be caught in a situation that would dictate the rest of his life, he couldn't tear himself away from her.

Just a few more moments.

He had purposely been trying to avoid her the past two weeks, hoping to clear his mind from all of his thoughts about her. He had strained mightily to convince himself that his attraction to her was only due to the fact that she represented Lismore Hall.

But deep down, he knew that to be a lie.

Graham drew back slightly and their eyes met. The light from the bonfire danced on the side of her beautiful face, and the oddest sensation tugged in his gut. There was something here, something powerful, and though he was eager to explore it, he knew the darkness surrounding them gave him a false sense of privacy.

This was too risky. He needed to be away from her before he

compromised them both.

Pulling away, he planned to leave, but when her fingers caught at the creases of his jacket, Graham's gaze dipped to her hands and then back to her face.

Her mouth opened slightly, as though she wished to speak, but no words came out. Her cheeks reddened as her expression became embarrassed and Graham was flooded with remorse for making her ashamed in his presence. Her hands released him and her fingers curled into her palms as she tried to twist away.

"I'm sorry—"

But Graham wouldn't have any apology from her. His well-thought-out plan to scold her and leave her was unravelling quickly. This was why he'd avoided her, because whenever he was near her, the all-encompassing need to be closer to her was too great to resist.

Unable to stop himself, he reached for her slowly. It was a mistake, he knew it, but he simply couldn't stop himself. He needed to touch her. To taste her. One strong arm curved around her; his hand pressed on the small of her spine while the other came up to cradle the back of her head as his mouth found hers.

A jolt pierced through his body as he kissed her, his mouth desperate to taste every inch of her. His tongue brushed against hers, sweeping and sucking as he pressed her soft body against him. She tasted like strawberries and tea and when she melted against him, he felt himself harden.

Damned if he didn't want to take her right now, beneath the stars.

The thought should have frightened him. Should have warned him of the dangers of the whole situation, but he couldn't pull away from her. It made no sense. Even though he knew of Belle's plot to force him into marrying Hope, and that he should therefore avoid her at all costs, his better judgment seemed to vanish when he was standing near her.

It made his skin crawl to be managed, but Graham liked her despite himself. Being alone with her, he could be himself.

Graham had been cranky and rude, yet she hadn't withered away.

Instead, she was kissing him back, almost as eager as he was, if not very skilled. Still, her earnestness made up for any lacking skill, and a primitive need coursed through him. For he was more than willing to teach her all sorts of things.

His mouth travelled down her chin as she tilted her head back.

"Graham," she whispered, and a building heat coursed through him.

"Mm?"

"What… We … Oh," she said as his mouth reached the hollow below her ear, breaking her thoughts.

He was glad to quiet her and yet regretted not hearing her speak. What a maddening desire this was. He needed to kiss her, to devour her entirely.

He dropped his hand from the back of her head and brought it down over her body, touching the front of her jacket and undoing the buttons of her Basque. All reason had left his mind as the need to touch her consumed him. When the last button released, her ribs expanded as she inhaled. Her billowy white habit shirt was thin and as his hands came upward, he could feel the hard boning of her corset. He longed to free her from it, but found that it didn't go all the way up as his fingers brushed against the round weight of her breast.

Hope's breath sucked in and Graham could feel himself harden at her reaction. Her kisses became increasingly aggressive, as if she were desperate for them to continue. Obliging her, Graham's head dipped down her neck as his mouth found the bed of her nipple through the white fabric. He sucked, his tongue wetting her shirt and her arms came around his head, holding him to her chest as he continued.

Hope moaned and Graham's grip tightened. He had lost all sense of time and place in the moment. His only concentration was on her. Her skin, limbs, and desire. He fought the urge to tear her clothes right there so that he could taste her skin. A single word echoed through the caverns of his heart.

Mine.

A desire to have, to conquer, had long been in his heart. He had wanted Lismore Hall for ages, but this? This yearning to possess another human being? He knew it was wrong, yet it felt so very right all at the same time.

Whatever it was, this craving, Graham ignored it and focused on the task at hand. To bring pleasure to Hope.

Her breathing had become short and shallow as his mouth teased her through the fabric. His hands moved down the center of her body, and before he knew what he was doing, he'd bent his knees in a preemptive attempt to hitch her leg up. But just as he was about to abandon all caution, he sensed another person's presence.

"Ah. Pardon me—uh, Graham?" A male voice, Jared, sounded from somewhere behind them.

Graham's entire body stilled as Hope froze in his arms. He should let her go, but he held her close to protect her from being seen in such a disheveled state. He glanced over his shoulder and glared at the intruder.

The hesitation in Jared's form and the tilt of his head let Graham know he was curious, if not cautious.

"What?" Graham said after a moment of heavy breathing.

"Um, nothing, I suppose," Jared said, unsure. "My father was correct, then? You and Miss Sharpe are set to wed?"

"Oh, well, actually no," Hope's muffled voice floated up from where her face was buried in Graham's chest, but he interrupted.

"Yes," Graham said.

A heavy pause followed as Hope raised her head.

"Graham?" she whispered. "What are you doing?"

He peered down at her. Her face was wrought with worry. The desire to protect her was too powerful. He couldn't deny it. He wanted Hope, all of her, just as she was and as soon as possible. If that meant caving to Belle's plan, then so be it, because if there was one thing he knew, it was that he would be damned if he let someone else have her. An uneasy peace settled in his heart as he looked down at her. If he couldn't stop himself from kissing her, perhaps a marriage between them was the only sensible choice.

But then he would have to tell her the truth.

He took a deep breath and brought his fingers up, grazing her cheekbone as he spoke.

"Would you have me, Hope?" he asked quietly.

Hope's brown eyes rounded, shining with shock.

"We're barely acquaintances."

"I know you well enough."

She made a face, unimpressed with his words.

"There's really no need for this. He is your cousin. Swear him to secrecy, and there will be no harm to my reputation."

"I have no doubt Jared could keep a secret."

"Well, then there you have it—"

"But I won't." Hope stared at him, wide-eyed. "The highlands may be a far more relaxed place than London, but we are not a people without morals. Now I've mishandled you—"

"You have not—"

"And I won't disrespect you or your family by ignoring what must be done. I'm offering for you, Hope."

He paused, still more than a little surprised to find himself trying to convince her, since he had been against this from the beginning. But he was not operating on logic or reason here. Graham was acting purely on instinct—and every one of his instincts was telling him that he had to have Hope.

"But ... but we hardly know each other."

He sighed deeply, oddly touched by her concern. He had already argued her points internally for weeks.

"I like you, Hope. And I think you like me, just a little bit. Don't you?"

Words seemed to catch in her throat, for all she did was nod in reply. Still, the small acknowledgment sent an explosion of gratitude through his chest. He faced Jared once more. "Aye, we are to be married."

Even if he hadn't been able to see it, Graham would have heard the smile in Jared's voice when he spoke.

"Fantastic news," he said, nodding. "Must be something in the air tonight. If you'll excuse me, I just, well…" He shuffled around them and Graham held Hope tighter. "I came this way to relieve myself." Jared waved his hand behind him. "Carry on."

Hope buried her face back into Graham's chest and he wrapped his arms around her, afraid that she was overcome with emotion. Was she regretting saying yes? Rubbing his hands up her back, he felt a ripple go through her body. His hands moved to her shoulders and pressing her back slightly, he discovered that she was laughing.

"Hope?" His voice was hesitant.

"Oh, goodness," she said, as laughter spilled from her lips. "How mortifying. How positively humiliating."

She continued to laugh.

"I'm glad you find this amusing."

"I can't help it. I always laugh when everything goes completely and utterly wrong," she said. An edge of fear entered her voice. "How could I have done this?"

"It wasn't all you," he said. "I had a hand in it."

"No, I know that. I just …" She bit her lip. "I should know better. The entire reason we came to Scotland was because of a scandal just like this. At the time, I couldn't imagine how it had happened, and yet here I am. Even after we were nearly caught at Elk Manor." Another nervous laugh escaped her lips. "Am I so completely careless?"

Guilt pushed its way into his thoughts.

"It isn't your fault, Hope. I shouldn't have taken advantage of you. I just," he said, shaking his head. "I couldn't help it. I'm sorry."

It wasn't much of an excuse, and Graham was surprised to see Hope smiling at his words.

"That's the second time you've apologized for kissing me,"

she said softly. "I might begin to think you don't like it." He opened his mouth to say something, but she held up her hand. "Besides. It's hardly fair of me to blame you when I was more than willing to participate."

Graham stared at her.

"You don't seem upset."

"I suppose I should be, shouldn't I?" A blush spread across her cheeks. It made him want to touch her cheek. "Given that I barely know you. But then…"

"What?"

"I don't know. It seems as though we've been pushed together, almost. As if it were fated or something."

Graham wasn't sure why, but her words chilled him. He needed to tell her the truth now before they went any further. He opened his mouth to do so, just as the booming voice of Laird McTavish echoed from beyond the fire.

"Hope, there's something I should—"

"Graham MacKinnon! Show yourself!"

They both looked toward the bonfire as a cheer erupted from the crowd. Graham cursed silently to himself.

"I think Jared must have told my uncle the news," he said. "He's always one for big shows."

"Oh dear."

"Yes," he said with a sigh. "But I want to tell you—"

"MacKinnon! Where are ya, lad?"

The cheers from the crowd grew louder, and Hope began to look nervous. Deciding now wasn't the best time to explain everything, Graham shook his head.

"Come. Let's go before they send a search party."

He helped her button up as they made their way out from behind the tents and carts holding hands. Hope and Graham received several knowing glances that made Graham cautious. He led her through the center of the crowd to where his uncle stood. After an exchange of words in his uncle's ear, the old laird stood back with a smile, eyes wide with delight.

"What fine news indeed!" Laird McTavish said, gazing between his nephew and Hope. "She works fast, doesn't she?" He winked at them both. "Fergus! Get the good wine. We have a celebration on our hands!"

"Who works fast?" Hope asked, as the old man took her hand and Graham's, wedging himself between them.

"Lady Luck, of course," the laird said. "Attention!" he bellowed across the crowd. "Quiet! My nephew, Graham MacKinnon, has just proposed to Miss Hope Sharpe, and she accepted!" The crowd broke into a series of cheers and whistled as the laird lifted their hands. "Let's have some proper music!"

"Uncle—" Graham protested.

"Ack, it's tradition, Graham," his uncle interrupted as the harps, bagpipes, and flutes all began to play.

The laird joined Graham's and Hope's hands before him, as some sort of show or display. Graham reluctantly pulled her toward him, as his other hand went to her waist. Several other couples hurriedly joined them as they began a simple waltz-like dance that Hope had never seen before.

"I don't know this dance," she said worriedly.

"No one does, except the McTavish Clan," he said, grasping her tight. "It's a clan tradition. Just hold onto me and follow my lead. It's fairly simple."

"Oh," Hope said. "Do all clans have a special betrothal dance?"

"No, but the McTavishes have always been a bit more willing to embarrass themselves than others."

His words caught Hope's attention.

"Embarrass? Are you embarrassed to dance?"

"I don't like attention," he said as they twirled out and came back together. "Dancing, announcements. All of it. I find it a bit ridiculous."

"You're rather a private sort of person, aren't you?"

He gave her a searching glance.

"Aye. Are you?"

"I suppose I am, though I've never given it much thought before," she said quietly. Hope glanced from side to side, watching the other dancers. When she looked back to meet Graham's eyes, though, she seemed nervous. "Have we made a mistake?"

The worry in her voice set his nerves on edge. He didn't want her to fear this partnership. He held her closer, ignoring the laws of propriety as they were betrothed now, giving them more leeway, especially since the rules of propriety were always relaxed during festival time. Graham leaned down, and his mouth found her ear.

"I don't think so," he said softly. "Do you think we have?"

She shook her head, and a tremor went through him as she smiled cautiously.

"No. I don't think so."

"Good."

Chapter Twelve

To Hope's amusement and Graham's embarrassment, rumors began swirling overnight about the circumstances of their engagement. After escorting Hope and her sisters back to Lismore Hall the night before, Hope and her sisters had stayed up late into the night discussing all that had happened.

"How did he do it?" Grace asked, her legs curled beneath her as she sat across from Hope on her bed. Faith was pacing before the fireplace, arms behind her back. Usually, Grace was more pragmatic, but something about the bonfire seemed to have captured her imagination. "Was it romantic?"

"It was different, I suppose, from how I always assumed a proposal would be."

"How so?"

"Well," she said, tilting her head. "I guess I always assumed it would take place indoors. In a sitting room or parlor. And the gentleman would be on bended knee."

"He stood?" Faith asked, her brow scrunching. "The whole time?"

"Yes, but there wasn't really an opportunity to kneel," she said defensively before turning back to Grace. "But it was rather lovely all the same."

Grace smiled.

"It just seems rather sudden, doesn't it?" Faith said, coming forward. "And serendipitous."

"How do you mean?"

"Well, Lismore Hall was his ancestral home once, wasn't it? Perhaps he's angling to get it back."

Hope's mouth fell open as she stared at her sister.

"Faith!" Grace chided. "How could you say such a thing?"

"No, no," Hope said, reaching for Grace's hand. If she were honest, Hope had worried about the same thing. "It crossed my mind too."

Faith had the decency to appear sorry, while Grace shook her head.

"Well, it's a foolish idea. Mr. MacKinnon has been taken with you since the day we arrived. Everyone has noticed it."

"Is that so?" Hope said with a smirk. Her gaze fell on Faith. "Do you think so?"

Faith shrugged as she leaned against the bedpost behind Grace. Her head rested on the dark wood.

"I suppose so. He has sought you out a number of times. And not very subtly."

Hope smiled, but even as her sisters assured her that Graham's intentions were true, she still felt unsure. Even if Graham was marrying her for Lismore Hall, that didn't mean that it was the only reason. The heat that lingered between them wasn't a facade. Was it?

Hope spent the rest of the night dreaming about Graham. In her dreams, she was constantly searching for him, but even when she caught glimpses of him in the distance, she could never reach him. When she woke the next day, she felt a deep restlessness in her bones. Belle had been asleep when they arrived the previous night, and though they had all slept in rather late that morning, she still hadn't risen by noon.

Thankfully, by the time Graham came for luncheon that day Hope had stifled her foolish worries. He had arrived to discuss the engagement with Belle but, upon realizing she hadn't woken yet, decided to eat with Hope and her sisters, all of whom had been listening to a very cheery Rose explain what had been said the night before, after the engagement had been announced.

"Supposedly, Graham serenaded you with a song, pledging his deepest love and loyalty for the rest of his life," Rose said before laughing. "Jeanne told everyone that Graham was smitten with his new English bride."

"It only happened last night," Graham said, appearing to be neither amused nor annoyed by the rumors, which pleased Hope for some reason. "How are there so many stories already?"

"Twelve hours is plenty of time for rumors to spread," Faith said over her teacup before taking a sip.

"Jeanne was quite happy about it," Rose said, forking her eggs. "She kept telling everyone you took up poetry to impress Hope."

Faith choked on her tea as Grace hid her face. Hope bit her lip, worried Graham wouldn't appreciate being teased. His coffee cup paused midair as he squinted at Rose.

"My cousins have a sense of humor," he said, surprisingly unbothered.

"It's not so bad, is it?" Hope said tentatively. "It's one of the better pieces of gossip I've been a part of and it's hardly vindictive."

He gave her a contemplative look, and she smiled at him nervously.

"Amusing, is it? To picture me groveling at your feet, reading some daft poem?"

If he had seemed genuinely angry, she'd have backed down, but she saw the twinkle of amusement in his eye, and it prompted her to let out a very unladylike snort. Her hand shot to cover her face.

"Yes," she said, clearing her throat. "It is. And since there's no stopping gossip, all you can do is laugh at it."

"Laugh at what?" Belle asked as she entered the dining room, followed as always by Andrews.

Belle wore a tangerine-colored gown with white floral embroidery and a gauzy overlay. Her hands were adorned in her usual emerald rings and a pair of teardrop pearl earbobs swung precariously from her lobes as she hobbled to her chair. She paused when she saw Graham, seated near the head of the table.

"MacKinnon. What are you doing here this early?" she asked. "Surely you returned home after you escorted the girls home last night."

"I did," he said, his voice serious as he stood up.

His gaze flickered to Hope, who stood as well.

"Aunt Belle," she started, coming around the table to Graham's side. "I'm afraid we have some news to share." Belle's eyes widened and the corner of her mouth pulled up in trepidation. "I think perhaps we should speak with you in private."

"Nonsense, my girl, nonsense," she said, moving around both Hope and Graham to take her place at the head of the table, her cane clicking loudly against the ground. She sat with deliberate slowness and squirmed slightly, making herself comfortable before giving them her full attention. "Now, my dear. What news do you wish to share?"

"Well—"

Graham reached for Hope's hand.

"We're to be wed," he said, interrupting her.

Hope's brow lifted as she turned to her side. Graham had a very serious expression on his face and Hope felt the same vague sense of worry she had felt last night creep into her heart. But the loud thwack of Belle's cane broke her concentration.

"Brilliant! Absolutely brilliant!" Belle said, her eyes locked on Graham's stoic face. "I have not heard such wonderful news in ages. We shall put it in all the papers. The *Herald*, the *London Times*, even the *Evening Standard*."

"The *Times*?" Hope said, a trickle of concern edging into her spine. "Is there really a need to announce to the entire country?"

"Of course there is. You're the granddaughter of an earl, my dear. The peerage should know."

Hope nodded, unsure why she was so hesitant. Perhaps she didn't wish for Pennington to know about her engagement.

Graham's large hand squeezed her fingers.

"If you'd rather not, we needn't post it," he said.

The expression on his face was veiled, but Hope worried that he mistook her hesitance for some sort of shame and that certainly wasn't it. She shook her head.

"No, of course we should," she said, facing her aunt. "Put it in all the papers."

"Wonderful!" Belle said. "Andrews! Set up my correspondence. I'll take breakfast in my office. I've a number of letters to write." Her cane wobbled slightly back and forth as she struggled to stand. "What is the date?"

"Oh, well, since our courtship was rather short, I think it would be fitting if we had a longer engagement," Hope said.

"How long?"

"A year I suppose," she said, only to be met with a deafening silence. Looking back and forth between Belle and Graham, both appeared stunned. She frowned. "It's not an unheard-of length of time for an engagement."

"Yes, my dear, but seeing as you've already experienced a long engagement prior to this one," Belle said. "I would assume you'd wish to be over with this rather quickly."

"They were never engaged," Faith said, earning her an elbowing from Grace. "What? They weren't."

"A year is far too long," Graham said, looking down at her, before adding softly. "A month is too long."

Hope's cheeks warmed as she grasped his meaning, but she still felt certain that they couldn't be married in a month. She pulled her hand away from his so that she could think straight.

"A month would hardly supply enough time to sort everything out. Dresses and flowers, invitations, licenses."

"We're in Scotland. We could go to the blacksmiths in Glencoe and be done with it today."

"I don't wish to be done with it," Hope said firmly, aware of their audience. She took a deep breath before explaining. "I was raised in large part by my grandmother, and she was a woman who believed strongly in propriety. Out of respect for her, I would like to adhere to a traditional length of engagement."

"I agree with MacKinnon," Belle said, lifting her chin. "To-morrow is good. Today would be better."

"We are not marrying today," she said, leaning around Graham's large frame to glare at her aunt.

"Two weeks then," Graham said, causing Hope's attention to snap back to him.

Her hand fell to the back of the closest chair to steady herself. Two weeks? Had he gone mad?

"Absolutely not. It is impossible."

"One week," he countered, taking a step toward her like some predatory animal.

"Half a year," she offered, pulling out the chair to block his advance.

"Tomorrow."

"Three months and not a day more," she said quickly. She glanced around the room, silently pleading for reassurance. "It's not unreasonable, is it?"

"No, it's not," Faith said firmly, for which Hope was grateful, but Graham was quick to disagree.

"It's too long."

"Yes, but it's respectable, MacKinnon," Belle said, causing both Hope and Graham to turn to her. Belle focused on Graham with an intent gaze. "And it's what my sister would have wanted. Very well. Three months it is."

Graham inhaled through his nostrils, which flared slightly as his eyes darted back and forth between Hope and Belle. For a moment, Hope wondered if he would refuse...but then he exhaled harshly and nodded.

"Three months." Putting his hands behind his back, he eyed the chair that separated him from Hope. She hastily pushed it back under the table. "Then I've some correspondence to attend to as well. Hope, would you see me out?"

"Ah, yes, of course," she said, following him out of the dining room without looking back.

A footman came up and handed Graham his coat and hat. A light rain had started sometime since his arrival.

"That's all, thank you," he said as the footman disappeared.

Hope thought that it was strange for him to dismiss the footman so abruptly. But she did not have long to dwell on it before a large hand wrapped around her wrist and whipped her around. Graham held her against his solid body and a noise escaped her lips.

"Three months?" he said, his mouth hovering above hers. He smelled like honey and she could almost taste it on her tongue. "You'll be the death of me."

"I-I'm sure I don't know what you mean."

"You will," he growled. "I'll not go through this torture alone."

"What torture?"

But her words evaporated as he pressed his mouth to hers, kissing her so deeply and earnestly that all sense escaped her. Without thinking, her arms wrapped around his broad shoulders, her fingers curling against the fabric of his coat that was spread taut across the muscles of his back. His mouth pulled and sucked at her tongue, luridly coaxing it out until she was a quivering mess in his arms.

Then he let her go.

Unsteadily, she tried to find her footing. After several deep breaths she looked at him. A wicked grin was playing at the edge of his mouth, his eyes dark with sensual tension.

"Good day, Hope," he said with the barest of nods before he turned and exited the house.

"Good bye," she said softly as the large wood door closed of its own weight.

Oh dear. What had she done? Three months seemed like an eternity now when she thought of how long she would have to wait before she could truly give herself to him. While a part of her was grateful to have so much time before their wedding to prepare herself, another part wondered if perhaps it was too long a wait.

Stop it. She needed to reel in her craving, lest she give any truth to her worry about being a wanton. Although Graham hardly seemed put off by her desires. The memory of all of their kisses, how he held her so possessively, made her long for things she barely even understood.

Shivering at the image she conjured up in her mind, she pressed her cold hand to her hot cheek and turned, going back to the dining room. If they were going to wed in three months, she needed to begin wedding preparations immediately. When she re-entered the room, she saw that her sisters were already discussing the event.

"Hydrangeas should be in bloom during the wedding," Grace was saying as she buttered a piece of toast. "A perfect flower for a wedding. Don't you agree, Hope?"

"Hmm?" she said, coming around the table to take her seat. The kiss she had shared with Graham had distracted her, but she shook her head to clear it. "Oh no, Grace. Hydrangeas aren't a wedding flower."

"They're not?" she asked, confused.

"Not according to Robert Tyas's *Language of Flora*. Hydrangeas represent a heartless boaster," Hope said. "I believe there's a copy in the library."

"I'll get it," Grace said, standing up from the table, hurrying out of the room.

Faith and Hope sat in silence for a moment before Faith spoke.

"Three months," she said, leaning back in her chair. "He's rather eager, isn't he?"

Hope felt a touch of uncertainty crawl up her shoulders at her sister's tone, but she tried to push it away.

"Yes," she said, finishing her tea. "One would want that in a husband, no?"

Faith didn't respond, and soon Grace was back with the book.

"I didn't know there was an entire book on this subject," she said, taking her seat again. "It covers everything from colors to blooms to seasons. Every flower has a dozen meanings."

"What do scarlet pimpernel mean?" Hope asked, pouring herself another cup of tea. "I've always liked them."

"Amusement," Grace said after searching the book for a moment. "I think that would be a clever flower to use."

"What about yellow roses?" Faith asked. "There's a dozen rose bushes in the garden."

Grace flipped through the pages.

"While roses are generally connected to love," she read. "Yellow ones represent jealousy."

Faith frowned.

"That's ridiculous."

"It's true. It says it right here," Grace said, before turning to Hope. "Which other flowers will you choose?"

Hope reached for her spoon and added a swirl of honey to her tea before mixing it in. The idea of what flowers to choose had been something she'd thought about for a long time. After all, she'd spent years expecting to soon be engaged to Jacob. She had her favorites, but it didn't seem right to pick the same ones as she had contemplated before.

"I think, perhaps I'll use goldenrod. Bees are supposedly very attracted to goldenrod."

"And you wish for a swarm to walk you down the aisle?" Faith asked sarcastically.

"No, of course not. But Graham is fond of bees and I think it would be nice to consider it."

"What does goldenrod represent, Grace?"

She winced.

"Precaution. But perhaps you could add some white roses and daisies to balance it out. Worthiness and shared sentiments."

"Do you share sentiments?" Faith asked, her tone unsure.

"Of course," Hope said with a frown. "Why do you ask?"

"It just seems to be happening a bit fast, all of this." She waved her hand in the room. "Don't you think? We only arrived her a few weeks ago and now you're engaged?"

"I was pre-engaged to Jacob for years and look how that turned out."

"Yes, but Jacob Pennington wasn't suspicious."

Hope stared at her sister, the pinpricks of defensiveness scattering up her spine.

"How is Graham suspicious?"

"I don't know," Faith said, putting down her napkin. "I just get a feeling from him. Like he's hiding something."

"Like what?" Grace asked.

"If I knew, I'd explain it."

Hope had long ago realized that Faith was firmly fixed in her beliefs that men were not to be trusted. But surely Graham had done nothing to deserve such distrust. Moreover, something in Hope made her feel rather protective of Graham and while she had her own worries, they were hardly Graham's fault. Jacob was the one who had discarded her so easily, who had shamed her for her desires. He was why she found it harder to trust now. But she didn't enjoy speaking about those doubts Jacob had planted in her heart. If she could smother them out of existence, she would. For the time being, she'd choose to ignore them.

"If you have no sound reason to suspect Graham of anything, I must insist you refrain from these suspicions. If you can't stifle them completely, at least avoid saying them out loud."

Though it wasn't exactly a demand, a tension fell on the room. Grace stopped reading the book as she looked between the two of them. After a moment, Faith stood.

"Very well," she said quietly as she turned to leave. It seemed as though she were offended.

"Faith, wait," Hope tried, but the hem of her violet skirts disappeared around the doorway. Hope sighed loudly and looked at Grace. "For someone who speaks her mind so freely, she certainly doesn't like to be challenged."

"Perhaps she thought you were being too dismissive of her suspicions."

"She has nothing to be suspicious about," Hope argued. "She's only trying to make me anxious. Faith has disliked men ever since that painter friend of hers, Donovan, ran away to Paris."

Grace shrugged.

"Probably. But you've never quieted her before."

"Well, perhaps she should learn to quiet herself," Hope said stubbornly, gazing down at her plate.

It didn't help that Faith was adding to Hope's own doubts. She wanted to believe that she and Graham genuinely got on, and they did—so there was really no reason to worry, was there?

Suddenly finding herself without an appetite, Hope stood herself and left the dining room, consumed by her thoughts.

— ❦ —

Chapter Thirteen

Although his uncle had offered to host the wedding at Elk Manor, Graham insisted it take place at Lismore Hall. Usually, a wedding would take months of preparation, but Belle had insisted on providing everything from the gown to stores of food for the festivities, as a wedding gift. And since money was no object, everything was gathered quickly. Hope had been slightly apprehensive at such a rushed wedding, but he would be lying if he hadn't wanted to marry Hope as quickly as possible. And not because of Lismore. Graham simply wanted her.

He enjoyed being close to her, hearing her speak and discussing things that he had never even brought up with the women he had known his entire life. For example, two weeks after their engagement was announced, he had agreed to a fishing excursion with Logan. Hope had expressed an interest in learning the pastime and soon he was teaching her how to cast a reel. Graham had been surprised to find that merely being in her presence made him happy. He thoroughly enjoyed teaching Hope all he knew.

It seemed every time their paths crossed, he became more and more interested in her and everything she did. But as the wedding day approached, the urge to tell Hope the truth weighed heavily on Graham. He didn't want to marry her without explaining Belle's offer, but the more he spent time with Hope, the further away he got from the truth. As much as he wanted to be honest with her, every time he was with her, he got so caught up in the pleasure of her company that the idea of uncomfortable confessions totally slipped from his mind.

For example, there had been the day he had travelled to Lismore Hall to tend to his bees. He had quite forgotten himself in his work when the old wooden door that led into the walled garden creaked out, catching his attention. He looked up and saw Hope, dressed in a cream-colored day gown with evergreen piping. She wore no hat or hair covering, her dark hair piled elegantly atop her head, and she smiled coyly at him, as though she were sneaking out to see him.

"Hello," he said, straightening from his hunched over position.

"Hello," she said, her hands behind her back as she craned her neck. Her smile deepened. "What are you wearing?"

Graham looked down at himself, realizing he was dressed very peculiarly, indeed. A long, white cotton canvas tunic covered his clothes. His hands were covered with thick leather gloves and a wide brim hat draped with a fine netting covered his head. All in all, he was certain she had never seen such a bizarre outfit.

"It's a beekeeper's suit. It prevents me from being stung," he said as he lowered one of the trays that he had taken out of the hive. A footman sprayed a cloudlike smoke over the bees.

"What's that?"

"A sedative, so they don't become angry at me for disrupting their peace." Her chin lifted as her mouth made a small O shape. "This needs all my attention just now, but I'll be with you in a moment," he promised.

She nodded cheerfully as he returned to his work. Graham was meticulous as he gathered a dark honeycomb and placed it into a glass jar. Assembling the hive back to its form, he replaced the top and backed away from the white box. He gave the jar to the servant who, removing his own specialized hat, appeared relieved to be finished with the task.

Graham removed the tunic he wore and handed it to the

servant who exchanged the jar of honey for the canvas bundle and hurried off through the creaky wooden door. Hope nodded at the man as he disappeared into the garden behind her. She stepped forward to get a closer look at the hives. She folded her arms across her chest.

"Inspecting my work?" he asked as he reached her.

"Somewhat," she said, tilting her head back. The sun shone in her eyes and she raised her hand to block it. "I realized yesterday that I don't actually know anything about what you do. I was curious."

"Curious about me?"

She nodded and a foolish thrill went through his body. It was human nature to find joy in telling others about oneself, but the fact that this particular woman was interested, well, it made him feel good.

Really good.

"Very well. This way," he said as he held out his arm. She took it and a sensation very close to pride filled his chest.

They returned through the gardens, but moved toward the northernmost part, where a small glass room had been attached to the back of the hall. It was covered in hothouse plants and only had two points of access—one leading out into the garden and one back into the house. Graham had set it up to be an office of sorts, where he could do his experiments in peace. No doubt it was wrong to be alone with Hope here, but they were already engaged and it wasn't as if they were in his private residence—merely his office which happened to be in *her* place of residence.

The private room was warm, uncomfortably so. As they entered, Graham looked down at Hope and saw a genuine fascination on her expression. Her dark eyes lit up with wonder as she gazed around the glass room.

"What is this place?" she asked, her hand grazing the rough, makeshift wooden desk where Graham would record his findings. Note papers and journals were scattered all about the tall table.

"It's a hothouse and my office of sorts. Although, technically, it's more of a records room. My office at the hunting lodge is far more organized."

She turned to face him.

"I should like to visit the hunting lodge. Is it far?"

Graham let out an unsteady laugh.

"It wouldn't be wise to bring you there."

"Why not?" The look he gave her must have been explanation enough, because her cheeks turned pink as she turned away. Taking a few steps toward the desk, she bent at the waist and pointed her index finger out. "What's this?"

Graham came up alongside her and reached for the little glass bottle that had captured her attention. He held up the golden, liquid treasure.

"Beautiful, isn't it? This is heather honey. The texture is different as it's more of a jelly until stirred. It turns into a syrup then, but will return to its former state if left alone. I have several dozen hives for it set up along the hills on the edge of my uncle's lands. There are fields and fields of heather that go on for miles. This is from there."

"Do you mean to say that the bees use the nectar of the heather flower?"

"Aye. The taste of honey can vary from place to place, based off of the flowers the bees have access to and the surrounding climate. The color changes too. You'll have every shade from white to dark amber."

"And do you produce a lot?"

Graham shrugged.

"Last year's numbers were good. We produced about nine hundred and fifty pounds of honey, fifteen hundred pounds of honeycomb."

Hope's eyes widened.

"Goodness, that's *quite* a lot."

"Not really. I have about thirty hives. I could have more, but I spent half of last year in Glasgow."

"Why is that?"

His brow quirked up.

"You really are interested, aren't you?"

"Of course I am."

He smirked.

"Well, I had been selling the bulk of my production to a confectioner, Duncan Thomas. He used my honey in his recipes—most particularly a hard, butterscotch like candy that sold out repeatedly in his shop. He asked for sole buying rights, but I had a different idea."

"What was your idea?"

"I asked his thoughts about building a sugar refinery. They're going up all over Glasgow and I thought why only sell to the people in the city? If we could sell his confectionaries nationwide, we'd have a proper business on our hands."

"You own a candy factory then?" Hope asked, her eyes widening.

"Aye—or at least, half of one. Mr. Thomas and I will share the profits fifty-fifty. Our first set of deliveries are going out next month."

"My goodness, you're a proper entrepreneur, aren't you?"

Knowing that Hope had come from the first of society, Graham was unsure if she was genuinely impressed. There were many in her class who would look down on a man for participating in common trade, no matter how profitable it might be. But with no lands of his own, he'd never been able to live a "proper" gentleman's life, earning his income from tenants. Not for the first time did he feel guilt swell in his heart. Hope should be marrying someone with something to his name. Someone who would inherit a title or land.

His gaze dropped to the honey jars.

"I suppose so."

The change in his tone seemed to catch her attention. Suddenly, Hope's hand came over his and he turned to see her staring at him with an impossibly caring expression, her dark eyes shining with certainty.

"You are an impressive man, Graham MacKinnon. Every day I learn something new about you and every day I'm stunned by it."

Her honest words and transparent feelings made Graham feel like a king and a heel all at once. She was so damn genuine and the more she said things like that, the more devoted he became. All he wanted was to carry her off some place and never let her go.

His hand came up to her cheek as his thumb ran across the edge of her cheekbone.

"Hope…"

Her cautious smile widened.

"Yes?"

He wanted to tell her everything in that moment. To lay out his entire life story. There was something about her that made him want to confess every wicked deed he had done, if only to find salvation at her feet.

But when he hesitated, she spoke.

"Will you take me? To see the factory, I mean?"

She could ask for the sun and he would provide it.

"If you'd like me to, I will."

She bobbed up and down on her heels and he smiled at her eagerness, unable to help himself.

"Yes, please."

Graham was pleased at how keen she was to see his work. "Then we will certainly go. But for today, there is something else I want you to try." He moved next to her and opened the jar, setting it on the table. Taking a long, thin wooden stick, one that had been sanded down, he dipped it into the honey. He lifted it out, setting the jar down, and with his hand underneath the string of honey as he pulled it away, he brought it to Hope's lips.

"This is why I brought you here," he said. "Taste." Obediently, she opened her mouth.

The rich clover scent was heavy in the air. He watched it melt against her tongue. Desire coursed through him as her eyes closed, savoring the flavor. He rolled the wooden utensil out of her mouth, grazing it slowly against her bottom lip as he withdrew it.

The stiffness in his trousers began to ache.

Hope watched him with undivided attention as he placed the wooden spoon back in the jar and settled it down on the table. Pulse pounding, he leaned in and kissed her.

Graham's tongue searched her mouth slowly and her eyes closed as her hands came up to his shoulders, steadying herself as he pulled her close. His kiss deepened, and Hope swayed to press herself against him.

He needed her. Never had he ever witnessed something so erotic and so chaste as her savoring his honey, and it had set him aflame. He pulled away slowly, her eyes fluttered open with confusion. Without a word, Graham's hand came up to her bodice and his two fingers tugged down on the neckline of her gown, lowering it until her breasts were revealed, while his other hand grabbed the utensil again. To Hope's obvious surprise, Graham drizzled a string of honey on her exposed nipple, causing her breath to hitch—though she made no effort to back away. Hope was a meal and he intended on finishing her.

His mouth quickly covered the tip of her breast, suckling at her as though she were his only source of sustenance.

Her arms wrapped around his head as his hands snaked down her backside, down her thighs as he hiked up her skirts. He was without reason, without any rational thought, as his mouth left the peak of her breast and come up to rediscover her mouth.

He kissed her urgently before lifting her onto the work table. His hands moved down her spread legs, gripping her calves and then thighs underneath her rucked-up skirts.

"Graham, what ..."

"Hush," he said as he leaned over her body, kissing her mouth before moving down her torso.

Graham was quick to find the opening of her drawers. Kneeling down, he drew his fingers over her sex. Hope gasped and he could feel the tension in her thighs as she tried instinctively to close them, but he wouldn't have her shy away from him. Instead, he licked her, long and slow, so that she might feel every bit of his tongue.

Hope let out a heavy breath, her legs relaxing—and then spreading even wider in welcome. Graham was happy to take advantage of the increased space to press himself closer and drive his tongue deeper. If there was ever a sweeter taste than honey, this was it. The tiny jerks that seemed to spread over her body only encouraged him and he feasted on her as if she were his last meal.

Hope's sweetness was his life's essence and as she reached her orgasm, she let out a cracked moan. Graham did not relent as she rode her ecstasy. By the time it finished, she was quivering and he was silently pledging his soul to hers forever.

Slowly, Graham stood up as Hope's skirts dropped over her legs. She was staring at him with a look of such hazy, heated desire that he knew he could take her right now if he wanted to, without a word of protest from her. The ache in his cock was almost too urgent to ignore, and it had him on the verge of giving in.

But whatever small part of him was still functioning on an honorable level stalled him. He wouldn't take his future wife in a greenhouse before he'd made his vows to her properly, even if every inch of his body screamed out for it.

He gently helped her down off the table and they stood there, panting for several minutes. Graham wrapped his arms tightly around her frame, and held her to his chest as if she were some sort of precious gift.

"You're too fine a woman to be taken in a makeshift green-house," he said into her slightly disheveled hair. "But I couldn't help tasting you." When she didn't speak, he pulled back and raised his hand to caress her cheek. "Are you all right?"

"Yes," she mumbled, pressing her face against his chest. "It's just… I never…"

Innate pleasure coursed through his veins. It was plain to see that no one had ever brought Hope to orgasm before, and he selfishly relaxed in the satisfaction that he was the only person to do so.

He dropped his forehead and rested it against hers.

"You'll not hold it against me, for doing so in a greenhouse?"

A short chuckle came from her mouth. She shook her head.

"No. I never want to be so fine a lady that I refuse to be taken in a makeshift greenhouse."

Graham chuckled, his laughter reverberating deep in his chest.

"I have to go to Uncle's house today to check on the rest of my hives," he said, his thumb brushing her bottom lip. "Come with me?"

She shook her head again.

"I can't. I meant to speak with Rose about something."

"About what?"

Hope pulled back slightly and the teasing glint in her smiling eyes made him hard all over again.

"It's a secret."

"Wives aren't meant to keep secrets from their husbands."

"Then it's a good thing we aren't married yet. But if you insist, I'd love to hear your thoughts on lace versus silks."

Graham sighed. Wedding preparations.

"Ah, well, perhaps you can keep this one secret."

She hit him in the chest playfully, but he caught her wrist and tugged her forward, planting a kiss on her forehead. It was tempting to capture her lips again…but if he did that, he might never leave. He needed to let her go before he lost control of himself.

"Very well," he said, releasing her. "I'll see you tonight?"

Hope nodded enthusiastically and Graham escorted her out of the greenhouse and into the garden where she climbed the stone staircase that led back up into her room.

He would have a devil of a time focusing on his work for the rest of the day. Deciding that his work could wait until tomorrow, he set out to return to the hunting lodge that served as his home when he wasn't in Glasgow.

Nestled in a copse of tall Scotch pine stood the gray, stone hunting lodge. It was a modest building compared to Lismore Hall, though it was certainly large enough to house twenty or so men comfortably. Graham kept a staff of four employed. A cook, a maid, a butler, and a stable hand. Each member of his staff was older than him by at least a decade and they all had chosen the job specifically because of the seclusion of the lodge.

Graham rarely hosted people there, given that he spent much of the year at his Glasgow residence. When he did visit his uncle and cousins, he had rooms at Elk Manor. Still, Belle had insisted that he make the old hunting lodge his own and he quite enjoyed the solitude of it.

After handing off his horse to Melvin the stable hand, he climbed the three modest steps and pushed through the green painted door, entering a bright hallway. The walls were whitewashed and adorned with dozens of antlers, trophies of men who had long since passed.

The floors were wooden and darkened by age and use. It was decidedly shabbier than Lismore Hall, but then the hunting lodge had always been a place for men to disregard the fripperies of elegant society. It had suited Graham's bachelor lifestyle for many years.

Turning into the third and last doorway on his right, he sensed another presence. Apparently, solitude would not find him today.

Upon entering the library, he found Logan Harris standing on the rolling ladder, searching one of the shelves for a book.

"Logan. I didn't know you were here," Graham said. "What are you doing?"

"McTavish mentioned to me that Lady Belle kept a rather extensive collection of society pamphlets and that she asked you to store them here since the Sharpes moved in," Logan said without turning around. "I'm trying to find someone."

"I'm only keeping them here because she didn't want her nieces to see them, in case there was something written about their scandal." He walked across the room to the side of the fireplace and opened a wooden cupboard. Pulling out a tall bottle of amber liquid, he grabbed one of the crystal glasses that sat on a tray above it. "Who are you looking for?"

"An artist."

"Why?"

"Because I've recently acquired a rather large painting—sight unseen, I might add—by a new up-and-coming artist out of Paris. Goes by the name Donovan." Logan pulled a handful of pamphlets off the shelf and climbed down. "Supposedly the fellow is beyond talented. The best painter the continent has seen in nearly two decades."

"So, you bought a painting by him as an investment?"

Graham knew of Logan's appreciation for art, but he himself didn't understand it. Art was pretty, he supposed but he wasn't terribly interested in paintings, sculptures, or the like.

"Well, usually I never buy a painting without inspecting it first," he said, coming around to a table to lay out the pamphlets. "But this one was too intriguing to ignore."

"Oh? What about it is so special?"

"The subject of the painting—a woman turned at the waist, surrounded by yellow velvet."

Graham shrugged. "That doesn't sound particularly special to me." He'd seen something similar dozens of times before.

"Ah, but the rumor has it that this one was not modeled by some London madam, but by a former lover of Donovan. Perhaps even a lady of first society."

Graham fought not to roll his eyes. It sounded like the sort of gossip someone would make up, just for the fun of having a scandal.

"So?"

Logan rolled his eyes.

"So, I was already in the market for a piece by this Donovan, and it felt expedient to act quickly. If the rumor is true, I may have procured a piece that someone might want back."

Graham turned to his friend, brow furrowing. "Are you hoping to get some sort of blackmail out of the situation?"

Logan shrugged.

"Not necessarily. Like I said, I was in the market for a piece by this young man anyway. However, if there is someone who wishes the painting to be out of circulation due to some personal reason, well, who would I be to deny a conversation with said person?"

Graham laughed.

"Always trying to make a deal," he said, shaking his head as he flipped through the pamphlets. "But I still don't understand why you're looking through these gossip pages."

"Lady Belle suggested it," Logan said, picking one up as he thumbed through the pages. "She had overheard my conversation with your cousin about the artist and mentioned that she had read about him in one of these papers."

"Did she?" Graham asked, instantly suspicious.

"Yes. Actually, I was debating between the Donovan or a pair of pieces from Marchelies—a French painter. Lady Belle told me about the rumor and rather persuaded me. You know, I've never been very fond of the old woman, but there was something about the way she spoke about it. Almost as if she were certain I'd be rich beyond my wildest dreams if I bought it. Made me curious." He picked up a pamphlet.

"She has some plot simmering in the back of her mind about something or other, mark my words," Graham said, now positive that Belle was up to something. "But if I know anything, she's probably correct that you'll make a pretty penny." Graham flipped a pamphlet over and added beneath his breath, "Though she might steal your soul in the bargain."

"What was that?"

"Nothing," Graham said. "Just be careful, is all."

"I will," Logan said, pointing a pamphlet at him. "Anyway, she suggested I take a few of these and read through them. I was just about to leave, but I'll not say no to a farewell dram."

"Fair enough," Graham said with a nod as he went to the far wall. He poured two glasses of scotch and handed one to Logan. "Did you talk to your sister about coming to the wedding?"

"Yes, but she isn't certain Father is up for the trip, even though he seems in better health these past few weeks. His cough has subsided."

"Is a recovery a possibility?" Graham asked. Logan's father had suffered from coughing fits for nearly two years.

"I'm hopeful, though Arabella is cautious," Logan said, sipping his drink. "But enough about that. How does it feel, MacKinnon? To almost be master of Lismore Hall?"

Graham stared at his glass, spinning it in his fingers as he watched the light glimmer through the cut crystal. To be honest, it was a thought that rarely even occurred to him when he thought of marrying Hope. He had been sure he would have had some sort of visceral reaction to finally obtaining his lifelong goal, but it had barely crossed his mind the last few weeks.

"It's daunting, I suppose. I think a part of me never really believed that I would ever get it." The corners of Logan's mouth turned down and he nodded, though he didn't seem to comprehend Graham's meaning. "How is it supposed to feel, do you reckon?"

"I would have guessed it would feel like you were finally home."

Home. What a simple, small word and yet it was an idea that had eluded him for most of his life. He'd always thought that home was what he wanted when he pursued the return of Lismore Hall, but now when he imagined home, what he saw was Hope. He was at home with her.

Finishing his drink, abruptly aware that he hadn't eaten anything in hours, he nodded toward Logan and turned to leave.

"Good luck with your painting," he said.

"Oh, before you disappear, Michael wanted to let you know that he's planning a stag stalk the week before the wedding."

"Why?"

"Something about male bonding," Logan said, returning to his search.

Graham grunted and left the library, unsure he wished to participate in whatever his cousin had planned.

Chapter Fourteen

HOPE READ THE paper in silence, her mouth slightly open as she read the ghastly announcement in the *Times*. It was the same one that had read in the *Herald*, as well as a dozen papers across the country that had arrived that morning to the dining room.

Hope, her sisters, Rose, and Belle all sat around the table in silence, each reading papers. It was evident that they were all thinking the same thing. To Hope's horror, the announcement hadn't been printed in the engagement section, but rather the gossip column.

...It has also been brought to this author's attention that one of the Sharpe sisters has finally made her match. Miss Hope Caroline Sharpe, eldest daughter of the Honorable Abbott Sharpe, has accepted a proposal from Mr. Graham MacKinnon of Glasgow. It was previously assumed that Miss Sharpe would marry her long-time beau, Mr. Jacob Pennington. The newly minted partner at Benton and Stanley Law firm rescinded his proposal after the scandal that took place at the Spotsmore Ball. One could only assume that Miss Sharpe was devastated, losing her dearest love, but it seems Hope springs eternal.

Though little is known about the would-be businessman, it should be noted that Miss Sharpe has been named primary beneficiary of her notorious aunt, Lady Belle Smith. A fortuitous match indeed for the unknown Scot and his lady love...

"A fortuitous match?" Hope said out loud, her voice breaking as she looked up. "Graham will be mortified."

"He'll be incensed," Faith said, shaking her head. "No one is going to read that and not understand what the writer is implying."

Hope's hand came over her face.

"Oh, why? Why did this have to be written about?" She turned to face Belle, who sat at the head of the table, reading one of the dozens of papers that had been brought in. "Is this what you asked them to write?"

"Goodness no, dear," Belle said. "I only mentioned the inheritance so that they wouldn't question MacKinnon's ability to care for you."

"So *who* wouldn't question it? The ton? London? The entire country?" Hope asked. "It reads as though I'm marrying a man who's desperate for money to finance his failing business." She hit the paper with her hand. "Would-be businessman? It makes Graham sound incapable."

"Well, that just isn't true."

"True or not, it's been written," Hope said, tossing her paper away. She groaned as she folded her arms on the surface of the table and dropped her forehead down. "He's going to be livid."

As if summoned by the mere idea of him, a thunderous noise came from the foyer. It sounded as though the oak doors had been shoved open, crashing against the walls behind them. Hope's head snapped up.

"Drats," Belle said under her breath as Graham came storming into the dining room.

Clutching a newspaper in one hand, he lifted his other and pointed menacingly at the old woman. Hope stood, determined to come between him and her aunt.

"You," he seethed, stalking down the side of the dining room table. He threw the paper in front of Belle and it landed on her half-finished breakfast plate. "Is it not enough that you've tried to force your agenda on me? You have to insult me, too?"

"MacKinnon," Belle hissed, her eyes flickering to Hope. "Hush."

Hope couldn't understand Belle's reaction, especially since Graham seemed completely focused on Belle. He leaned over her, one hand gripping the top rail of her highbacked chair. He hunched over her, ominous in his stance.

"What the devil do you mean to do to me? Eviscerate every part of my pride?"

"You're being ridiculous—"

"And you're nothing but a conniving old—"

"Graham," Hope said loudly, her voice cracking as she tried to stop him from saying vicious thing that he wouldn't be able to take back.

The urgency in her voice seemed to catch his attention at last, but as soon as he turned to her, Hope began to question her decision to be on the receiving end of his glare. He stood up and came around the table, stalking her as though he were some disgruntled hunting dog and she were an injured rabbit. Her hand came up to her throat as she took a step back.

"'Dearest love,' was it?" he said as he came to crowd her, but Hope would not be cowed. "Had I known how desperately in love you had been, I might not have bothered."

Hope knew he was hurt. But she was not in the wrong here, and she would not let him make her ashamed. Though she was shaking slightly, she held her chin up, confident in herself.

"I will not deny my feelings for Mr. Pennington, or what I believe I felt. You knew as much when I came here."

"Oh, aye, I did," he said sarcastically, his dark eyes baring into hers, as though he were trying to see into her core. "I know he threw you over the moment it was convenient."

Hope inhaled sharply, and her sisters stood, evidently dismayed by the distress she was clearly in.

"Girls," Belle said, standing with the help of Andrews's hand on her elbow. "Let's leave these lovebirds in peace."

The term "lovebirds" sounded heavily sarcastic, Hope noted

as her aunt walked the length of the table. Still, neither Faith nor Grace moved until Belle struck the ground with her cane, shaking both of Hope's sisters from their trance. They turned to follow Belle, though Hope knew neither wished to leave her.

Once they were alone, Graham took several deep breaths. For several long moments they looked at one another, Hope searching his face for any crack in his anger that might show he was capable of being reasonable about this.

"Graham—"

"She's made me out to be some fortune seeking beggar," he snapped, though his voice seemed defeated. "I should have never have even come here."

Hope's heart sank. She reached out to touch his arm, but he pulled away and turned his back on her.

A stone on her chest might be more comfortable than the pressure she felt in that moment. She opened her mouth to speak, but her throat felt tight. She felt ill at the thought that his next words would be to end their engagement. If he did that, she would be ruined.

"Do…" She started after a long moment. "Do you wish to… to end this?"

Graham circled back slowly, the fury displayed on his face somehow even more intense than it had been a moment ago.

"So, you can go back to your precious Penton?"

"No," she said quickly, not bothering to correct him. It would do no good, since he never seemed to be able to remember Pennington's name. "No, I just thought—"

"Thought that I'd abandon you? Like he did?" he asked, taking a step toward her. The space that separated them was eliminated in seconds and she had to crane her head back to look up at him. "Unfortunately for you, I'm nothing like him."

That irritated her.

"I don't want you to be like him."

"And yet the author of that article—"

"The author wrote what he wanted to write. He writes for a

gossip column—he's not interested in the truth but only in what will sell papers," she said, shaking her head. "Whatever I felt for Jacob before, it's not… It doesn't compare…"

The words stuck in her throat and she curled her fingers into her palms. Why was it so difficult to tell him how she felt about him? Was it possible that Jacob's abandonment had hurt her so significantly that she couldn't he honest?

No. She wouldn't let her past ruin her future.

Her hands came up to the lapels of his coat and though he tried to pull back, she held on tightly.

"I trust you, Graham. I believe in you and I… I care for you a great deal."

A silence followed and Hope half expected him to say something similar. Except in the next moment, his large hands came over hers and to her misery, pulled her grip from his coat.

"Don't say that," he said lowly.

Hope frowned, unsure why he would reply like that. Was he worried that she might still have feelings for Jacob? It wasn't true and she needed to tell him.

"It's true—"

But Graham wouldn't listen. He took several steps away, his back expanding and contracting heavily, as if he was laboriously breathing. Concern filled Hope and though she was worried he'd pull away again, she went to him.

Her hands reached up and moved over his back. She wanted him to hold her, as he had in the greenhouse, and tell her there was nothing to worry about. That he wasn't angry at her for foolish things, like her past. But instead of taking her into his arms or saying anything to comfort her, he visibly flinched beneath her palms.

"Graham," she said, her voice cracking with emotion. "Do you… Do you still wish to marry me?"

"Aye," he said instantly, though he wouldn't face her.

"Then can't we… put this behind us?"

But Graham only shook his head and moved out of her reach.

The cracks of Hope's heart seemed to fill with doubt and she balled her hands together as anger flared up within her.

"It isn't fair," she said quickly, the words refusing to be buried within her. "You cannot be mad at me about loving someone before I ever met you."

He spun around and Hope half expected him to yell about something or other. Instead, he grabbed her and pressed her body against his. Bending his head down he spoke harshly into her ear.

"You shouldn't be so damn certain of things, Hope," he said, his hands roaming over her body. She closed her eyes, eagerly accepting his touch. "You believe too easily in people."

She frowned.

"So what if I believed in Jacob?" she asked. "I believe in you now, don't I?"

The words seemed to burn him and he released her with a violent curse. She stumbled backwards, unsure what meaning to give to the shadows that passed over his face as he held his hands up, to bar her from coming toward him.

"This changes nothing," he said gruffly, more to himself then to her. "A month from Monday."

They were set to marry the following month and while he didn't sound exactly pleased by the idea, Hope nodded. After which he turned on his heel and left the dining room as though the devil was chasing him.

Hope stared at the space he'd disappeared from for longer than she would have liked to admit. The wedding announcement had been poorly done, but why had he been so angry with both Belle and with her? Surely he didn't believe that was what they'd wanted to have printed.

She folded her arms across her chest as her hands crawled around her, holding herself in a half embrace that she wished she could have gotten from him, instead. Was her past really so terrible that Graham couldn't forgive her for it? A large part of her wanted to argue, to tell him that he had no right to blame her for having fallen in love before, and yet she was afraid to challenge him because she was still worried that he would abandon her.

Unfortunately for you, I'm nothing like him. His words had been cold, but she had felt a distinct comfort in them. No. Graham was nothing like Jacob.

And for that, she would be forever grateful.

Chapter Fifteen

T HE INCIDENT IN the dining room had created a detachment between Graham and Hope in the following weeks. Though they had maintained an uneasy truce that prevented any additional outbreaks of shouting, neither had addressed the article since that morning. Where they had once been able to talk to each other so freely, there now hung a strained silence.

It had been decided that a stag hunt would take place the week prior to the wedding. Having set out with his cousins on their hunt before the sun rose, Graham was churlish, unable or unwilling to leave his dark mood.

The growing guilt seemed to be pressing against him from all sides. While Graham's initial reaction upon reading the articles had been to rage at Belle and Hope, the truth was, he was angriest with himself for the part of the article that stated the plain and simple truth: it *was* a fortunate match for him in that it would allow him to inherit the property he had always seen as his birthright. Graham had tried to reason, to argue with himself that he wouldn't be marrying Hope if he didn't like her and his marriage to her was simply a fortunate happenstance, but the fact remained that he was receiving enormous benefits from this match—and he had yet to share that particular detail with Hope. Her trust in him made him feel all the more wicked.

I trust you, Graham.

Trust. As if he were ever deserving of such a thing.

It grated him to realize his weaknesses when it came to Hope.

Now to put his faith in her when she was so oblivious to her power over him, well… It made him more than uneasy. It terrified him.

Graham's deepest wish, his only want in life, was to belong somewhere. He had always believed that place was Lismore Hall, but he was beginning to believe that it was not a place that truly mattered but rather who was by his side. Anywhere could be home, if Hope was with him. Which would only make her dismissal of him that much worse. It would create a chasm in his heart and he wasn't sure he would survive it.

He belonged to Hope, but he hadn't realized how much until he was stalking a red deer.

"What is it?" Logan asked as they walked. Each of the men was paired off, set up strategically around the glen to flank their prey through the glen. The thick fog that laid in the valley wrapped around them, cold and wet, akin to being embraced by a specter. "You're quiet today."

The rolling green hills around them appeared nearly black due to the dampness of the morning and though the sun had begun to rise, the mist was so thick one could hardly see where it stood in the sky.

"Am I?" Graham said, neither admitting nor denying anything.

"Aye, you are," Logan answered. "Not regretting your upcoming nuptials, are you?"

Graham gave him a warning glance.

"Watch your mouth."

Logan lifted his brow and shook his head.

"I mean nothing by it."

"Good."

"Still, I'm curious …"

"About bloody what?"

"What it will be like. Marrying an English woman," Logan said, visibly disgusted by the idea.

"Why not ask your father?" Graham asked sarcastically.

"I have," he said, seemingly amused by it all. "And he's as daft about his bride as you seem to be about yours."

Graham grunted as he walked, unwilling to have any sort of conversation about Hope with Logan.

"Blast Michael," Graham said, turning around and seeing no one. The sun had risen behind gray clouds as they continued to trudge through a low-lying mist. Fog was good for stalking deer, particularly once they found a spot to set up and stop moving, though the fog made it slightly more dangerous, but this haze was almost too dense. "Where is he? He and Jared should be here by now."

"Who knows?" Logan asked, unimpressed. "I swear, some English lassies appear out of nowhere and everyone's upside down. I'd swear the Sharpes had put some sort of enchantment on everyone since coming here."

Graham cocked his head at Logan's dramatics and his ongoing, irrational dislike of every English lass as a matter of principle. But enchantment was a perfect word to describe it. He had felt bewitched the moment he first laid eyes on Hope. Even separated from her, he couldn't deny that he was still under her spell.

"There you go again," Logan said, stepping over the thin stream as they made their way down into the glen. "Miserable and brooding. No doubt because of the Sharpes."

"What is your aversion to them?" Graham asked, annoyed. "They have no sway over you or your life. Is it simply because they're English that you can't stand them?"

"It would be enough." Logan trod carefully over marsh-like ground. The squelching sound of his steps would spook any animal within a mile. "And I can't say I find any of them particularly worse than the other, except perhaps the middle one."

"Faith?"

"Yes. She's always trying to correct me. It's rather infuriating," Logan said.

Graham shrugged.

"I don't mind Faith. She's a bit stodgy, no doubt, but there's a sense about her that she isn't a fool. She seems more relatable than Grace."

"Really? I would have thought Grace was the friendlier of the two."

"She is, but there's a reserve to each of them. Grace is friendly, but there are ways in which she remains wholly unapproachable. I can't quite put my finger on it. While Faith, who has a barrier first and foremost, relents eventually. Though she hasn't been entirely pleased with me since witnessing my argument with Hope."

"They're a tightly knit family," Logan said. "But I have to disagree. That Faith woman thinks I care what she has to say and insists on informing me on topics I'm quite well-versed in."

"Such as?"

"Well—"

A loud bang echoed in the glen as a flock of birds flew up into the sky several yards away. Before either Graham or Logan could react, a searing pain cut through Graham's flesh. With a guttural yell, he grasped his side and fell to the ground.

"Graham!" Logan shouted, falling to his knees beside Graham. "What the devil…"

A rustling of footsteps sounded from somewhere behind Graham's head, but he could barely focus. It was the strangest thing, almost as if he knew he had been shot, but couldn't quite comprehend it. Agony emanated from the place he had been hit, but the shock was settling in.

"Oi!" Logan shouted. "Over here!"

"What's this?" Michael's voice was faint in his ears as darkness edged Graham's vision. "Oh, God, no. Did I hit him?" A second figure stood over him, but he couldn't see who it was. "No. Oh, Graham, I'm so sorry!"

"Get the horses," Logan ordered, before peering down at Graham as his vision blurred. "Stay awake. Can you hear me? Graham? Can you hear me?"

But as Logan's voice faded, a cool darkness wrapped around Graham, engulfing him completely.

Chapter Sixteen

THE DAY HAD become hot and the air was heavy. A storm was moving in.

"Stalking deer," Grace said, shivering at her own words over breakfast that morning. "I find it a ghastly thing to do. Hunting poor, defenseless animals."

"You've bacon in front of you," Faith pointed out. "You've no problem eating that."

Grace glanced at her plate and made a face. She pushed it back.

"Perhaps I should stop altogether. You know, I've just finished reading a fascinating book by a doctor in London to talk about the benefits of a vegetarian diet."

"A what?" Belle asked.

"It's the idea that one should refrain from eating meat."

"For how long?"

"Well, forever."

"Good gads, no," Belle said. "What's one to do if there's no meat? You'll become sick, no doubt."

"Actually, there's an argument that it's better for one's digestion."

As Grace and her aunt bickered over the benefits and disadvantages of such a diet, Hope's mind drifted back to the tension that still lingered between her and Graham. Was he still upset with her? When would things finally get back to normal between them?

Still feeling rather glum after breakfast, Hope searched out the gardener, Mr. Fitzpatrick, to talk with him about the lavender plants. For over an hour or so, she helped dead-head certain flowers and had worked up quite a sweat as the clouds above them became darker.

A crack of thunder boomed above just as a fat raindrop landed on her wrist. Then another. And another.

"Drat," she said, turning to Mr. Fitzpatrick. "It seems as though our lesson will be cut short."

He nodded, and Hope started to turn to head back inside, but then another sound echoed through the air. Horse hooves. Wiping her hands on the apron tied around her waist, she came around the garden to the front of the house and saw six or so horses galloping toward her. It seemed the men were back from the hunt, but why they were coming here made no sense. And why would they be riding with such speed, such urgency?

"What in the world…"

But then she saw Graham, head slumped as if he had lost consciousness, body held in place by whoever was braced behind him.

Something was wrong.

Without another thought, she sprinted toward the steps, arriving just as the group reached the front of the house.

"What's happened?" she asked, her voice panicked. Logan Harris jumped off his horse and came to Graham's side.

"There was an accident," Jared said. Graham rolled himself off the horse with a guttural sound. Hope was glad to see that he was conscious after all, but he certainly didn't sound well. Nor did he look well, though she couldn't tell right away exactly what was wrong.

"What accident?" she demanded as she went to Graham. Her hands went immediately to his chest, but he hissed at the contact, causing her to pull back. Peering down at her hand, she gasped when she realized it was covered in blood. Her head snapped back up. "Graham?"

"I've been shot," he grumbled, his face wet with perspiration.

"Shot?"

"Fetch a doctor," Logan was telling one of the groomsmen. "See if Dr. Hall is home. If not, get Barkley."

"Yes sir," a groom said, taking a horse.

"We have to get him inside," Logan said, pulling Graham with him.

Hope had never experienced such panic before in her entire life, and it was all she could do to stay steady on her feet and follow the crush of men as they entered Lismore.

"What's all this?" Belle asked. Jeanne, Rose, Faith and Grace came out of the drawing room. "What's wrong?"

"Graham's been shot!" Hope followed her husband-to-be and Logan on quivery legs. "Have cook—"

"Yes, dear, I know," Belle said, her usually cheerful face drawn and worried. She hobbled forward appearing to struggle more than usual. "Andrews!"

As Belle barked orders, her cane caught in the lip of one of the flagstones and she let out a yelp of fear as she fell to the ground.

"Aunt Belle!" Hope shouted, dropping to the floor to help her. "Are you all right?"

"Gad, blasted floor!" she barked. "Andrews!"

Hope turned around and watched Logan help Graham up the stairs. She was desperate to follow, but Belle's breathing was becoming labored and a strange sort of whizzing was emanating from her throat.

"Is Aunt Belle all right?" Grace asked, dropping to her knees.

"Faith, follow the men, please," Hope said, ignoring Grace as Andrews appeared, rushing to his mistress. "I'll be along in a moment."

"But—"

"Please, Faith."

She must have heard the desperation in Hope's voice, because Faith nodded quickly and turned on her heel, rushing up the stairway as Andrews lifted Belle with apparent ease. Grace followed Belle to her room while Hope began ordering the servants about. She needed hot, clean water brought up to Graham where she suspected Dr. Hall would perform some sort of extraction of the bullet, if he could. Belle would need a bath as well as a poultice made for the bruises she undoubtedly gained during her fall.

It was so unlike her to fall, but Hope suspected the commotion that morning had been enough to distract her from her footing. When the servants were all hard at work on their tasks, Hope went to Belle's room to check on her. She found Andrews and Grace had taken things into hand.

Grateful, Hope left and followed the sounds of commotion up to the room where they had taken Graham. She focused on the great wooden bed where several men had helped Graham to, along with Faith, who was standing back, her face scrunched with what looked like disbelief.

"Faith?" Hope said, coming up to her and reaching out to touch her elbow. Faith flinched and turned, apparently having just realized Hope was there. "Are you all right?"

"Yes, of course," she said unconvincingly.

Hope frowned, but was distracted by a guttural noise coming from Graham.

"Thank you for keeping an eye on things for me," Hope said as she moved toward the bed, but Faith's hand wrapped around her wrist. Hope turned back, her frown deepening. "What's wrong?"

Faith's mouth opened, but no words came out. She appeared torn, and a moment later, she dropped Hope's wrist and shook her head.

"Nothing."

Hope gave her a quick nod, assuming that she had simply been worried about the sight of blood.

A sweat had broken out over Graham's brow, and his breathing was strained. Logan loosened his collar. His hair stuck to his forehead and his eyes were closed tightly as he winced at the slightest movement.

The storm clouds in the sky made the room appear darker than usual. It was also noisy and crowded, buzzing with maids and footmen delivering swathes of towels, boiling water, sheets, and extra pillows. Logan was helping Graham remove his coat and vest, though he ordered one of the maids to cut the shirt.

At first, it looked like he might be shot in the chest, and Hope unwillingly let out a small gasp of fear.

"Oh God," she whispered into her fingers covering her mouth with her hand.

"It only nicked me," Graham said, his gaze flickering to her.

"It did a bit more than that." Logan pressed a fresh towel to the wound, causing Graham to gasp. Logan nodded toward Hope. "Hold this here."

She nodded, replacing his hand as Logan set out to mix something that the maids had brought up.

"How did it happen?" Hope asked as he leaned back into the stack of pillows behind him.

"It was an accident. Michael wasn't paying attention where he was bloody shooting," Graham grumbled.

"He's lucky he didn't kill you," Logan said, mixing his concoction. "Damn fool's aim is miserable."

"I don't know about that," Graham said. "A few more inches that way and he would have got me right in the heart. Augh!"

Hope hadn't meant to lean into his wound, but the thought of Graham being shot in the heart had made her woozy.

"Sorry," she said, glancing at Logan, who was mixing a bowl of brownish liquid. "What's that?"

"Soap, salt, and scotch." He gently brushed her hand from Graham's chest and poured the mixture onto the wound.

"AGH! DAMN IT!"

She pressed her chin to her shoulder, attempting to keep herself from getting even more lightheaded. Taking a bracing breath through her nostrils, she felt a wave of nausea slam into her as the scent of blood overpowered her.

"Hope? I need more of the mixture," Logan said.

Fighting to breathe through her mouth, she turned back and handed it to him. As he dipped the soapy alcoholic mixture into Graham's injury, another frightful grunt came from the bed. Hope's hand instinctively went to Logan's forearm as she tried to push his hand away.

"Maybe you shouldn't do that."

Logan gave her a quizzical stare.

"It hurts, but we must clean the wound out," he said slowly. "I promise you; he would be in far worse pain if we let it become infected."

Hope nodded and removed her hand from Logan's arm as he continued to clean the bullet hole. He proceeded to pour the rest on, which caused Graham to curse again.

"Easy," Hope said, her palm coming to his forehead. She pushed back the hair that stuck to his skin. Beads of sweat rolled down his temple. "Be easy."

Graham's gaze locked with hers as the his wound was cleaned. Though he flinched and snarled, he did not curse. Hope fought the growing tremors in her body, struggling to remain calm. Though she watched this massive bear of a man writhe in pain before her, she wouldn't let him notice any of the fear that was gripping her. All she could do was stare at him when a knock at the door grabbed her attention.

"Well, let's get to it," a man said, coming into the room.

Though Hope had never met him, she was sure this was Dr. Hall. He was taller than both Graham and Logan—which was saying something, as both men were quite tall—but he wasn't quite as broad. His dark brown hair was clipped short in a way that was popular with most young professionals, and while his face was handsome, it was partially hidden by a close-cropped beard. His serious, hazel eyes flickered from person to person as he observed the situation.

"You cleaned it out?" he asked Logan as he came forward to

assess the wound.

"Yes."

"Good," he said, opening his leather bag on the bed. "Stay still." Wrapping his hand in a white cloth, he hovered over Graham's prone form. Reaching up, he pressed into the wound.

Graham flinched and let out a slew of vicious curses that Hope had never heard before.

"Do that again," he snarled at the doctor. "And I'll put yer teeth out."

"Not with your right arm, and not for some time," Dr. Hall said, removing the soiled cloth from his hand. "It seems the bullet passed through, but it's not a pretty wound. It's shattered your skin being this close to the edge of your body."

"What does that mean?" Hope asked.

"Well, I'm going to sew it up best I can, but I won't be surprised if the edges blacken. It'll be imperative to keep this wound clean so infection doesn't set in." The doctor rummaged through his bag and began removing formidable silver instruments, lining them up on the bed. Hope shuddered. "The bandages must be changed once every four hours, I think."

"Yes," Hope said, as if she were taking orders.

"Will a maid or someone need to be informed?"

"No, I'll do it," she said.

The doctor paused in his movement and gave Logan a quick look. She wondered if the doctor didn't believe she was capable of managing a wound, but if he had his doubts, he didn't state them aloud. Still, Hope became slightly defensive. She notched her chin up when his gaze landed back on her.

"Very well," he said. "You must pay attention once I've sewn him up to understand how to clean it properly. Logan, assist me."

Logan came around and put a gentle hand on Hope's shoulder.

"You'll not be wanting to see this," he said, nodding toward the door. "It won't be pretty."

"I'm not leaving," Hope said.

"Madam, I must agree with Logan," Dr. Hall said. "It's not for the faint of heart."

"I'm not leaving this room," she said firmly, her eyes on Graham.

"I really must insist—"

"No."

"Hope," Graham said. For a tense moment, all three men looked at her. "Sit down," he said, nodding to a chair by the fireplace.

Sitting as quickly as possible, she watched the two men work on her husband. For nearly a half hour, they operated on him. The entire time, Hope was engulfed in excruciating worry. With every grunt and every shift, she had to fight not to leap up and rush to her beloved's side. As she watched Logan and the doctor work together, Hope realized that they barely spoke. It was almost as if Logan had firsthand knowledge of what needed to take place. Though Hope couldn't remember anything being said about Logan being a doctor, she remembered that he had been in the war. Perhaps he had learned something about medical treatment there.

When they finally finished, they cleaned the wound once more, put a slave on it, and wrapped their patient in bandages. Graham was offered a drink, but not more than one since the doctor didn't want him to bleed through his wraps. Apparently the doctor believed that alcohol made wounds hemorrhage.

She followed the doctor and Logan to the doorway.

"Thank you, Doctor. Mr. Harris," she said. "I can't begin to tell you how much I appreciate it."

"It was nothing," the doctor said. "But I'm afraid I need to depart. I was supposed to be on the way to Glasgow hours ago."

"Of course," Hope said. "Thank you again."

Dr. Hall nodded and turned to leave, with Grace at his heels.

"Where was he shot?" Grace asked, following the doctor down the hallway. "Was it the triceps or the latissimus dorsi?"

"The what?" Hope asked.

"It was an external wound through the latissimus—wait, who are you?" the doctor asked as he left, just as Faith, who had melted back into one of the corners of the room, stepped forward.

"Hope," she began, her voice unusually small. "Can we talk?"

"Miss Faith," Logan said loudly, coming around Hope. "A word, if I may?"

"Perhaps in a bit, Faith," Hope said, peering over her shoulder. "I wish to stay with Graham for a little while."

Faith bit her lip as her hands came together. It seemed she wished to say more, but when Logan came toward her, something surprising flashed across Faith's face—a look of pure loathing. With a jerky nod to Hope, she turned quickly and disappeared through the door, followed by an impatient-looking Logan.

Shutting out the madness of the world behind, Hope leaned her back against the door and observed Graham from a distance. Though the darkness of the room caused dozens of shadows to stretch out across the bed, especially with the storm raging outside, a small, orange glow of light coming from a series of oil lamps that had been lit for Dr. Hall cast Graham in an almost unnatural aura. She could see that he was staring at her through a thin veil of pain, alcohol, and worry, and it hurt her heart to think of him in any sort of discomfort. Still, she remained where she was, unsure if she should go to him.

He, however, was not unsure.

"Come here," he ordered.

Hope pushed off the door and came over to the side of the bed. He seemed exhausted, and she wondered if he shouldn't attempt to sleep rather than talk.

"How does it feel?" she asked, watching him with concern.

"Wonderful," he said sarcastically. His good arm crossed over his chest and he reached for her hand, which she willingly gave him. "Listen, Hope, about the other day. I'm sorry—"

"Oh no, Graham, you don't have to—"

"Aye, I do." He tried to sit up, but he winced, which caused Hope to lean closer. "I shouldna been acting as I did after our argument. It was wrong of me."

The slur of his speech made his accent sound thicker, his brogue broadening. Was it the wound that caused it or the alcohol she wondered.

"Graham, really, it's fine—"

"Will you hush so I can apologize?" he said. She snapped her mouth shut and he continued. "I know the announcement in the papers wasn't your fault and I shouldna snapped at you as I did." Hope's heart fluttered at his apology. He *had* been wrong to snap at her, but it pleased her to know that he wasn't the sort of man that was too stubborn to ever admit to his own faults. He inhaled. "As for Penedragon—"

"Pennington."

"Aye, him," he said, taking a breath. He flinched slightly and, though Hope tried to comfort him, he batted her hand away. "I suppose I canne be angry about things that happened before we met."

"No, you certainly can't."

Graham scowled, and it reminded Hope of the face a child would make when he was being scolded.

"But I'm not pleased about it either," he continued. Hope gave him a strained smile. He went on. "I know it's not good of me, but imagining you with any other man makes me irrational. And I think it's unfair of you to say I shouldne get upset—"

"Is this an apology?"

"—but know that I won't be letting my temper get the better of me anymore. You don't deserve it, even if Pottington deserves to have his throat ripped out for hurting you."

He was never going to say Jacob's name correctly. Hope's hand crept up his neck and she brushed the stubble on his chin.

"But Pennington and I were never together. Not the way you and I..." She trailed off.

"Aye, which is almost worse. Ye and him shared something

special, something more than physical, and I know it's wrong of me, but I hate it."

Hope leaned forward and put her hands flat against Graham's warm cheeks.

"You, Graham MacKinnon, are the only man I have ever shared anything special with. Do you understand?" He stared at her for a long moment, seemingly hypnotized by her. He nodded slowly. "Then know there is never a need for you to be jealous. Ours will be a marriage built on trust, and you will never have any reason to doubt me. I promise."

His gaze dropped and Hope assumed that speaking so honestly about her feelings made him uncomfortable. He coughed into his hand and she leaned back, giving him some space.

"I want you to know that I do care about you, Hope," he said, his voice strained slightly. Probably due to his injury. "Even though I might have started this wrong, believe me about that."

A tingling sensation swept across the back of her neck, making the tiny hairs stand on end. What was he talking about? His eyelids dipped and Hope assumed the medicine was making him drowsy and perhaps a little confused.

She leaned her body carefully over his and brought her mouth to his ear.

"I care about you too, Graham MacKinnon. More than you know."

A satisfied smile spread across his face as she leaned back. Graham squeezed her fingers and sighed deeply as his eyes fully closed and he fell asleep.

Chapter Seventeen

Having spent nearly four days sleeping in a chair in the sickroom where Graham was recovering, Hope had practically been pulled out to bathe and sleep in her own room. She had been diligent in her nursing Graham back to health, and had flatly refused to leave his side until Graham himself had ordered it.

Still, as soon as she awoke in her own room, fully rested and recharged, she wanted to check on him. She crawled out of bed and rang for a maid who helped her dress into an unpretentious day gown. Doing her hair in a simple braid, she wrapped it around her head in a halo style, pinning it in place and then quietly opened the door. She stole down the hallway to Graham's room just as Una the maid was exiting.

"Oh, my lady, he's awake, but says he wants to sleep," Una said. "His bandages were changed an hour ago. Dr. Barkley was just here as well, poking and prodding at him."

Hope smiled.

"Thank you, Una," she said, putting her hand to the brass knob. "I'll only bother him a minute."

Una nodded and bobbed a curtsy before scurrying away. Hope gently opened the door, which creaked slightly. She moved into the room as quietly as possible.

One of the things Hope had discovered over the last few days was that Graham preferred to sleep in while she was always up with the dawn. She had enjoyed waking up before him as it gave her plenty of time to gaze at Graham without disruption.

He appeared younger while he slept, as the scowl he so often wore disappeared. She was tempted to stroke the stubble of his jaw as she watched him breathe, but she was sure he'd try to pull her toward him if he realized she was there.

But alas, she was already too late on that front. Seeming to sense her presence, Graham opened his eyes and a small grin crawled across his face. Hope's heart fluttered beneath his gaze.

She came around the small table at his bedside that held his medical supplies. A brown jar sat unopened next to the alcohol bowl they had been using to clean the wound. Picking it up, she brought it to her nose and sniffed. It smelled of honey and turpentine.

"Graham?"

"Mm-hmm?"

"What is this mixture?"

"It's honey and pine resin. It's a concoction the doctor is trying out. Honey cleans out wounds and the resin can draw out dirt. You're supposed to swathe it over a wound to prevent infection."

"Really?"

"Supposedly. The bee hives I have at Elk Manor are particularly good at producing dark honey. Dr. Hall got it from my own hives."

Hope's brow lifted in surprise as she lifted the jar. She held it up to the light of the window, examining its contents.

"I didn't know honey could be used as medicine."

"There's plenty of uses for honey," he said, resting back against the pillows.

She smiled at him.

"Did he say if you were able to get out of bed today?"

Graham frowned. "No. He says I should wait until the end of the week, even though I feel just fine."

Hope lifted a finger. She had been following both doctors' orders religiously and Graham had suffered beneath her command.

"If the doctor said no, then you shouldn't. I'll have a tray brought up immediately."

"Give it an hour or so," he said through a yawn. His eyes closed. "I shouldn't want to be a bother."

Hope smirked and left the room, letting him sleep. She sighed with contentment as she made her way down the main staircase. How much life had changed in only a few short weeks, she mused. Had she been able to go back in time and tell herself, only months earlier, that she would soon live in the highlands with Aunt Belle and her sisters, on the verge of marriage to a handsome Scot and set to inherit an estate, she was sure her younger self would have laughed profusely.

Shaking her head, she went to search for Dr. Barkley to inquire about what sort of food would be best for Graham to eat as he recovered.

That week's activities had certainly distracted her, but now that Graham was well on the mend, Hope had never been happier. Graham certainly seemed to feel the same way.

Hope searched the parlor, and then the library, only to find both empty. Deciding that Dr. Barkley was probably in her aunt's office, she headed there. She was just about to round the corner when she heard the disgruntled voice of Belle whispering so harshly that it caused Hope to stop in her tracks.

"And furthermore, I will not have you or anyone else tell me how to live my life," she spoke as the soft 'thud' of her cane tapped the floor with finality.

"Lady Belle, I must insist you reconsider."

"Absolutely not."

"I've seen this in several other patients. Peritonitis is not an easy disease. It will only get worse. Now, there are beliefs that a warmer climate could help—"

"For the last time, I will not remove myself from this home," she continued. "Now, are there no other treatments?"

"Besides the morphine, no. Dr. Hall and I have discussed your condition at length and I must reiterate—"

"I've heard quite enough. After you attend MacKinnon, you are dismissed."

Hope's hand covered her mouth.

"Dismissing me won't change your diagnosis," he said evenly.

"I believe you said it would be a good idea to get a second opinion."

"Correct me if I'm wrong, but aren't I the third doctor you've seen for this? See a dozen doctors, see a hundred if you like. Perhaps you'll find one or two who disagree with the prognosis, but it won't change the fact that unless you leave Scotland for a considerable amount of time, your decline will be rapid and irreversible."

Hope's brow furrowed.

"You may leave, Dr. Barkley," Belle said stiffly.

The doctor sighed. "Very well."

Footsteps sounded from the room. Suddenly aware of how incriminating it would appear for Hope to be caught eavesdropping, she stood up and walked directly into the room, slamming into the doctor.

"Oof!" the older man said, dropping his bag.

"Oh! Dr. Barkley! I didn't see you there," she said, bending to help him gather his things. "I came rushing down the hallway without thinking."

"Not at all," the doctor said stiffly. He stood up and straightened his coat. "Good day, Miss Sharpe."

"Of course. Good day," Hope said, swiveling sideways to let him pass.

She turned back to face the office door. Hope entered the room fully and saw Belle sitting in a winged back chair, one hand clenched around her cane tightly. She smiled at Hope, though it didn't reach her eyes, and she tried to stand. Hope instantly came toward her, kneeling before her to prevent her from rising.

"Oh, there's no need for you to get up, Aunt Belle."

"Nonsense," she said swatting at her hand as she stood, forcing Hope to stand as well. "How does MacKinnon fare?"

"Very well," Hope said, watching her aunt carefully. "The wound is clean and the edges seem to be healing."

"That's good."

"And how are you feeling? Surely the doctor wasn't pleased to see you in your office so early."

"Bah, Barkley simply isn't used to seeing such a healthy woman."

Hope nodded slowly, though she kept a close eye on her aunt.

A stilted silence followed, and Hope wondered if she should tell her aunt that she had overheard her talk with Dr. Barkley. Taking a tentative step forward, she held her hands together, her thumbnail picking at her forefinger.

"Aunt Belle, are you well?"

"Yes, of course," she said evenly. Hope was silent and Belle gave her an inquisitive stare. "Is there something wrong, dear?"

Hope shook her head quickly.

"No, Aunt Belle, it's just…"

Hope didn't want to upset her, but she needed to know what was happening. The decisiveness in her aunt's tone might have dissuaded her from pressing the issue when she first arrived, but Hope was determined.

"Just what, dear?" her aunt asked.

"I want you to know that if you were ever not well, we—my sisters and I, that is—would do anything and everything to help you get better."

Belle squinted.

"Is that so?" she asked. Hope nodded. "My dear, why don't you see if Dr. Barkley needs any assistance?"

Hope didn't move.

"Aunt Belle, if you are sick—"

"If I am sick, it is my own business. Not yours."

"It is very much my business," she said coming forward. "Aunt Belle, you must let someone help you."

"I've lived many years on my own, my dear girl, and I'm not about to have anyone start dictating my life now. You should go."

Hope sighed. Belle could be the most stubborn woman in the world at times. Annoyed at accomplishing nothing, she left Belle's office. If she would refuse to accept help, there was little Hope could do about it.

Upon reaching the dining room, Hope saw Grace and Faith, staring at one another rather intensely. When Grace noticed Hope, she stood up, somewhat frantic.

"Hope, good morning," she said, her hands coming together before her. "How is Mr. MacKinnon faring this morning?"

"Well," Hope said, coming into the room. Both sisters appeared as though they were hiding something. "Are you all right, Grace?"

"Me? Yes. Very well," she said, looked down at a stony-faced Faith. "We both are. Aren't we, Faith?"

Faith sat quietly, apparently unwilling to say anything, which gave Hope pause. What was going on?

"Are you unwell, Faith?" she asked, collecting a plate at the side table.

After scooping some poached eggs over two pieces of toast, Hope came around the table and took her seat. Still, Faith wouldn't meet her eyes.

"I don't think we should lie to her," Faith said to Grace when Hope finally sat down.

"It's not lying," Grace said. "You simply misinterpreted—"

"I did no such thing!"

"Wait, wait," Hope said, holding up her hands to stop her sisters from arguing. "What are you two going on about?" When neither seemed willing to speak, Hope pressed. "Faith?" She turned her head. "Grace?"

Wringing her hands together, Grace tipped her head nervously.

"Well, Faith believes she heard something—"

"I don't believe I heard something. I know I did."

"Be that as it may," Grace continued. "It's rather an unsettling thing, and I'm not sure quite how to share it with you."

Hope's brows pinched together as she looked back and forth between her sisters, her gaze finally settling on Faith.

"What is she talking about?"

"Listen," Faith said after a moment. She exhaled a long breath before continuing. "I know I wasn't exactly pleased about coming here and that I've made several comments about him already that might make you doubt my account, but I'm not making this up. I know what I heard."

"Well, please, share, because I'm not sure what either of you is talking about."

A short silence followed before Faith continued.

"The other day when Graham was brought here after being shot, you asked that I accompany him and Mr. Harris to one of the rooms upstairs," she said, glancing up. "And I did. I tried to be as helpful as possible, but I also didn't want to get in the way. And everyone was so frantic, I'm not sure they even noticed I was there. When Mr. Harris helped Mr. MacKinnon to his bed, I overheard Mr. MacKinnon whisper something about how ironic it would be to die in the same house where he was born, having never once lived here since that day, and Mr. Harris said... Well, he... I'm afraid..."

"What?" Hope asked, a twisting sort of warning snaking through her body. "What did he say?"

"He said he only needed to hold on a few more days and it would be his." Faith's gaze met Hope's as she looked her squarely in the eye. "He said, *remember the plan, old boy.*"

Hope stared at her sister for a long time before a humorless snort escaped her mouth. She shook her head and looked at Grace, who had stopped wringing her hands and appeared rather pale.

Plan? What plan? Hope shook her head again, trying to unstick some thought that wouldn't leave. The plan to what? Marry her to gain ownership of Lismore Hall?

No, that couldn't be…

"That's preposterous," she said breathlessly, not to anyone in particular. "Graham didn't ask me to marry him because of this house." She looked back and forth between each sister. "He didn't want to marry me. Remember? At Elk Manor, he was furious—"

"—that you and he had nearly been caught alone together," Faith said. "Rose came to your aid and kept you from being compromised. You thought he was angry that you'd nearly been caught, but what if he was angry that you *hadn't* been caught—hadn't been forced to get engaged right away? What if that was his plan?"

"There was no plan," Hope said, her anger getting the better of her. Closing her eyes, she tried to breathe steadily. She felt as though her body was being pulled beneath the earth, as though she were in a sort of quicksand. "What sort of plan would there be?"

"A plot to regain this house by marrying the woman who will inherit it," Grace said gently.

"No. There isn't any plot," Hope started as she stood up, suddenly without appetite. "But if there was one, Graham certainly wouldn't be a part of it. He couldn't."

Though neither of her sisters argued any further, neither appeared convinced. Hope swallowed back the bile that rose in her throat, replaying the words she had just heard. An uncomfortable heat crawled up Hope's spine. *This isn't happening*, she thought miserably. Surely it wasn't true. It couldn't be true.

But then, cold and uncomfortable zings lit up across her skin. It was like being pelted with bits of hail. Why did the truth always hurt so much? Her fingers braced against the back of her chair, painfully digging into the wood.

Hope wondered why she hadn't realized it before.

Of course, Graham would want to marry her so he could regain Lismore Hall.

Her stomach turned with nausea as she pressed the heel of

her palm to her head. Oh, could she have been so blind? So blatantly foolish? She should have known better.

Her heart beat erratically. What an idiot she was. Turning, Hope headed toward the doorway that led out into the hall. She needed to speak with Graham.

"Hope?" Grace called from behind, but she didn't stop.

Glancing up to her left, she saw the massive painting of Graham's grandfather staring down at her. He seemed rather annoyed, as if he didn't appreciate her, and a furious burst of animosity echoed in her heart toward the long dead man. Frowning, she glared at the painting.

"You've no right to glower at me," she said.

"I wasn't glowering."

Hope jumped, terrified at hearing that voice she knew all too well. It was Jacob Pennington, standing next to an annoyed looking Una.

"Begging your pardon, Miss Sharpe, but Mr. Pennington only just arrived. I was coming to tell you."

"Uh, yes. Of course, It's all right," Hope said blinking, as if she was seeing things.

Una bobbed her head and left. He come forward quickly, obviously distressed to have frightened her. He reached for her hand.

"Hope, I didn't mean to scare you." His golden flax hair was perfectly fixed, his intent brown eyes showing worry. "Are you all right?"

"Jacob," Hope said, lifting her hand to her throat. "What on earth are you doing here?"

"Well, after I read the announcement in the *Times*, I was stunned, to tell you the truth. Knowing you as I do, I knew such a swift engagement must be at the behest of someone else. Over the past several weeks, I've grown more and more worried, and eventually I couldn't help but to take the harrowing trip north to see you and make sure that you were all right. Tell me, has your aunt forced you into this? Has she compelled you to live here, in this remote part of the world?" He peered around her into the dining room, noticing that they weren't alone. Still, he didn't release his grip on her fingers and instead drew Hope back into the dining room. He bowed his head. "Miss Faith. Miss Grace."

No, this was not good.

"Mr. Pennington," Faith said, stalking down the room, her fists clenched at her sides as she walked, followed closely by Grace. "What the devil—"

"Ah, Faith, perhaps we should leave Hope and Mr. Pennington alone," Grace said quickly, encircling her arm around her sister's elbow. She pulled her away toward the door. "I'm sure Aunt Belle or perhaps the staff might wish to be informed about our guest. Come along."

"But—ow!"

Faith was practically pushed through the doorway. Grace's mouth pulled up into a pained smile, her eyes lingering on Hope's hand held by Jacob. With a nod, she was out of the room.

Turning back to face Jacob, Hope pulled her hand swiftly from his and moved carefully around him. The shock that fizzled through her veins at the sight of him was beginning to settle, but she still had questions. First and foremost: What on earth was he doing here?

"Jacob, what are you doing here?"

"To save you from what so obviously is some sort of hack marriage," he said. "The Hope I know would never agree to such a quick wedding. Why, we weren't even engaged and yet our courtship lasted well over two years."

"Yes, because you wished for it to last so long," she said. "What exactly do you intend to do here?"

"I'm here to save you."

"Save me? From what?"

"From making a terrible mistake. I was positively flooded with worry when I read about your engagement and it's tortured me these many weeks to think that our estrangement might have pushed you into an unwanted situation. I've wrestled with my better judgment, but in the end I lost. I realized that I love you, Hope Sharpe. And I intend to bring you back to London."

Hope's mouth fell open at his proclamation. Then, she sent up a silent prayer for strength before she spoke.

"Oh, Jacob, that is, er, generous of you and it was kind of you to come all this way just to check on me, but I'm afraid your journey has been for naught."

"Because you're being forced to do this?" he asked. Hope stared at him, bewildered. "The marriage, I mean."

"No," she said. "Jacob, no one is forcing me to marry anyone. Mr. MacKinnon and I have decided to wed because that is *our* wish, without any sort of pressure from anyone else."

The word stuck in her throat as she remembered what Faith had said. Was she lying to herself? Did Graham truly wish to marry her—or was his only concern to inherit? Had Graham really ever been interested in her?

Jacob scoffed. Pity appeared on his face, annoying her. But she struggled to swallow that annoyance down. He had traveled so far to see her and offer his assistance, and she did not wish to be rude.

"Are you quite sure?" he asked, his tone doubtful. "There is no, well, underlying reason for you two to be forced into matrimony?"

Hope did not understand his question until she saw him examining her body as if he could see through her clothes. Mortified at the implication that a pregnancy had required her to marry immediately, Hope instinctively folded her arms around her body, as if to shield herself from his intrusive gaze. She held her chin up high.

"As I said, I am *quite* sure."

"I see," he said, frowning a bit, and Hope had the distinct desire to kick him.

She came toward him and tried to shoo him from the room. But he didn't move.

"I think it would be best if you left now," she said.

"I'm not going anywhere until I know you are safe," he said. "To think that when I ended our courtship that you would have to marry a Scot—"

"Really, it's all right," she said, waving her hands to get him to leave the room. "As I said, I am quite happy with the match."

"You didn't seem very happy when I first entered the room."

"I had just finished discussing a misunderstanding with my sisters. That is all."

Jacob watched her for a moment before sighing. He put his hand over his heart.

"I shouldn't have tossed you off as I did," he said. "Oh, Hope. If I could go back and change things, I would."

Hope's thoughts drifted up to Graham. What would he do if he found Jacob here? He had been thoroughly upset even knowing that he had once been her suitor.

"That's all very good of you, Jacob, but really, you must leave. There is no space for you here."

"Not even in some corner of your heart?"

Hope stared at him as though he were mad. He gazed back at her with a longing expression in his eye, as if he were besotted with her. What on earth was wrong with him? Never in their entire courtship had he ever looked at her like this.

"Jacob, I'm very grateful that you came all this way and I thank you for being such a devoted friend, but you must know that there is no changing things. I am m-marrying Mr. MacKinnon," she said, stumbling over her words. "And I'm quite happy about it. So please, please. You must refrain from asking about my feelings for you." She shook her head. "Those feelings stopped when our relationship ended. And if Mr. MacKinnon were to hear any of this, he would have you quartered."

"Because he is a cruel man?" Jacob asked hopefully.

"Because he is a *loyal* man. Now, I beg you to leave this house, right this very moment."

"Then there are no feelings left for me? None at all?"

Hope had to restrain herself from rolling her eyes.

"You were the one who cut me loose, remember? Now as I've told you—"

"Why are you in such a rush to be rid of me? Is it because you fear that if we spend more time together, you might find that somewhere deep inside, you might still have feelings for me?" He reached for her hand again, gripping it tightly. Uncomfortably so. She tried to pull away, but he wouldn't let her go. "Forgive me, Hope. I was a fool to let you go." He brought her hand up to his mouth and began peppering her knuckles with kisses. Her mind whirled at the idea of Graham walking into this. He would murder Jacob. "And I will never let you go again."

"Yes, you will, right this instant," she whispered harshly, finally yanking her hand free. "What's come over you?"

"I love you," he said, coming toward her. "Run away with me."

Hope gasped, legitimately shocked. "Good lord, you have gone mad," she said, more to herself than to him. "Jacob, you need to leave right now. I insist. If Gra—uh, Mr. MacKinnon finds out that you were here, he'll be very upset."

"Damn him," Jacob said, with a false bravado that made Hope exasperated. "He doesn't care for you—I'm sure of it. His only interest is in your windfall."

Hope tilted her head and her brow furrowed.

"My windfall?" she repeated. "What windfall?"

"You do not have to be coy with me, Hope," he said, recapturing her hand. "It was all over the papers in London. It's what made me so worried about you in the first place."

Hope squinted.

"You thought my fiancé only wished to marry me because of my supposed future inheritance?"

"Well, I must admit—Uh, did you say supposed inheritance?" he said, his stance shifting slightly.

"Yes. It was only revealed to me a few weeks ago, after reading that article, that Aunt Belle was set to name me as her beneficiary. But I declined."

"You… You what?"

"I asked that her estate be divided three-fold so that I might share with my sisters."

Breathing a sigh of relief, the worry in Jacob's eyes vanished as he squeezed her hand tighter.

"Oh, my dear, you mustn't worry about that. As the sole beneficiary—which is only proper, given that you're the eldest—you would be able to allot your sisters a yearly allowance. But we needn't discuss that just now. Now, we must leave."

"Leave?" Hope repeated, utterly confused. "Have you completely lost your mind, Jacob?"

"I love you, Hope. I always have and it was my own foolishness that separated us, but no more," he said earnestly, pulling her toward the doorway. "All that matters now is that we can be together, with financial independence."

Hope kept shaking her head. She wasn't sure if she should laugh or cry or scream as she sorted through a dozen emotions. She tried to tug her hand out of his grasp.

"You really must let me go."

"But Hope—"

"Let go, Jacob."

"Get your fucking hands off my wife," a dark, threatening growl sounded from the doorway.

Chapter Eighteen

THE SEARING PAIN in Graham's side could not compare to the rage he felt at the sight of Hope's fingers crushed in another man's hand. Hope's head snapped up, her mouth agape at the sight of him.

Everything that happened next was a whirlwind. In an instant, Graham had the man by the throat, pushing him back against the edge of the dining room table as a chair fell to its side on the floor. Jacob was gasping, scratching, and clawing at the large hand that threatened to strangle him. Graham bared his teeth, his heart pounding with determination.

"Graham! Stop!" he heard Hope yell, but he barely registered it, even as she came up around to his side and wrapped her hands around the arm that pinned the sputtering Englishman in his place. She seemed to pull with all her might, but the solid muscle of his arm would not budge. "You'll kill him!"

"So?"

"For heaven's sake," Hope said, fighting against his strength. "Let him go."

"No."

Hope let out a horrified gasp, causing him to look at her. Hope's mouth had tightened and her nose had crinkled. He felt exposed beneath her appalled expression.

"Graham, please," she said softly, releasing his arm. "I'm not going anywhere. Don't kill him."

The gentleness of her voice finally pierced through his rage.

With a final squeeze, he flung the Englishman to the floor. The man gasped, rubbing his neck as he coughed.

"Assault!" he croaked after a full minute of gasping. "You should be in prison. You are a menace!"

"Get the hell out of my home or I'll give them a real reason to send me to the gaols."

At Graham's threat, the Englishman's eyes went wide and, after a fleeting gaze at Hope, he bolted out of the dining room. When the front door was slammed shut, Hope breathed a sigh of relief, but there was a hesitation to her as she came face to face with Graham.

He had scared her, he assumed. Well, too bloody bad. He wouldn't stand for any man touching her and if she was going to try and lecture him about such things, she might as well be talking to a pile of stone.

"I'm not apologizing," he said roughly as he stared at her. "I'll not let you be accosted and I don't give a damn what you say about it." Hope's brow drew together as she faltered a bit beneath his furious glare. She watched him with a strange curiosity, as if she were trying to read parts of his soul.

"Graham—"

"What the bloody hell was he doing here?" he bellowed, seemingly unable to control his temper.

Hope opened her mouth to speak before closing it, her eyes locked on his face. Why wasn't she talking? Why wasn't she trying to defend herself? Graham knew that Hope would never lie to him, yet the longer he stared at her, the more he felt exposed.

"What?" he bit out.

That seemed to snap Hope out of her puzzling silence. She shook her head before explaining.

"He read about our engagement in the paper and couldn't believe that I would marry so quickly. But," she said, her voice dropping. "It sounded as though he were really only interested in the inheritance part of the article."

"Sniveling little cretin. I should—"

"Graham, did you plan to marry me only to gain ownership of Lismore?"

The words fell from her mouth like a hammer on an anvil. In that moment, everything stopped. Graham's heartbeat, the passing of time, the world turning on its axis—all seemed to freeze. For a sickening moment he felt Hope being snatched away from him and he wanted to rage against it, but the small, slight woman standing before him made him go still.

It was time to tell the truth.

He took a step toward her, but instinctively she took one back, her hands coming up to stop him. The ache in his heart from not being able to touch her was unbearable.

"Hope, let me explain."

A sharp inhale of breath.

"Oh no," she said so softly that he barely heard her. He had confirmed that there was something that needed to be explained—which apparently had the same effect as if he'd simply said "yes." The pain written across her face made him want to set the world on fire. He had caused it and he would walk backwards through hell to take it back, if he could.

Unable to stop himself he reached for her again, and though she tried to pull away, he refused to release her. He needed to hold her, to push out all the doubt and pain he had caused.

"Let go."

"Hope—"

"I can't believe this."

"I want to marry you," he said, his hands coming up to the sides of her face. "I wouldn't have agreed unless I wanted you."

She let out a bitter laugh as tears filled her eyes.

"Well, of course you did, when you had all of this to gain," she said, gesturing to the building surrounding them. "Was the house all Belle offered you? Or was there more? The townhouse in London, perhaps? Or maybe she included the vineyard in Italy?"

"Hope, stop it—"

"Or maybe she begged," Hope said, a humorless smile on her face. "Maybe she was so desperate to marry off her silly, spinster niece that she outright begged you to marry me. Because of what a complete and utter failure I am—"

Graham's fingers dug into her arms, shaking her slightly as the poisonous, self-deprecating words fell from her mouth.

"Stop it," he barked, furious and ashamed. "You're not a failure."

"Aren't I?" she said, her eyes unfocused as her head bent downward. "I never could manage to do anything right. That's what my grandmother always told me. Lord, how she must have pitied me. The way I spoke, the way I acted. My inability to focus," she said, frowning. "Over six seasons in society, and the best I could manage was Jacob Pennington. And even he didn't want to marry me. Not truly," she said, her mouth contorting into a brittle half smile. "Not until I was finally worth something."

Graham's anger toward himself was mounting.

"Don't say that, Hope. You're worth everything." A sob escaped her lips and a knife might as well have gone through his chest. "Hope, please stop crying."

"I can't."

"I know you're angry, but you have to believe me. I wouldn't have done any of this if I didn't feel so strongly about you."

"Angry?" she repeated the word, her brow furrowing. "You think I'm angry?"

"Aren't you?"

"No. No, I'm not angry." Her voice dropped to a whisper. "I am mortified." She dropped her head, covering her face with her hands as she cried.

Graham hadn't realized how much he had hurt her until that very moment. Quickly, he gathered her up into his arms and pressed her toward his chest. She fought him at first, but when he refused to release her, she finally gave in, crying softly into his chest as he held her close.

What sort of man am I? Graham wondered. Was he really a

man who would stop at nothing to get what he wanted—regardless of who it hurt? Perhaps he wasn't so unlike his father after all. He had been so determined to gain ownership of Lismore Hall. He had plotted and twisted his way into Hope's life and hadn't even the decency to tell her about one of his driving motives. No, instead he lied and cheated her. He was a bastard, but even now, through all of it, Graham couldn't regret it because if he had Lismore Hall, it meant he had Hope too.

Finally, she pushed away from him.

"What a fool I am," she said, her arms wrapping around her torso in a protective way. "I've completely ruined myself and for what?"

Graham didn't like the sound of her words. Ruined? She wasn't ruined at all—particularly since they were still going to be wed. He took a step forward, his large, looming form standing over her. He half expected her to cower in response, but then again, that wasn't Hope. Even as a tremor racked through her, she refused to flinch as she glared up at him.

"You're mine. Do you understand?" he all but growled. "We're to be married and not you or your Pendenton or God himself will be able to undo it."

"Do not insult me, Graham. There are other options—"

"You have no options. You're mine."

He was being bull-headed and intransigent, but he refused to give her up. Even if he had to sacrifice everything he owned, he wouldn't let her go.

"Listen to me, Graham MacKinnon," she said, squaring her shoulders. "I may be a fool—in fact, I know I am—but I'm not the sort of woman who can live unhappily for her entire life. I thought I could once, but..."

Hope shook her head, seemingly unable to explain. It was as if she were slipping away, right through his hands, like a rope he couldn't hold on to and it shook him to his core.

Reaching for her once more, he gathered her tightly to his chest. The gentle scent of rose water perfume wafted against his nostrils and he had to fight to remember his intentions. Though he had never experienced addiction, he wondered if this was the feeling others experienced when their unattainable need broke over them.

"Graham, please let me go."

"Over my dead body," he said, his words rough and angry as he bent his head low. "I won't ever let you go. You belong to me, Hope."

Triumph surged through him as he felt the softest of pressure from her, leaning against him. She wanted him still, despite everything, and it was the single most important thing in his world. She wanted him. And he wanted her, was desperate to possess every inch of her.

Didn't she understand? She was his as much as the leaves were to the trees, as much as the rain was to the land. He stroked her cheek and kept a steady gaze on her.

"Ye belong to me because you're mine," he rasped as his mouth came down on hers.

His hands drifted down the front of her dress and he pressed his hand into the folds of her skirts, between her legs. Her eyes fluttered closed as he moved his mouth down the edge of her jawline to her ear. He felt a desperation to mark every inch of her for himself. It was intoxicating.

But just as he felt the pull of his own need, she tore out of his arms.

"Stop it," she said, holding her hand up to stay him. She was breathing heavily. "Please, just stop. Someone will see."

"As well they should. In case there was an ounce of doubt left in anyone's mind about whom you belong to."

He reached for her once more but she sidestepped him.

"Insufferable man." She pushed past him. "I am not an object or creature you can own." She gestured up at the ceiling. "I am not Lismore Hall."

"I know that."

"Do you?" she asked, her heart pleading. "I'm also not some

idiot who will be swayed by kisses and empty words."

"What words have I spoken that are untrue?" he challenged.

"What words have you spoke that were fully honest?" she countered, tears rolling down her cheeks. "I think, perhaps, that you should go."

Every inch of Graham seemed to turn to stone as he watched her pull on the lock of hair. Though his heart beat furiously against her words, his head wondered if he hadn't earned her condemnation. He had kept an essential truth from her from the beginning and even though his feelings for her were genuine, he knew to deceive was to kill any and all feelings she might have for him.

He stood and took a single, shaky step forward.

"I don't want to," he breathed, his words broken.

Hope closed her eyes tightly, her entire face crumbling with pain as she inhaled in unsteady breaths. He knew in that moment that it was over. He had caused her too much heartache to be forgiven.

What sort of man deceived the woman he loved?

"Please, Graham. Just go."

Without another word, he stepped around her and left the dining room. Out of the corner of his eye he saw Belle, Rose, Grace and Faith standing some yards away, huddled together like some gaggle of geese. He wanted to say something, to blame Belle for everything, but as he stalked away to the foyer, he knew it was no one's fault but his own.

As he shoved his way through the front doors into the mid-morning air, Graham felt well and truly cut off. The doors slammed behind him and he turned to give the pile of rocks a final glare. Lismore Hall had been lost once more by a MacKinnon and it should have been a torturous realization, but all Graham could see was Hope's heartbroken face.

He turned his back on the cursed castle, on everyone who had ever lived there and left without a single look back.

Chapter Nineteen

FOR THE NEXT few days, Hope stayed in her room, unwilling to venture down to the rooms below. She had nearly confronted Belle the day Graham left, but she had felt too humiliated to face the woman who had all but tried to sell her in marriage. Instead, she had sequestered herself in her bedchamber. Grace and Una had to inquire if she was eating or sleeping, but Faith didn't come and Hope wondered if Faith was feeling sorry or smug for having been right from the beginning.

Hope certainly felt like a fool for not believing her. What an idiot she had been. She was far too willing to believe in people, especially men she fancied and it blinded her to their faults.

Graham had been right. She trusted people too much.

How she hated his arrogance, the sureness with which he spoke. His possessiveness both irked and aroused her and she was sure that he would bully his way back into her life. Instead, he had disappeared, breaking her heart even further. Although she had asked him to leave, she hadn't believed that he truly would, and it felt like a fresh betrayal.

Now, locked away in her room with the curtains drawn, she could remember every touch, every kiss from his mouth. She could no longer be sure any of them had been sincere… but that didn't change how they affected her. She hated herself for longing for him, for wanting him despite everything he had done.

This wasn't how life was supposed to go. Hope had long believed that marriage would be a pleasant enough event. One where she and her husband would be cordial and respectful to one another while not sharing too much of themselves. She'd had years of fantasies of being Jacob's wife and never in her wildest dreams had she ever believed that there would be a great amount of passion between them.

But Hope's entire world had changed the moment she met Graham.

Ever since their first kiss, Hope had felt a part of her awaken, as if she had been half asleep her entire life. Graham had made her feel things that she had never conceived of and the end result was that she had grown and changed since first coming to Scotland. Hope would never shrink herself to fit into another person's world again.

No. Hope would know happiness. Loud and wild and beautiful happiness. That was what she demanded from life, and she would never let anyone else deter her from it.

Not even Graham.

A soft knock sounded at the door and Hope barely lifted her head. The morning sun fought through the cracks in the drapes from the windows, creating sharp lines of light across the dark room.

Someone pushed the door open, coming into the room a few steps before turning around.

"Come on," she heard Grace whisper.

Hope could see Faith enter the room behind Grace, who came up to the side of the bed.

"Good morning," she said softly. Hope didn't move, and instead looked up at her, upside down as she laid on her back. "How are you feeling today?"

"How should I feel?"

"I don't know," Grace said, sitting on the bed next to her. "Well rested perhaps?"

Hope snorted and rolled to her stomach before pressing herself up to a seated position. Faith stood several feet away, hands behind her back. Her face was drawn and her mouth pressed into a thin line. Hope wondered why she seemed so nervous.

"Come to tell me I was wrong?" Hope asked, her hands coming together in her lap. She began to pick her thumbnail. "That I should have believed you? Well, you needn't bother. I'm already aware."

Faith's head snapped up and she came forward, reaching for her sister's hand.

"No, Hope. I… I wanted to tell you how sorry I am."

"Sorry?"

"Yes. I didn't want to be right. Well," she paused, looking sheepish. "That's not completely true. I do like being correct, but I didn't know how you felt about Mr. MacKinnon, not truly. I thought you fancied him as much as you used to fancy Pennington."

"But I didn't just fancy Pennington. I loved him," she said.

But Faith just shook her head.

"No, you were fond of Pennington, but I don't think you ever truly loved him because deep down, you knew he was never worthy of it. He represented a way for us to carry on, but when he discarded you, you didn't suffer any true heartache. Only a worry that Grace and I would have no one to care for us."

Looking back, Hope could see that she had cared more for her sisters' wellbeing than for Jacob's dismissal. Perhaps Faith was right and she had never loved Jacob at all. She knew what she felt for Graham was worlds apart in comparison, but that only made her situation so much worse.

How could love be so painful? Perhaps it would be smarter to marry someone who couldn't hurt her so much.

Hope moved toward the edge of the bed and gingerly swung one leg over the end.

"So?" she said, knowing nothing could mend her relationship with Graham. "What difference does it make in the end which of the men I loved most? One is still willing to marry me and the other… has gone away."

"But you told him to go."

"Yes, because I couldn't let him stay. Not after learning the truth," she said bitterly, closing her eyes to fight back the tears. She shook her head. "Perhaps I should reconsider Jacob's offer."

"No!" Grace said, her hand coming to her mouth. "Why on earth would you do that?"

"Because at least with Jacob, I won't have to be forever reminded that Graham lied to me."

"You can't, Hope," Faith said. "Pennington doesn't care about you. Not the way MacKinnon does."

"You don't understand, Faith."

"I understand you love MacKinnon and he loves you, despite all this business about the silly house," she said earnestly. "Please. Don't marry Pennington just because MacKinnon made a mistake."

But Hope had already made up her mind. An image of her future with Jacob played out before her eyes. They would live in a suitable townhouse in some fashionable district in London, such as Mayfair or Belgrave. He would go to work and she would care for the house. They would have dinners with his colleagues and friends and every day would be the same. There would be nothing painful or hurtful because Hope would never give her heart to him and they would live the next forty years or more in utter, peaceful mediocrity.

Yes, she thought sadly. There would be no room for any hurt in her life with Jacob.

"Please, Hope," Grace begged, shaking her from her thoughts. "Don't make any rash decisions."

Hope wanted to laugh, but it stuck in her throat. Rash? Rash had been believing in Graham. Rash had been searching him out every time she had been close to him. Rash had been falling in love with a man who only wanted to marry her to gain a house.

She forced a smile to her lips.

"No, of course not," she said, though she didn't believe it. "Perhaps I should get dressed today."

Grace's eyes lit up. "A wonderful idea. Let's go down to

breakfast."

"I should like to speak with Aunt Belle first," Hope said as she clambered off the bed. "Alone."

Both sisters watched her as she walked across the room to the wardrobe. Yes, she would say her piece to Belle. Straightening her shoulders, she selected a burgundy gown, one that reflected her somber mood.

Her sisters helped her dress in silence, apparently too anxious to ask what she would say to Belle when Hope confronted her. She had refused to speak with her since Graham's departure, but as she laced up her ankle boots, she had a fair idea of what she would say to her elderly aunt.

As she marched down the hallway, the walls of this castle seemed confining. She wanted to be away from this place, from all the people within.

Hope found Belle in her office, hunched over her desk as she usually was, writing a letter as Andrews stood behind her. When she knocked on the open door to announce her entrance, Belle looked up and a faint smile touched her lips.

"Andrews, if you'll excuse us," she said as the butler nodded, moving past Hope, who waited for him to close the door behind him before she spoke.

"Aunt Belle."

"How are you my dear?" she said, struggling to stand. "Do sit down."

"No," Hope said, as her aunt paused, partially up out of her chair. "Thank you, but I'll only be a moment." Belle gave her a nod and sat back down. Hope took a deep breath. "I would like to know when you and Graham first came up with the idea of marrying me off."

"My dear, it was never some wicked plot to marry you off."

"Please," Hope said, holding up her hand. "No more lies."

Belle watched her for a long moment before finally exhaling.

"It was my idea," she said, sounding defeated. "I presented it to MacKinnon the day after I received news about my sister's death."

"And you assumed he would be eager to marry me so that he might gain ownership of Lismore?"

"Heavens no," Belle said, but Hope squinted at her. "Well, yes, I suppose, but it was never about Lismore."

"Wasn't it?"

"No, my dear. Your grandmother was so worried that she had failed in making you a proper match and she wanted me to help."

"She… What?" Hope asked, confused.

Belle reached across her desk and pulled a pretty, maple wood box toward her. It was beautifully carved, with a painted rose on top. Lifting the lid, she pulled out a stack of letters and pulled the top one off the pile.

"My sister and I may have been very different women, but we were still sisters. We wrote to each other weekly for forty years," she said, looking down at the letter she held. "Her last letter was a jumble of worries and sadness. She wasn't particularly pleased with your Mr. Pennington, for having dragged his feet for so long. She worried that he might not follow through. She wanted you married and protected and asked if I knew of anyone who might be a suitable match for you."

"And you thought of Graham?"

"I did. He is as fine a gentleman as any I have ever known and I had grown quite fond of him. I thought you and he would suit greatly and so I wrote her that I knew of someone, but she died before she received it." Belle's eyes misted over. "It was the last thing I could do for my sister, to see you married to someone who would love you."

"But he doesn't love me."

Belle gave her a queer smile.

"Of course he does, my dear," she said. "He wouldn't have proposed if he didn't wish to marry you."

"Wanting to marry me is not the same as wanting *me*. He only wanted to marry me because of the castle."

"Lismore was an incentive, yes, and I may have tried to manage it a bit heavy-handedly at first, but a man like MacKinnon would never commit to a lifetime of misery for a house. Not even if he was desperate to own it."

Hope was silent for a while, unable to believe it. The wound was too fresh and too raw for her to be practical in this moment. More than that, she didn't *want* to be practical and forgiving. She was done being hurt by men.

"No," Hope said, turning to leave. "I cannot forgive him."

"Hope, wait."

She left the room quickly, despite her aunt's pleas to stop and come back. She didn't want to be tricked and manipulated by her anymore. As she made her way down the hallway, fighting tears, a footman approached, holding a silver tray topped with a letter.

"For you, miss," he said.

Taking it, she heard Jeanne's cheerful voice coming from the dining room. Stuffing the note in her pocket, she came into the dining room to find her sisters, Rose and Jeanne all seated around the table.

Several plates of poached eggs, steaming puddings and bacon and towers of toast lined the table. Everyone quieted as Hope entered. Trying to appear cheerful, she gave them all a brittle smile.

"Good morning," she said, heading toward the buffet table. "I didn't expect you this morning, Jeanne."

Jeanne was wearing a smart yellow day gown with a lavender sash. Her hair was even fixed with some violets. She looked as pretty as the day was new.

"Good to see you, Hope."

Hope made a plate from the side table and came around to sit next to her. Faith leaned over the morning paper as she ate her toast and while Hope fixed her cup of tea, she sensed Jeanne's gaze on her. She lifted her head and stared at the woman.

"Yes?"

"Are you all right?" Jeanne asked in a low tone.

"Yes, of course," Hope answered. "Why do you ask?"

"Only that when I saw Graham, he looked terrible."

The entire room froze at her words.

"Y-you saw him?" Hope asked, staring at her plate.

She wanted to know how he was faring, but she also didn't wish to appear as though she cared. Jeanne wouldn't let it drop, however.

"Yes."

"How is he?" Faith asked.

"Not well at all," Jeanne started. "Jared found him two days ago, drunk as a skunk in the bee yard."

Hope turned to face her.

"Oh dear," she said under her breath, but Jeanne heard her.

"Oh yes. Nearly killed himself knocking over the hives. My brothers had to lock him in the larder overnight."

Everyone seemed to be looking at Hope, but she didn't wish to be dragged into this conversation. Clearing her throat, she turned to Rose.

"How is your Mr. McTavish, Rose?"

"He's well," she said cautiously. When no one spoke, Rose continued, a blush rising to her cheeks. "Actually, he's asked my eldest brother Ryan if he could ask for my hand in marriage."

"Marriage?" Jeanne said, her brow lifting with surprise. "My brother doesn't drag his feet, does he?"

"Well, in some respects," Rose continued, her shoulders dropping. "But he said since we've known each other for so long, that there's no point in a long courtship."

The conversation turned to Rose's relationship and the local happenings. Hope shifted in her seat and felt the small, pointed edge of a letter press into her thigh. Taking out the letter from her pocket, she recognized the handwriting immediately. It was from Jacob. Sighing, she opened it up.

My dearest Hope,

I am beside myself with grief at having not been able to express my deep devotion and love for you when last we spoke. I pray you reconsider my offer. I am staying at the Cock and Sparrow Inn and have plans to leave by month's end. I hope you find me there so that we can pursue a life together.

Your faithful servant,
Jacob Pennington

Hope stared at the note, reading it over several times. Jacob was obviously pretending to be in love with her for her inheritance. Well, she would not be fooled again into trusting a man when he claimed to love her. Still, the idea of remaining here, in Scotland, in Belle's home after what her aunt had done… Well, it was just too much.

As the others ate, Hope weighed her options. Since she was now an heiress, if she went seeking a husband, she would likely have her pick of gentlemen—though they would surely all be fortune hunters. If that was to be her fate, perhaps it would be better to marry Jacob, a man who did not love her and a man she did not love, but one who offered her some sort of dependability, some familiarity akin to her old life. Hope doubted she would ever marry for love now anyway, so why not Jacob? She could return to London and eventually her time in Scotland, Graham and everything in between would become nothing more than a sad dream from her past.

Her heart had broken a dozen times since confronting Graham. She wished she could cast her feelings aside and run right back into Jacob's arms, but even entertaining the idea made her stomach twist into knots. The truth was that regardless of everything that had happened between her and Graham, she would not, could not, marry a man she did not love. Not now that she knew what love truly was.

Folding the letter up, she wondered if she should have an honest conversation with Jacob. She could write him a letter, but that seemed insufficient. She had known Jacob for years and while he hadn't always been the most attentive person, he was still a person and deserved to hear the truth from her in person. After all, they had cared for each other once and Hope wanted to tell him just how much she appreciated his coming north to offer his assistance.

Yes. She would go to the Cock and Sparrow Inn today.

━━━━━━━━━ ❯❮ ━━━━━━━━━

Chapter Twenty

THE HORSE'S HOOVES beat against the earth, heavy and fast, as Graham wrapped the reins tightly around his fists. It had still been dark that morning when he woke, mouth dry and head splitting in his uncle's lard. After several bangs and shouts, a sheepish footman had let him out. Groggy, ashamed, and miserable, Graham had headed to the stables with an idea to return home, but once on his horse, he hadn't found his way there. The path he took had winded and turned and he'd followed it without caring. Hell, it could have taken him to the edge of the Inner Hebrides and he wouldn't have been concerned.

He had lost Hope.

She had asked him to go and though it had tortured him to heed her, he had. He would not bully or berate her into staying with him. Graham had already done enough damage and though he needed her desperately, like the pines needed rain, he couldn't bring himself to cause her any more pain.

He rode hard across the harsh landscape, as if he were trying to outrun his mistakes. The thundering of the horse's gait across rock and dirt was nearly loud enough to block out his own thoughts. A hard rain had begun, stinging against his skin as he rode faster, desperate to distract himself from his own thoughts. But no matter how far or how long he went, Hope was with him. She had become a part of him. He could go to the end of the earth, and still, she would be there, deep in his heart.

It was nearly noon when his senses seemed to return, and having a care not to ride the horse to death, he decided to return to his hunting lodge.

Cutting through the forest via the northern road, he tilted his head up and watched the grayish sky disappear beneath the long pine branches. The woods engulfed him in a dark, cold embrace. *If only I could explain everything to her*, he thought bleakly as his horse trotted down the dark, rain-soaked path.

He hadn't wanted to hurt her, but he had managed to do so and it tormented him. Images of Hope danced across his mind as he rode. Her kind, accepting eyes, her dark hair that she often played with when she was deep in thought. How she would drift off sometimes, only to snap back to herself with a new perspective. She was thoughtful, smart, too beautiful for his liking. He wanted to hold her against his chest and grab fistfuls of her hair. He wanted to bury himself inside of her and breathe her in for always.

But she had sent him away and he had no right to her. Not now, not ever again.

Turning the corner of the last crop of trees before reaching the house, he saw a group of people—no, a group of women—standing in the rain before his front door. His butler stood before them, seemingly arguing. He frowned. What the devil was going on?

"What's this now?" he asked, swinging off his steed as he reached them. Belle, Rose, Faith, and Grace turned to face him, each with a different expression. Belle appeared apologetic, as did Rose, while Faith looked furious and Grace worried. Something was wrong. "What's happened?"

"Sir, these ladies are looking for their sister," his butler said. "I've explained that neither she, nor you, have been here for days, yet they still refuse to leave."

"Why should we take your word for it?" Faith asked, glaring back at the butler before snapping her head back to face Graham. "Where is she?"

"What do you mean, where is she?" he asked, his own temper flaring at Faith's accusation. "I'm not the one in charge of her."

"No, thank heavens for that," Faith said. "Or lord knows what sort of fiendish things you'd force her into."

"Faith, that's not fair," Grace said, stepping forward. She moved to stand in between Faith and Graham. "Please, Mr. MacKinnon. Hope left this morning and hasn't returned. We thought at first she might have come to see you. but..."

"But what?"

"But we found this note," she said, her hand dipping to her side. She pulled it out and handed to Graham. "None of us believed she would really go see him. After all, he had hurt her terribly when we were in London. But at this point, I think it's safe to assume that that's where she's gone—to see Mr. Pennington. And to that end, we need your help."

The mere mention of that man's name made Graham want to clench his teeth and snarl, but to hear that Hope had potentially gone off with him, well that deflated him. Reading the note in his hand, he noted the familiar way the man addressed her, as if he felt entitled to such intimacy. Hanging his head, he pushed through the women and entered his house.

"Mr. MacKinnon?" Grace called out from behind him.

If Hope wanted to run off with Pennington, who was Graham to stop her?

He shrugged off his soaked overcoat and tossed it to a waiting butler and headed toward the library. Much to his annoyance, the sound of wet leather boots followed him. *The hell with them*, he thought as he reached the library. He crossed the room in seconds and began pouring himself a drink.

With his back to them, he swallowed the first quickly and then poured himself another.

"For heavens sakes, MacKinnon, what is wrong with you?" Belle finally spoke, striking her cane on the carpeted floor. "Go get her."

Graham turned, glaring at all four women who stood in the

doorway, watching him like he had lost his mind.

"No."

Belle actually gaped at him. Pulling her shoulders back and lifting her chin with withering scorn, she scowled at him.

"What the devil do you mean 'no'?"

"Exactly that," he said, taking another bracing, burning sip of the scotch. "I'll not be bothering Miss Sharpe anymore."

"But why? Don't you care about Hope?" Grace asked worriedly, stepping forward. "You must go after her."

"It's her prerogative to go off with Mr. Pennington, who am I to interfere?"

"Her fiancé, for one," Faith said, her tone cold.

"A fact that has bothered you from the beginning," he countered, looking at her.

"Yes, when I thought you meant to use her," Faith said pointedly. "But since she is not here, and the alternative is that she ran off with that coward Pennington, then I must insist that you go after her at once."

"She doesn't want me."

"Oh, but that's not true," Rose said, stepping forward, in line with Grace. "Hope is very fond of you."

"She was. Until she learned of our little plan," he said sarcastically, raising his glass to a bitter-faced Belle.

"You prideful fool," Belle snapped. "So, you'll let her be carried off by Pennington? A man not worthy of her? A man who once asked her to refuse to acknowledge her own sisters?"

He glanced at Grace. And then Faith.

"Not an unreasonable request."

"Why you—"

"Mr. MacKinnon, you don't mean that," Grace said, silencing her sister with the wave of her hand. "Regardless of how you feel about us, you would never make Hope choose. Would you?" He wanted to say yes, if only to cast these banshees from his house, but even if he said the words, he knew they wouldn't believe them. Even Faith rolled her eyes, knowing the truth. So, he remained silent. "Please, Mr. MacKinnon. Please, you must go after her."

"She doesn't want me," he said again, his eyes searching the nearly empty scotch glass in his hand as he brought it up to finish. "She told me to leave."

"For a time, not forever," Rose said earnestly. "Please."

"You must," Belle said, striking her cane once more, as if it were some magical staff that could command him to do her bidding.

Daft old woman.

"Surely you know she doesn't belong with Pennington," Grace said. "Don't you?"

The pleading in her tone was nearly enough to turn Graham's heart, but the fact that Hope had dismissed him was enough to ignore all their pleas. She didn't want him and—

"Mr. MacKinnon," Faith said, causing him to look up. "My sister does not deserve a lifetime with that man. And you owe her a debt." She paused, looking as if she was bracing herself to do something deeply distasteful, her throat bobbing up and down as if trying to swallow her own tongue. "Will you, *please*, go and return her to us?"

Graham stared at her.

"She may want to be with him. Return to London and all that."

"And if she truly does, we will accept it," Faith said, peering around her to the others. "But we need to hear it from her own mouth first."

"So why not go after her yourselves?"

"Why indeed." Faith let out a bitter laugh. "I told you, Aunt Belle. Coming here was a waste of time."

"I was hoping to be proven wrong," Belle said, her judgmental stare locked on Graham. Then she added loudly. "But I suppose it's fitting that two innocent, young ladies and an elderly woman using a cane would find no help from the likes of a MacKinnon!"

He knew he was being goaded. Belle's blatant attempt to guilt him into going after Hope was weak at best, but it didn't matter. He'd likely never hear the end of it if he didn't go. And truth be told, he wanted an excuse to see Hope again.

But he wouldn't give Belle the satisfaction of seeing him eagerly run off. So, he rolled his eyes and slowly put down his unfinished drink.

"Very well," he said, stalking toward the doorway. The women parted quickly. "I'll go now. But if she tries to throw something at me, I'll be coming to you lot for restitution."

"Mr. Pennington was staying at the Cock and Sparrow."

"Yes, the note said as much," he said, searching his pocket for the crumbled piece of paper. He handed it to Grace, who was at his heels.

"Oh, but sir, should you change?" his butler asked. "Your clothes are…" Graham gave him a piercing glare. "Very good, sir."

Graham was out of the house and mounting his second draft horse, a buckskin-colored horse named Honeycomb in a matter of minutes. He was tired and his head was pounding. His muscles were sore and he was wet, filthy from the rain and the mud he'd accumulated from his morning ride, but none of it mattered.

Turning Honeycomb, he gave out an angry YAW and heeled his side. They took off like a shot, just as the rain stopped. The southern skies seemed to open as the clouds parted slowly, leading him toward the Cock and Sparrow Inn.

$$\text{---}\!\!\blacktriangleright\!|\$|\!\blacktriangleleft\!\!\text{---}$$

Chapter Twenty-One

HOPE ENTERED THE old building with the faded sign over its door cautiously. The Cock and Sparrow Inn seemed dark and dangerous and she soon realized that Rose had been right. It was not the sort of country inn she and her sisters had stayed at during their journey north. Though there were plenty of south-facing windows, they were so grimy and dirt-covered that the only light came from candlesticks on every other table. Scents of sour beer and unwashed bodies assaulted Hope's nose, but she tried to keep her face expressionless.

The barman and two other men glared up with suspicious scowls immediately upon her entering and watched her as she made her way toward them.

"Excuse me," she said, trying to sound brave. "I'm searching for a man—"

"Piss off," the barman growled at her.

Hope inhaled sharply, taken aback by such hostility. Never in her life had someone spoken to her so rudely.

"Excuse me?"

"Yer heard me, ya damn English pidgin," he said, attempting to clean out a dirty glass with a soiled rag.

Hope's eyes flickered to the man's hands before lifting back to meet his gaze. Swallowing hard, she held her chin up and tried again.

"Mr. Jacob Pennington?" she pressed on. "He is supposedly staying here for a few days."

The barman shifted closer to the two suspicious characters. Hope followed his gaze, but the two only huddled together, covering their faces with their hands. Hope considered going over to confront them, but the barman's voice sounded behind her.

"Ack, is it that," he tipped his chin across the room, "English prat you be wanting fer?"

Hope's head whipped back around to see the feet of a man descending the stairs.

"Hope?" Jacob said as he saw her.

The crisp, cultured accent was so drastically different from the barman that Hope nearly didn't understand him at first.

"I can't believe you're really here," he said, coming to her with his hands outstretched, looking behind her. "Did you come alone?"

"Yes," she said as he pulled her toward a table. She sat down as he pulled out the chair for her and then moved around to sit down himself.

"That wasn't very smart," he said, frowning. "It's dangerous around here."

His gaze traveled past Hope's shoulder. She looked back and noticed the barman and the two other individuals staring at them.

"It's all right," she said, facing him again. "I've been back and forth on the main road many times in the past few months."

"Still. Perhaps we should find some privacy," Jacob said standing as he nodded his head toward the stairs.

An internal self-preservation alarm immediately sounded within her. Besides, she wasn't all that excited to be alone with Jacob. In fact, she would much prefer to stay in the view of others while they spoke.

She remained seated.

"I'm not sure that is a good idea," she said. "This is just fine."

Jacob bent forward.

"I don't think it would be wise to continue this discussion here," he said in a low voice.

Hope frowned, but followed Jacob's darting eyes. The two

men who were sitting in the far corner seemed very interested in her. They were staring intently and a sick feeling began to crawl up her spine.

"Very well, but only for a moment," she said, standing and following him up the narrow staircase.

The inn was ancient and not well-kept. There were four doors along the hallway upstairs, and Hope followed Jacob into the first room on the left. It was a dingy, sparsely filled room, but there was a length of yellow and blue plaid slung over a chair in the corner. Hope wrinkled her nose at the stench of smoke in the room.

"Jacob, what are you doing here?" she asked, only to be stopped by his raised hand.

"I'm so happy you've reconsidered my offer, Hope. I knew you would eventually come to your senses."

"Come to my senses?"

"Yes. My letter convinced you."

Hope frowned.

"Your… oh, no," she said as the realization dawned on her. "No, Jacob, that's not why I've come here."

"Isn't it, my love?" he asked, coming toward her, hands outstretched. "I thought I lost you forever to that brute."

"Graham isn't a brute. And he's actually the exact reason I've come here."

"He is? How so?"

"Well, while I'm very grateful for your loyal friendship in coming all the way to Scotland to make sure I was all right, I wanted you to know that I do still intend to marry Mr. MacKinnon, that is, after we have a very long discussion about what has transpired between us. You see, I'm not as smart or as spiteful as I should be. I love Mr. MacKinnon, and I know it is a true love because I'm not willing to give up on it. But that said, I wanted to come here and tell you how much I appreciate your concern for me and my wellbeing."

Jacob paused in his packing as Hope swallowed. Graham had

hurt her deeply and while she didn't intend to forgive him so easily for his deception, she had concluded that morning that she loved him and she truly believed that he loved her, despite everything. It wasn't a great feeling, loving someone who had betrayed her, but it made marrying anyone she didn't love seem impossible.

Graham had deceived her and even though she knew it was foolish, the optimist in her believed him when he told her his feelings for her were genuine and that he knew he had made a grave mistake.

Jacob turned to face her, his expression stony.

"You know he only wants you for your inheritance, my pearl. Ever since it was published in the papers that you would inherit your aunt's entire estate, it's all anyone in London has talked about. Everyone knows he's using you."

That stung, but Hope squared her shoulders.

"And you decided to come here strictly because you love me?" she asked, unconvinced. "You left me in my hour of need, Jacob, and while I've been more than understanding as to why, you didn't believe that I would rush back to you, now that I'm some sort of heiress, did you?"

Jacob scowled.

"Now, see here—"

"And Graham doesn't need my inheritance. He has a very successful business. Bee hives, actually."

"Bee hives? What a plebeian pursuit."

Hope took a deep breath and ignored him. He would never understand the work Graham did, and she would not waste her breath trying to explain it to him.

"So, you didn't come here to run away with me?"

Hope tried to look sorry.

"No."

"Ah. Well, that does change things, I suppose." He shifted back toward the door. The distinctive sound of a click reverberated through the room, and Hope's heart sank before she even had a chance to realize what was going on.

"Jacob—"

"You see, I had hoped to convince you in person to reconsider our relationship. When that brute attacked me and forced me to leave, I had hoped that my words, written out in expertly written prose, would help convince you, to remind you of my love."

"Jacob, there was never any love between us."

"But now I see that I have no choice," he continued, rotating around to face her. "This is for the best. You will realize that and will forgive me one day."

"Forgive you for what?" She backed away as her skin prickled with a warning. "What do you intend to do?"

"To take you away, just as I told you before," he said. "Far enough away where your MacKinnon can't find us, though I doubt he'll go through the trouble. Once settled, we'll petition for your inheritance and live as we always hoped we would."

A sinking feeling settled in her stomach. He was mad. Surely he didn't believe that she would willingly go with him?

"Jacob, there isn't a place anywhere on this green earth where you could keep me without me immediately running back here, I assure you that."

Hope backed away with her hands behind her back. An oil lamp on the table behind her tipped slightly as she bumped into it, but she steadied it.

"Well, perhaps after our wedding you won't feel that way," he said, his eyes roaming over her body.

Hope's fingers grazed the glass oil lamp, and she clasped it in her hand.

"I shan't forgive you for any of this," she said, and as quick as she could, she rounded her arm around her body and slammed the oil lamp into the side of Jacob's skull.

"AUGH!"

Hope dodged around him as he screamed. She reached the door, but he lunged after her, his hands clawing around her waist.

"Let me go!" she yelled as he fisted his hands in her skirts to keep her from getting away.

Jacob pulled her back, tearing one of her sleeves nearly clean off her gown and tossing her on the straw-filled bed behind them. Hope watched in horror the streams of blood coursing down his face. The glass must have cut him.

"You little bitch!" he seethed.

Flinching, she tried to remember if Jacob had ever cursed in front of her before. He stomped toward her, and Hope instinctively pulled her legs up. In a last-ditch attempt to keep him from reaching her, she had begun to kick with all her might when a voice from somewhere downstairs called her name.

"Hope?"

"Graham?" she whispered to herself before yelling out loud. "GRAHAM!"

Jacob, apparently in a panic, tried to lodge a chair against the door to block any entry, but his efforts were stymied when the entire thing began to creak and break as it was torn off its hinges. Hope scrambled back further onto the bed as Graham burst through the door. His eyes searched her form, and though she didn't think it possible, his furious face contorted even further. He emanated pure rage.

Jacob tried to climb out of the filthy window, but Graham grabbed him and slammed his fist directly into his jaw, holding him up off his feet. Hope screamed, her hands flying up to cover her face in an attempt to hide from the brutality of the scene before her. A thud followed, and Hope peered through her fingers. Graham had dropped Jacob, and she realized he had been knocked unconscious.

Frozen for a moment, Hope stared at Graham's profile. His chest heaved up and down as he glared down at the heap on the floor. Nostrils flared and a deep set of vertical wrinkles between his brow told her he was furious.

Slowly, his head turned, and his eyes locked with hers. The breath went out of her beneath his gaze. Pushing off the bed to stand on unsteady legs, Hope moved toward him.

"Graham?" she said shakily.

"What the hell were you thinking?" he snapped at her, causing her to freeze. "You could have been raped! Or maimed! He could have bloody well killed you!"

"Graham, I—"

"Have you lost your ever-loving mind? Riding off without anyone knowing where you've gone to—"

"Graham, please—"

But he didn't let her finish. In the next second, Graham grabbed her wrist and hauled her roughly against his chest. A gust of breath escaped her, and before she could speak, his mouth found hers.

Hope's mind was swimming as his hands roamed gently all over her body. His kiss was deep and desperate and her arms wrapped around his neck, unwilling to let him go. His arms wrapped around her waist and back, lifting her out the door as he backed out of the room.

"Forgive me, Hope," he begged, his voice raspy as he leaned his forehead against hers. "I should have told you about Belle's offer from the beginning." Hope searched his eyes, unsure how to respond. She had planned to be angry and standoffish with him, but all her plans had gone out the window. Instead, she stayed silent—and he continued. "I love you for you, Hope. Not for Lismore, or your inheritance or anything. Just you."

"I love you too, Graham," she said softly, planting tiny kisses across his mouth as he sighed.

"Will ye forgive me?"

She paused and looked deep into his eyes.

"I don't know if I can just yet," she said. Her words were shaky, but she forced them out. She needed to say them. "But I think I could, with time. I think I will."

He was quiet for a moment and she worried that she had upset him, when he squeezed her.

"I understand," he whispered against her mouth. "I do."

Hope's heart expanded with gratitude. "How long do you think it might take, though? For you to forgive me, I mean." She nodded, doubtfully, but the look in his eye seemed to edge her on. "Sixty years or so?"

Hope let out a surprised laugh and nodded her head slowly.

"Yes, possibly," she said as he smiled down at her.

"Good. Then I should like to spend the next sixty years or so in your debt."

Tears falling down her cheeks, Hope nodded as Graham leaned in and kissed her again. In her heart, she had already forgiven him.

She was sure she was melting into him when he turned and carried her down the first two steps. She forced herself to pull away.

"G-Graham," she stuttered, knowing they would soon be in full sight of the guests below. "We'll be seen."

"Aye."

She thought for a moment that he might concede, but in the next second, she saw him bend before her, and suddenly his hands gripped her around her thighs as he heaved her over his shoulder.

"Graham! Let me go this instant!"

"Never again."

He ignored her frustrated huffs, not seeming fazed at all despite the inherent ridiculousness of their positions. Hope hid her face as he walked her down the stairs, ignoring the hoots and hollers from the barman and his customers. He marched her out of the tavern and into the twilight. Finding her horse, he took the reins and walked it to his. Lifting her up on his own steed, he sat behind her, and they left in a fast trot.

Hope frowned as she realized they weren't heading back to Lismore Hall.

"Graham, where are we going?"

"To see Rory."

The name was vaguely familiar, but Hope couldn't place it.

"Who?"

"The blacksmith."

"Why are we going to a blacksmith?"

"Because we have some business to tend to."

Realization dawned on Hope.

"Do you mean… Are we to be married? Tonight?"

"Aye."

"But the church! And the flowers and all the guests."

"Aye, we'll do that too," he said, holding her tightly to him, his mouth warm on her ear. "But I'll not let you go one more day without being my wife."

A swell of satisfaction popped in her chest and she snuggled back into his strong body.

"Aye," was all she said in response.

Chapter Twenty-Two

T HE MOON WAS just beginning to rise when they reached Rory's blacksmith shop, but the building was completely dark. The blacksmith was known to turn in early, as he was an early riser, and it cost Graham several favors to rouse the old man from his bed, but once he finally set himself to the task, they were married in quick fashion. Rory's knowing smirk seemed to irritate Graham, but Hope's hand on his arm was enough to keep him well enough in check.

After sending off a missive to Lismore Hall to inform the family that Graham had indeed rescued Hope, they rode through the evening to the hunting lodge. Upon their arrival they found the estate completely quiet.

Glancing around the foyer once she'd stepped inside, she noted the antler decorations that seemed to be in every Scottish home—though here, they were in even greater profusion than she was accustomed to seeing. Sighing, she followed Graham as he led the way down the hall, fighting off a yawn. Graham led her to a library, with a pair of French doors that led out into a courtyard.

"Here," Graham said, bringing her to a lounge. "I'll be right back."

Hope nodded, letting her eyes close as she laid down. When she opened her eyes, a cool light emanated through the French doors. She had fallen asleep.

Sitting up, Hope looked around the room. Her shoes had

been removed and a heavy knit blanket had been draped over her. Graham's jacket was draped over a velvet sitting chair. There was no sign of where he'd disappeared to, but she guessed he hadn't gone far.

Hope noticed the French doors slightly ajar. Tiptoeing barefoot, she came out onto the courtyard and looked around. There, under a single apple tree that sat in the middle of the garden, was Graham.

He was sitting against it, his back pressed into the trunk as one long leg laid straight and the other bent. It was strangely light out, and Hope saw a full moon shining just above the western horizon. The vague scent of burnt tobacco carried on the gentle breeze. Her attention was pulled back to Graham who held the faint glow of red embers blazing in his hand. He was smoking a pipe and before she knew it, she was coming down the staircase and walking toward him.

The night air was surprisingly warm so early. Hope could smell a dozen intermingling flower scents as she entered the garden.

He seemed aware of her approach as he shifted his position, though he remained seated. Hope was curious why he was awake still or if he had recently woken up. He glanced up at her as she stopped only a few feet away.

"Hello," she said softly.

The hand that held his pipe came to rest against his bent knee. He watched her. Though it was bright for the night, she couldn't quite make out the expression on his face so she came closer. He seemed contemplative.

"Hello," he replied.

"I'm sorry I fell asleep," she said, nodding back toward the house. "I'm sure you had expected to … well …"

"I didn't expect anything," he said, his tone gentle. "Do not worry yourself about that."

"Oh," she said, biting her bottom lip uncertainly.

She needn't be obvious in her disappointment, so she lifted

her chin and squared her shoulders.

In a sudden and swift motion, he was standing. She nearly took a step back, but stopped herself. She knew there was nothing to be afraid of. Not from him.

"You were tired," he said, his hand coming up to her face. The pad of his thumb pressed against her cheekbone. "Are you still?"

"No," she said as she stared at him. "I'm not."

"Good."

His hand caressed her cheek and inched down her neck and further still, as his fingers pressed firmly into the tightness in her shoulders. She let her eyes close as he massaged muscles she hadn't even realized were so tense.

"That feels nice."

"Does it? Turn around."

She obeyed, rotating slowly to face away from him as his second hand came up to rub the other side of her neck. He kneaded and worked out the knots of her neck and upper back, his large hands warming her skin.

Though he handled her so readily, Hope sensed he meant this contact to be more healing than amorous, though her body seemed to react of its own free will. After a profound point of tension finally released, a moan escaped her mouth, and his hands stilled. Worried that he might have found her tawdry in her uninhibited reaction, she spun back only to see his heated gaze.

Graham's bottom lip dropped, as if he wanted to tell her something, but in the next instant, his hand slid to the base of her skull and he reeled her against him in a searing kiss. Hope met his urgency with equal fervor as her arms wrapped around his neck.

His other hand held her lower back in a nearly painful grasp as it drifted down her body, kneading at her bottom most deliciously. His kisses were deep and purposeful, as though he were discovering every inch of her. Hope gasped as his mouth dragged away from hers.

He was panting heavily as he stared at her. Though she

wasn't sure what he saw when he looked at her, he appeared confused.

"Graham," she whispered, breathing unsteadily.

"Aye?"

"Don't stop."

In the next moment, he was on her again, holding her and kissing her as though she were some sort of life essence. Hope's mind swam with half-thoughts as she moved with him. He gently pressed her back against the tree he had been leaning on. Hope's hands trembled slightly as they came up and landed on his shoulders. He let out a low sound, something between a growl and a hiss. It was audacious to be taken beneath the stars, outside, but Hope pressed her cheek to his fingers as they trailed against her face.

His hands skimmed down her sides, pinning her as he kissed down, reaching the tops of her breasts that threatened to spill out of her dress. With a gentle tug, he slid down the front of her dress, exposing her pale flesh to the night air. She gasped as his warm mouth fell over the taut skin of one of her nipples, sucking and feasting on her.

Hope began to wrap her arms around his neck, but he was quick to reach for her hands. He dragged them slowly above her head as her skin scraped against the rough bark of the tree trunk. With one hand, he held her hands above her head as his other hand stroked down her abdomen to her hip. Gathering her skirts as best he could, he yanked them up as he continued his campaign.

Hope could barely make sense of what was happening when he began to speak in words she didn't understand.

"Mo ghraidh," he murmured against her skin as he kissed her.

She didn't want to ask what he was saying, but hoped it was an endearment because it felt like one. A steady stream of unfamiliar words fell from his mouth as he lowered himself in front of her. Her hands rustled through his hair as he slipped lower until he was kneeling before her, gazing up at her with a lustful expression.

Slowly, he lifted her skirts. She wasn't sure why she trembled, but something made her petrified and eager. It was almost too much to bear. When the hem of her garments came up to her knees, she clamped her hands onto his shoulders.

"What are you going to do?" she asked breathlessly.

The hint of a smirk passed over his mouth and Hope was grateful to have the support of the tree behind her.

"I'm going to taste you," he murmured, disappearing beneath her skirts.

Hope brought her curled fist to her mouth as his tongue dived inside her. She tried not to yelp in surprise and pleasure. Her eyes closed as his mouth worked at her, tasting her hungrily, and her knees buckled as a tremors began to swell within her.

Her breathing became short and shallow, and her fingernails dug into his shirt, raking into the skin beneath as a frenzy slammed into her, sudden and raw.

A guttural cry escaped her lips as her body trembled with aftershocks. Graham's strong arms circled her as she slumped against the tree. She was pliant in his hands as his hand hooked beneath her knee and brought it up.

A hard length pressed into the center of her where his mouth had just been. Her body clenched at the pressure, but he pulled her into his arms as his powerful legs stood wide.

"Hold onto me, mo ghraidh," he said in a harsh whisper, a desperate tinge to his voice.

She clutched onto him with all her might as, with a single, swift plummet, he pushed into her. The invasion was intense; for an instant, it was hard to breathe. After a moment, the pain subsided, and he began to grind into her, excruciatingly slowly at first and then faster as he fell into a primitive rhythm.

"Graham," she whispered, her voice cracking with emotion.

"Don't," he said roughly as his movement intensified.

Don't what? She did not know. What she did know was that she *needed* to speak. Needed to let him know, somehow, that another deeper, softer build of emotion was welled up within her.

"Graham, I think … I think it's happening again," she said slowly as the fingers of one of her hands dug into his thigh.

Her words seemed to affect him profoundly, for in the next moment, he gripped onto a low-hanging branch above them as he thrust with conviction, pinning her against the tree in a final push.

A deep quiver coursed throughout his body. She wasn't sure if she was shaking too, but she held onto him as their bodies quaked and settled, coming to uneven breathing, then finally peace. They held onto one another for a long time and when they finally separated, Hope was both grateful and sorry, though she couldn't understand why.

His hand came up to her face and stroked her cheek as he studied her with awe.

"Did I hurt ye?" he asked, his voice softer than before.

"No," she reassured him.

He grinned before his forehead dropped to hers as he leaned gently into her. In one single motion, she was brought up in his arms. "Come."

As if she had any say! He was carrying her again. She didn't bother to struggle this time—she just let her arms come up around his neck. He brought her back across the garden and climbed the stone staircase to return inside, this time leading her to what she realized was the bedchamber. Graham undressed her and Hope tried to cover herself with her hands. Of course, the whole of her couldn't be shielded from his attentive gaze, especially when he came to wash her with a piece of cloth that he dipped in a basin that sat on a small table next to the fireplace. Although the fire only housed a few burning embers, the water was lukewarm.

"I can do it," she said as she tried to take the towel, but he heaved away.

"It'll be my pleasure." He pressed the damp cloth against her shoulder.

He ran circles around her entire body, becoming extra gentle and vigilant with her most private areas. She was sure her whole body was red with embarrassment. Graham must have noticed, because he paused halfway through his work.

"You're not ashamed of me seeing you like this, are you?" he asked.

"No," she lied.

Surely a wife shouldn't be embarrassed of being nude in front of her husband. Hope knew that. But then, she had never been fully naked in front of anyone before, not even maidservants. To be so exposed to someone made her aware of her own vulnerability.

"I think you are." Graham dipped the cloth into a bowl of warm water. He brought it down between her legs, and she closed her eyes as he cleaned her. "You needn't be."

"I'm not."

"Good." He slowly pressed against her and she felt a jolt of pleasure. "Because you're the most stunning creature I've ever seen."

Her eyes opened. When they met his, she saw he spoke the truth.

"Really?"

"Aye," he said quietly. "And if I were a better man, I'd let you get some rest."

She stared at him.

"What do you mean to do instead?" she asked, barely above a whisper, as a single finger stroked against the bud of her.

She shivered.

"I'd like to tease you into saying my name again," he murmured, his mouth close to hers as he spoke. "But I shouldn't. You've had too much for one night. And against a tree, no less."

"I didn't mind," she said quickly, which seemed to please him even though he gave her a guilty glimpse, like a puppy who had ruined a favorite slipper.

"I shouldn't have done that. Someone might have interrupted

us. But I couldn't help myself," he said as he pulled away from her.

"Oh."

He shifted to the side of the table and began to peel off his shirt. Hope's mouth was oddly dry as she watched the muscles of his long back ripple as he lifted his arms. His hands came to his hip and he undid the pin that held his kilt together. Without warning, it fell away and Hope's eyes went wide at the sight of his taut backside.

His entire body was a mass of tightly bound muscles, shaped into curves and divots that looked all the more pronounced in the dim firelight. Her polite upbringing begged her to look away, but when her eyes drifted down and she saw the front of him, she audibly sucked in a breath.

Her gaze snapped to his, and though he was no longer grinning, he appeared amused.

"Yes?" he asked after a moment.

"Nothing. I didn't say anything," she said quickly, her attention darting in spite of herself from his face to his member standing straight and impossibly rigid.

Had that been what was in her? It didn't seem possible.

"Are you sure?" He came toward her. "I could have sworn you asked to touch it."

"What?" she said loudly, until she saw the playfulness in his face. She let out a shaky laugh. "You're teasing me."

"I am," he admitted. He grasped her hand and led her toward the bed. "Come. I won't accost you while you sleep."

"Are we to sleep naked?" she asked, a little surprised.

"Of course. Why wouldn't we?"

"I never have before."

"Really? I do so every night."

"Truly?" she asked. He nodded. "I never imagined that someone would do so."

He held up the covers, and she crawled beneath them. He cuddled next to her and gathered her against his body. She felt sore enough that she was slightly worried that he would seek to make love again, but he only kissed her shoulder.

"Easy, darling," he said. At that, her muscles began to unwind. "I've only plans to hold you."

Hope relaxed against him, their bodies fitting comfortably together beneath the cool sheets. Her eyes closed, his breath warm against her neck.

"I think I was right," she said dreamily as her tired body nestled closer to the comfort of his. "We shall have a lucky marriage indeed."

"Indeed," he said, as Hope drifted off to sleep.

Hope had never slept more peacefully or more profoundly than that night. It was as if every worry or sorrow that had ever plagued her had dissolved and she was only left with wonderfully pleasant musings. All past troubles had left her and when she woke the next day, she could hardly believe her luck at waking up as Mrs. MacKinnon.

By early the next morning, Graham returned to Lismore Hall with Hope as his bride. In the message they had sent the previous day, they'd said they would return the following morning.

Hope mused that she was not a bit sorry that they had been married in a hurry, though she did wonder if perhaps they should keep it a secret.

"I don't want to spoil everyone's fun for the wedding," she said as Graham held out his arm for her. "The McTavishes were so excited for a party."

"They always are," Graham said as they made their way through the front door of the castle. "They wouldn't be disappointed though. I think they'd be glad about our getting married."

"I'm sure they would, but it's quite fun, don't you think?" she said, smirking up at him. "To a have a little secret?"

Graham's warm glance sent shivers down her spine.

"Aye," he said lovingly before nodding down the hallway.

"Come. We'll at least need to confirm with Belle that we truly are married."

Hope playfully slapped her palm against Graham's arm as they passed the dining room. The sudden scratching of chair legs against the floor caused them to turn as Faith and Grace hurried out into the hallway.

"Hope!" Grace said, wrapping her arms around her sister. "Thank goodness you're home!"

"Oh, yes," Hope said, struggling against Grace's assault. "It's good to be home." She gave her sister a squeeze before peeling away from her. Faith just stood there, arms folded against her chest. "Hello, Faith."

For a moment she thought Faith would turn away, but then she found herself wrapped in her middle sister's embrace.

"Foolish Hope," she said with a teasing warmth. Pulling back, she held her with her hands at arm's length, her gaze flickering to Graham. "Then I suppose you've forgiven this one?"

"Not quite yet," Hope said, reaching back to hold Graham's hand. "But I will. One day." Graham gave her a gentle smile before Hope looked back at her sisters. "Do you know where Belle is?"

"Her office, most likely," Grace said.

"Have no fear. I've given her a piece of my mind," Faith said, winking.

"Er, thank you," Hope said, turning to Graham. "We should go speak with her."

"Aye."

They continued down the hallway and entered the office. As ever, Belle sat hunched over her desk, simultaneously writing a letter and dictating another to Rose, who sat at her own desk against the window. Andrews stood silently against the back wall, waiting for instructions.

"—and furthermore have the…" The footfall against the flagstone floor caused the mountain of grayish white hair piled on top of Belle's head to shift as she looked up. Her eyes widened at the sight of them. "Ah! My darling Hope. MacKinnon. Returned at last." She put down her pen as Andrews came forward to help her up. It seemed she was unable to walk unaided now that she held tightly to her butler's arm. She squinted her eyes at Graham. "Took you a bit long to return her, didn't it?"

"We were detained," Graham said simply, refusing to be baited.

"Hmm, well, hopefully our dear girl isn't too tired from her ordeal," she said, turning to eye Hope. "You shouldn't have run off like that without at least taking Andrews here."

A solitary brow on the butler's forehead reached up, as if he found the idea of leaving his mistress absurd.

"Aunt Belle," Hope said coming forward. "I want you to know that I haven't forgiven Graham. Nor you for that awful idea you had."

Belle looked offended and then, glancing at Hope's hand gripped in Graham's, she smirked.

"Keep your forgiveness as long as you like, then. All that matters to me is that I got my way," she said smugly. "And both you got what you deserved as well."

"Be that as it may," Hope said. "Graham and I would like to ask you something."

"Oh? And what is that?"

Hope opened her mouth, unsure how to phrase what she wished to ask. Turned to Graham, she gave him a helpless look. He came forward.

"We want to know," he started in a low voice, "how much time you have left."

The question seemed to catch Belle off guard. Her grip on Andrews's arm tightened noticeably and the gulping noise she made exposed the truth. Belle was dying and she had likely known about it for some time.

"Who told you? Did that Dr. Barkley tell you something? Or perhaps it was your friend Hall."

"Hope deduced it."

"Hope?" she repeated, somewhat surprised, gazing at her niece. "But I never told you."

"Told her that you were dying?" Graham continued to ask, noticing her flinch at his indelicate language. He shook his head. "How long have you known?"

"Several months now, I suppose."

"Months? And you didn't think to tell anyone?"

"If I had my way, I'd have been dead before anyone even realized I was ill," she said as she struggled to come forward. Andrews helped settle her into an overstuffed wingback chair. Graham came toward her to help, but she swatted at him with her cane. "Leave me be."

"Let me help you."

"I do not need anyone's help."

The noise of shuffling paper caught everyone's attention. When they looked up, they saw Rose trying to carry several papers with her out of the room.

"I think I should just be going," she said softly.

"No, Rose. Stay. You'll need to hear this," Belle said, her ring-clad fingers clanking against her cane as she tightened her grip. Taking a deep breath before she continued. "Dr. Hall was the first to suspect it. I had been dealing with a significant amount of discomfort since last summer and Dr. Hall insisted on a full examination. He discovered a growth near my hip. Apparently, it has grown significantly since then, which means I'm not long for this world. It's why I insisted that I only deal with Dr. Barkley from now on. At least he allows me to bully him. He'll let me die in peace."

Hope felt her throat tighten.

"Are you in much pain?"

"Yes, but I'm made of tougher stock than most."

"The doctor mentioned something about a surgery," Hope said. "Not Dr. Barkley. Dr. Hall."

"Yes, he wants to filet me. Well, my answer to that is 'absolutely not,'" Belle said stubbornly. "I've no wish to be carved up by anyone, especially Dr. Hall." Her clear gray eyes pleaded in her disgruntled face.

"What about a trip to the continent? Perhaps to your vineyard?" Hope said. "Would a warmer climate help at all?"

Belle sighed.

"Please, let's not speak about this anymore. It's far too morose for my liking."

"So, you wish for everyone to go about their lives as if your own life isn't slowly fading away?" Graham asked.

"Yes."

"No," Hope interrupted. "How can you expect any of us to do such a thing?"

"Because I demand it. Now," she paused, glaring at them. "What's all this from your letter last night about already being married?" Belle asked, her tone authoritative again. "We've already ordered hundreds of flowers and it cost a king's ransom for the amount of food we're preparing for the event."

Hope bit her lip, feeling ashamed for not thinking of all the work and expense that had gone into the wedding planning.

"Um," the gentle voice of Rose piped up. "I might have a suggestion."

"We can't just toss it all away. I'm rich, not wasteful," Belle continued, ignoring Rose. "There has to be something we can do with it."

Rose cleared her throat.

"I said, I might have an idea."

Everyone turned to Rose, who appeared rather nervous. When she didn't speak again right away, Belle let out a sigh.

"Well? What is it?"

"Oh. Well, you see, Jared—er, I mean, Mr. McTavish—asked me to marry him just the other day," she said. "And if Hope and Mr. MacKinnon wouldn't mind, I'm sure we would be very grateful to help, um, take everything off your hands."

Hope smiled broadly.

"That's a brilliant idea. Can it be done?" She eyed Rose's

figure. "You're slighter than me in the waist, but I'm sure the dress can be altered. What do you think, Aunt Belle?"

Her crinkled cheek pulled up at the corner, and her eyes seemed to twinkle.

"A brilliant idea, indeed. Yes, of course it can be done."

Epilogue

THE WEDDING OF Jared McTavish and Rose Ryland took place on September 23rd. It was a joyous affair, and a great many family and friends came to join the celebration. The men prepared themselves in Belle's office, laughing and offering Jared advice while plying themselves with good Scottish liquor while the ladies made ready in Rose's room at Lismore Hall.

Graham rode his horse behind the carriage with the other cousins as the entire party made their way down the glen to an old private chapel that had been used by the MacKinnons for generations. While Jared had wished to marry Rose on McTavish lands, she had explained that her family had descended from the MacKinnon Clan, and as it was such a sweet church that sat in front of a woodland stream, surrounded by bluebells, Jared had conceded.

Gavin, Jared and the rest of the McTavish men entered the church, which was filled by guests sitting in their pews. An old man dressed in dark robes, with white whiskers on the sides of his face, stood before a small window at the back of the building. After an exchange of words with Jared, the priest nodded to someone at the doors and the bridal party began their march down the aisle.

Graham never imagined being sorry for not having a church wedding, but as he stood next to Jared, he thought he might have felt a little remorseful, if not for that fact that he was terribly pleased that Hope was already his wife.

When she entered the church ahead of the other bridesmaids, Graham's breath caught. She wore an ivory gown with a gauzy overlay, like the other ladies in Rose's processional, but to Graham's surprise, she also wore a swath of MacKinnon plaid across her chest, from shoulder to opposite hip. His heart pounded with pride at the sight and all reason went out of his mind. God, how he loved her. Utterly and completely.

Hope took her place at the back of the church as the rest of the bridesmaids followed. Everyone stood the moment Rose appeared in the doorway, but Graham kept his eyes steadily on Hope.

When the bride reached the priest, he began his speech with such a thick brogue that made Hope frown occasionally, evidently unsure what he was saying. Graham had a hard time keeping himself from smiling. The ceremony was over quickly, and as the bride and groom hurried out of the church, Hope came to Graham's side. As she took his arm, a genuine feeling of peace came over him.

She was his.

A ball was held later that day in Lismore Hall. Several hours after they returned from the church, Hope and Graham found Belle, seated on her throne-like chair at the head of the ballroom. She was frowning as they approached, seemingly perturbed about something.

"What's wrong, Lady Belle?" Graham asked. "The festivities not to your liking?"

"Festivities indeed. This might as well be my going away party," Belle said. "I suspect this will be the last time I'll see a ball taking place here."

Graham tried very hard not to roll his eyes while Hope bent at the waist and kissed the wrinkled cheek of her great aunt.

"Nonsense. You'll be back in the spring," she said.

"Talking about our trip?" Grace said, coming forward after dancing with one of the McTavish brothers. "It's terribly exciting, isn't it?"

"Hardly," Belle said sourly.

The plan for Belle to travel had been discussed at length. After asking the opinions of both Dr. Barkley and Dr. Hall, it was decided that a trip to a warmer climate would be beneficial. Faith and Grace would accompany Belle to Italy, where they would spend that coming winter. Laird McTavish would join them as well.

Grace had an alternative motive though. She intended to convince Aunt Belle to visit an Italian physician, Dr. Bassi, who was making groundbreaking advances in surgical medicine.

"Oh, we'll have a splendid time," Grace said. "I'm sure of it."

"We will miss you, Belle," Graham said, though his heated gaze was on Hope. "When do you leave again?"

Hope elbowed him.

"A fortnight," Belle answered. "A fortnight until my doom."

It would be Hope's first separation from her sisters, but Graham was excited at the prospect of spending an entire season alone with his wife. A blush spread across her cheeks as he watched her, imagining wrapping her up in a length of MacKinnon plaid, laying before the fire.

The musicians began to play a lively song, and Graham bowed.

"Shall we?"

Hope smiled.

"Yes please," she said, taking his hand.

Graham twirled Hope onto the floor, spinning her around to several loud whistles and cheers. He pulled her close.

"You seem particularly spirited today," she said as they righted themselves.

"I am."

"May I ask why?" she asked. To answer, he leaned down to kiss her. It was a decidedly improper thing to do, but she hardly seemed fazed. Instead, she leaned forward and whispered. "What was that for?"

"No reason in particular," he said, smiling down at her.

"Come along."

Graham held her against him as the music played and silently thanked the lord above that he had found Hope.

He was at home at last.

The End

About the Author

Matilda Madison lives in the Pocono mountains of Pennsylvania. A history lover, she finds immense joy in knowing useless facts, exploring the woods around her home, and drinking copious amounts of tea. When she's not writing, she can be found researching obscured periods for her books, refurbishing old furniture, and baking.

Catch up with me anytime on my socials.
Website – www.matildamadison.com
Instagram – matildamadisonbooks
TikTok – @matildamadison